A Lesson in Patience

Jennifer Connors
A Lesson in Patience

Published by J Connors Publishing, LLC
Gilbert, Arizona

This is dedicated to the winner of the bet. Richard, you didn't think I could do it, but it has been done. Congratulations!

Chapter 1

Ginny could feel herself moving, but didn't want to open her eyes. Judging by what her senses were picking up, she knew she wasn't home. Once she opened her eyes, the illusion would be gone. But which illusion? The one she just left, her handsome husband leaving the room to order her bath? Or the one where she was back in her own body, living in her own house, and working as a physician's assistant? But of course, that wasn't an illusion, at least it shouldn't be.

Moving her hands down her body, Ginny knew she was definitely not in the 21st century. For one, she was wearing a dress. Ginny could count on one hand how many times in the past year she'd worn a dress. And two, she was on a train. With the amount of rocking, it wasn't the high speed train between London and Paris.

With a deep sigh, she finally relented and opened one eye. The first thing she noticed was all the wood. Definitely not Arizona, definitely not even close to her own time. Ginny had seen trains like this one, even been on one. They were antiques, used as props at train parks.

Dammit, she thought with another sigh. Begrudgingly, she opened the other eye and turned her head around to take it in. Hopefully she wouldn't be kept waiting with the information on who she was and why she was on a train. Beside her, sat another woman, looking excited. The woman's eyes were wide, looking out the windows of the train as if anticipating their arrival.

Confirming her suspicions, Ginny noticed the dress. Using her limited knowledge of history, she guessed the time period to be in the mid to late 1800's. Glancing out the window, she knew she had to be in America. England did not have this type of open plain landscape. The woman next to her would shortly confirm her guess.

"Henny, you awake?" the woman spouted, bouncing in her seat with excitement. "I figure we should be getting there real soon."

Henny? What was that short for? Henrietta? *Oh great.*

"How do you figure?" Ginny had to keep it simple until she knew what the hell was going on.

"Looky out the window. Surely we must be coming toward Denver."

"Denver?" Ginny whispered. *What the hell is in Denver?*

Turning toward Ginny, with a serious look on her face, the woman spoke desperately. "We will stay together, right? You won't be off getting married, leaving me behind, will ya?"

Ginny's eyes took on a bewildered look. Getting married? Again? Hadn't she been there and done that? The woman started looking like a deer in the sights of a rifle. Not wanting a crying woman on her hands, she said the first thing she could to reassure her. "Of course, we'll stick together."

Releasing a huge hiss of air that the woman had been holding, she smiled. "I knew you would be a good friend, Henny. I knew it like I know my name is Priscilla Younger." Nudging her elbow into Ginny's shoulder, she added, "But not for long, hopefully. I know we took a big chance coming out here, but what else could we do?"

"Indeed." Ginny hoped Priscilla would continue to babble on and give her more information. She wasn't disappointed.

"I knew when we met on the platform in St. Louie, that we would be the best of friends. Maybe we can find men who live by each other. That way, we can stay friends after the weddings, and all." Priscilla turned to her for confirmation.

"Yeah, sure. That would be great." Ginny's head was spinning. Were they going to meet men to marry? Who does that?

Staring out the window, it came to her in a flash. At least, a few memories came to her. A man, walking up to her as she slept in an alley, claiming he could give her a better life. *Come with me,* he said, *and I will find a nice man to marry you. You can live on the frontier.*

How in the hell had she fallen for that? There was, of course, a catch. Ginny could remember the man telling her that if no man would offer for her, she would be sold to a brothel. She would have to pay off her debt to the owner, and then she could do as she pleased. *Yeah, right*, Ginny thought.

Fruitlessly, Ginny tried to search her memories for more information. She could only remember the man in the alley, and everything that had happened since. She had no idea where she was from, if she had family or friends or if she was rich or poor. Presumably, she was poor, since this offer was attractive enough to get her to sign on.

The more she thought about it, she realized that the man who made the offer had also given her the name, Henny. The body she now possessed, clearly had no memories beyond a few weeks ago. As if it weren't hard enough living someone else's life, now she got to live as an amnesiac.

Grasping the bridge of her nose with her two fingers, squeezing tightly, Ginny felt the pressure of her situation. She was a young woman, with no resources, heading towards Denver with another woman, trying to find someone to marry her or end up as a whore. Rubbing her face in her hands, she had only one simple question left. What had she done to deserve this?

Priscilla continued her chatter all the way to Denver. Normally, it would have driven Ginny crazy to listen to it, but she used the time to consider her situation, as Priscilla rarely needed a response.

Finally, the train entered a large station. The weather was warm and humid, leading Ginny to believe it must be summer. The sky was azure and there were few clouds about. The weather looked fine, unlike Ginny's newest situation.

They departed the train, each with one small bag and were swiftly directed toward a cart. It was then that Ginny realized how many women were participating in this "bride" auction. At least twenty women sat in the back of the cart, like some deranged hayride. It occurred to Ginny that women during this time period, with no resources, would probably be desperate enough to do this. Anything had to be better than starvation or exposure.

Thinking about the past, Ginny knew that the frontier was much like Alaska today: many men, way fewer women. With such odds, every girl out here would probably be picked. But what kind of life were they getting themselves into? Living in a home without running water, bathroom or electricity? Sounded like hell on earth to Ginny, who in her previous lives at least had servants to handle all the hard stuff. Here, she would be the servant, without many skills where she needed them most.

Ginny could cook and clean, but cared for neither. Not having a microwave would put a damper on her food preparation skills, as would no refrigerator or gas stove. Her expensive cookware, a Christmas gift from her mother, would be irrevocably destroyed in this

7

environment. And what about washing clothes? Beating them against a rock and using lye soap, she assumed. *This is really going to suck*, she thought grimly.

Turning her attention to her surroundings, Ginny was surprised to see what a bustling city Denver was. She didn't have any idea exactly what year it was, but she always imagined the "frontier" being one line of buildings surrounded by a whole lot of nothing. Maybe she shouldn't get her history from old John Wayne movies or *Blazing Saddles*.

The roads were paved and there were many intersecting streets. To Ginny, it looked like any modern city, except that the buildings weren't as tall. *Are those telephone lines*, she thought to herself, looking up at the telephone poles with dozens of intersecting wires. She had to find out the year, but didn't know how to ask without looking crazy or stupid.

The cart was taking the women out of the town limits, entering an area of woods. It seemed like they traveled for over an hour. When they arrived at a clearing, Ginny saw a dozen men standing around awaiting their arrival. The men were all different heights, weights and sizes. Mostly, they were short and unattractive, but who was Ginny to say, since she hadn't seen herself yet.

Her mega-hunk had to be in this crowd, but so far, Ginny hadn't seen a single man who would even come close to good-looking. At this point, she would settle for anyone who had all their original teeth. Many of the men were covered in dust, as if they'd rode night and day to be there on time. They wore worn flannel shirts, dirty denim, and everyone had a cowboy hat.

The man driving the wagon and the man who first approached Ginny, came around and unhooked the back of the cart. The women, trying to look their best, smoothed out their skirts and pinched their cheeks in an attempt to look more healthy. A line was formed just outside the back of the cart, when the women began to display their personal best attributes.

Ginny stood at the end of the line, next to Priscilla, who was making strange pouty looks with her lips. *So this is what it's like to be cattle at auction*, Ginny considered her situation. *All this to go home with one of these guys. Or, become a whore in a brothel. Fantastic.*

The men walked up and started sizing each women up. Feeling her cheeks going red over the humiliation of it, Ginny took on a defiant look. As if it wasn't bad enough to be put in a situation where you had no choices, then she had to parade around a bunch of dirty cowboys. The indignity was too much to bear, and Ginny could feel herself turning away when Priscilla took her arm.

"Henny, stop. Do you want to end up as a whore?" Her whispered plea reminded Ginny of what was at stake. Somewhere among these "gentlemen" was her mega-hunk. She just had to bide her time until he showed up to rescue her.

"Remember our agreement..." Priscilla persisted. "Don't you dare go anywhere without me."

"I know, Priscilla." Ginny took a deep breath and began to examine the men anew. There had to be one among them that would fit the "romance novel" type.

As each man passed, Ginny noticed that their looks were nothing compared to their smell. Body odor and horse mingled freely with dust and dirt. Giving up on the men, Ginny watched the women. All the girls began to turn and twist, showing their best sides and sultry looks. It brought about a new feeling of anger thinking about the fact that these women's options were so limited that these men appealed to them.

Silently chastising herself, Ginny realized how shallow that was. Some of these men might make great husbands and caring fathers. Ginny had to remind herself that judging the package was not only empty, but usually not entirely accurate. With this new sense of righteousness, Ginny decided to give the men a chance.

One of the men stopped in front of her. He was about the same height, with a strong build like he was no stranger to hard work. With his hat on, Ginny could see wisps of greasy hair escaping the sides. His intense black eyes were taking in every inch of her and Ginny felt her blush coming back.

Suddenly, his hand whipped out and grabbed hers. In that moment, Ginny wondered if he would throw her over his shoulder, grunt a few unintelligible words and carry her off to his lair. Instead, he examined the stolen hand.

"You ain't never done a days work in yer life, have ya?" The odious man had the nerve to sneer at her.

"Excuse me?" Ginny put all the force of her sarcasm behind those two words, which were completely lost on the man.

"Look at yer hands. Soft as a baby's ass. Did yer rich daddy put you out for fooling around with the coachman?" With that, the man let out a cackle, shortly joined by the other men in the group.

"I wouldn't touch you with a ten foot pole." Turning towards the audience of men, he continued, "This woman be'd too much trouble. Probably wouldn't do a damn thing. Expect to be waited on, no doubt. Not to mention, she ain't likely too pure anymore."

Ginny smiled. Before she could think better of it, she said, "Somehow, I doubt that would really be an issue for you. Seeing how the only women you've ever had were bought and paid for."

The man's eyes got darker and meaner. He took a step towards Ginny, pushing his foul breath in her face. "You better watch that pretty mouth of yours or I just might come and buy some of you when you become a working girl."

With a shiver, Ginny turned away first. The thought of that man touching her made her skin crawl. She had better find her mega-hunk soon, or she was likely going to have to try and escape the men who brought her here. And judging by their look, she wasn't likely to succeed.

Chapter 2

The wooden cart rolled along at a painstakingly slow pace. The weather was perfect, with clear, blue skies and just a few fluffy clouds. Usually, this kind of weather always brought a sense of calm to Colby, but not today.

"Damn wheel. We're so late I doubt there will be anyone left," Colby Miller said with a sense of both anger and trepidation. "Why the hell of all days did the damn thing have to go today?"

"I'm sure it will be fine," his best friend and ranch hand, Tim, said. "How many men 'round here could be looking for a wife?"

Turning in his seat at the head of the cart to stare at his friend, Colby replied acerbically, "Gee, Tim, how many ya think? Just about every damn ranch owner out this way needs a woman. It's not like there are that many to choose from."

Deciding it would be better not to reply, Tim kept his mouth shut. It wasn't long before Colby decided to start in on the same argument they'd been having since they set out. Although, argument would not quite describe it, since it was entirely one-sided.

"This wouldn't be necessary if you hadn't stole my governess," Colby stated, bringing up the reason for his journey.

"I said I was sorry. I can't help that the poor woman fell so deeply in love with me. You know I'm known for my... abilities." Tim smiled and winked in Colby's direction.

"Abilities? Damn. I figured you just bribed the poor girl. You know how much it cost me to ship her out from St. Louis. Hell, what it cost me to just convince her to come out here to teach the children."

"I told you I would pay you back any expenses."

"Yeah, you told me alright. Hell if I've seen any of that money."

Sighing deeply, Tim did truly feel bad. When the governess, a Miss Eloise Jamison, came to live on the ranch, he never imagined he would fall head over heels at first sight. The two had made a love connection from almost the first time they spoke to one another. That had been nearly three months ago and his friend had yet to forgive him.

"I swear Colby, as soon as I can, I will pay you back. Plus, Eloise has been tutoring your brothers and sister for free. It's just with her pregnant, we know she's gonna be awful busy in the next few months..." Tim let the rest of his thought go. It didn't matter, Colby would either forgive him or not.

"What if I can't find someone? The summer is busy and autumn worse with harvest. With all the cattle, you and I will scarcely be around. I'm not so worried about Georgia, but Frank and Nate need a woman around to care for them. Nizhoni has too many chores around the ranch to keep the boys in line."

"My ma used to always tell me to not borrow trouble. We'll be there soon and we'll see for ourselves if there are any acceptable women left. If not, maybe we could spend the night in Denver and see if there are any rich men's daughters looking for a little adventure in the backwoods of Wyoming Territory."

"As a man about to be a daddy, would you let your daughter go live with some stranger in Wyoming?" Colby liked to ask questions he already knew the answer to. It was one of the reasons he wanted to become a lawyer. But some dreams die hard, like at the hands of a flash flood.

"Hell no, but then again, I know you." Laughing at his own joke, Tim felt the glare more than saw it. "Well still, ain't nothing you can do until we get there."

"True enough."

As if being displayed like cattle weren't humiliating enough, being ignored by filthy men was worse. Priscilla slowly began to distance herself from Ginny's side, instead moving herself down the line. So much for sticking together. Priscilla saw the writing on the wall. Ginny was headed for the nearest whorehouse, to be used and abused, and have her virginity stolen by the highest bidder.

A feeling of heaviness fell on Ginny. Despair? Not yet, but very close. This was the third time she'd had to live with this. What was the point? Was this some sort of punishment for not being the best person she could have been? *God, you know I tried... and I wasn't really that bad*, she mused as she stood alone at the end of the line.

The men went about picking their women and paying their captors. Priscilla, who was obviously ignoring her, was chosen by the nasty creature that had insulted Ginny. *Good riddance! Hope you have a great life together.* Ginny realized it was uncharitable, but couldn't help it. She wouldn't have abandoned her friend as easily. No, she probably would have gone down in a blaze of glory just to prove a point.

Slowly, as hour after hour went by, the girls were chosen and left with their new husbands. One of the men even performed a "wedding ceremony" for each new couple. As far as legality, it probably didn't mean much, but who was going to check or even care? It was doubtful that any of the women were already married and if they were, their husbands weren't likely to come searching for them.

Sitting on the back of the cart, Ginny wondered what her guardians next move would be. Would they try again tomorrow, wait around to see if anyone else showed up or just dump her off at the most convenient brothel? As the crowd left, it became obvious that they would wait, just in case.

The two men weren't completely unkind. They offered Ginny some bread and meat. They made sure she had water and a comfortable place to sit and eat in the shade. They even made polite conversation with her. The man who had originally approached her was named John, and he had been transporting women out west for the better part of a decade. Jack, the assistant, was also named John, but to keep things easy, he went by Jack. Both men were of average height, but that was where the similarities ended. John, older by at least fifteen years, was balding and what was left of his hair a salt and pepper color. Jack, young and strapping, had wavy brown hair that reached his collar.

"So, guys, what now?" Ginny figured that information was power, so she shouldn't put her head in the sand.

John, being the senior partner, answered, "Well, we'll wait around here for a few more hours. 'Til dark, I reckon. Then we can make camp and see if anyone shows up in the morning. After that, well... we'll just wait and see."

"Do you have many women who end up in the brothels?" In for a penny, in for a pound.

"Nah. Once in a blue moon, but I haven't had any in a few years." Ginny was beginning to like his drawl. It was comforting, especially in the light of such an uncertain future.

"Gee John, I think the last one I remember was Dory. You suppose?" Jack was also twangy, but not in a comforting way. His accent was more bold.

"Oh, yeah... Dory. Too bad about her." John let it go at that, but Ginny wasn't about to.

"And what happened to Dory?" Ginny's eyes were wide with the possibilities. John noticed her uneasiness and set out to make her feel better.

"Now, now, you ain't like Dory. She was a sweet girl, but she wasn't really right, ya know? Said she heard voices and all. No man wants to bring home that kind of crazy, not when you want to have kids and all."

"Why did you bring her out here, then?" Ginny tried to temper her exasperation, but knew she was only human.

"Didn't know at first. Seemed okay when I met her in St. Louie. Didn't start with the crazy until we were halfway here. Investment was already made by then." John was so matter-of-fact, Ginny almost winced. Once again, she had to remind herself that this was a very different time, with very different rules.

"So, what happened?" she asked, truly curious.

"Brought her to a nice place, just north of here. The madam is a friend of mine and she treats her girls real good. Gave her a good deal, since Dory wasn't gonna be any good as a 'working girl' if you know what I mean. Anyway, Dory didn't like being cooped up, working as a housemaid, so she went and hung herself a few weeks later. To keep things right between me and Nadine, I gave her the money back, minus the cost of a few weeks work."

Ginny stared at the man as if he had grown a second head. John hardly noticed, as he was working on releasing some dirt under his fingernail with a knife.

"So... Nadine... she's a nice woman?" Just like Ginny, get to the point.

Jack answered this time. "Aw, yeah, she's great. Treats her girls real nice. Makes sure that the men know how to treat a lady. I like her a lot." Rolling her eyes, not so either man could see, Ginny thought, *What a ringing endorsement!*

"If you gentlemen would excuse me for a moment, I have to take care of my needs." Ginny was surprised when both men stood up as she did. Jack even used his hand to steady her, when she swayed on her feet.

Smiling at both men, Ginny walked away and found a quiet place in the woods to take care of her business. Oh how she truly hated having to pee in the woods. And she didn't even have any toilet paper to boot. Just as she finished up and went looking for some water to wash her hands, she heard a cart approaching. *Maybe this is it,* she thought excitedly. Then she realized how silly it was to get her hopes up. At the least, she was still going to have to live some other life, not her own, just to move on to wherever she was set to go next.

Chapter 3

When the cart came around the last bend, Colby saw the two men best known in the area for obtaining wives. Word always spread pretty fast when the next "shipment" would be in, so men from hundreds of miles away could make a special trip to marry a woman. Most women in the outer reaches were either already married, too old or already had employment that made them less than stellar candidates for the job of wife and mother.

Colby was looking around, not seeing a single woman around. His heart sank, as this was the last time in a while he would have time to find a wife to watch his siblings. After both his parents were killed in a flash flood late last summer, he had been forced to give up his position apprenticing with a lawyer in Denver. He had hoped to work with the attorney for a few years, then go to college back east somewhere and get a degree. The law fascinated him, and he even hoped that one day he could use his job as a way to get into government.

But after the accident, he was needed back home. Colby wasn't the oldest. He had an older brother, RJ, who had left home at eighteen and hadn't been back since. Colby wasn't even sure where he was. They received a letter every six or so months detailing the adventures of the older sibling. Colby had sent a telegram to the last known address for his brother, but didn't even know if he knew that their parents were dead.

So, Colby had to return to take care of the ranch that his parents had built together over the nearly thirty years they'd been married. The couple had left behind five children: Robert Jr, Colby, Georgia, Frank and Nate. The youngest being only ten, and his next oldest brother only thirteen. His sister, Georgia, was eighteen and would be courted soon by every available and imaginable bachelor in the territory. Women were rare, but appropriate women were even more rare.

It was because of the two youngest that Colby needed a wife. He cared little for companionship for himself, but needed someone who could raise his little brothers and keep an eye on his sister and her many callers. He cared little whether the woman was good looking, just that she was responsible and could help around the ranch.

Pulling his cart alongside the one already parked in the field, Colby jumped out and walked over to the two men. Tim came up beside him, smiling at the men now rising from under a tree. Whispering to Colby, he said, "Maybe you could strike a deal to have them deliver a woman to ya with the next shipment."

Colby recognized that Tim was trying to placate him. It was obvious that all the women were gone and he was screwed. Removing his hat, Colby held out his hand to the older of the two men.

"Good day to you, gentlemen. My name is Colby Miller and it appears I'm too late." His voice was even, although he was seething inside. It certainly wasn't these men's fault that his wagon wheel broke.

"Howdy. My name is John and this here is my assistant, Jack. And despite what you see, you ain't too late." John smiled, happy that he was going to be able to unload his final ward. He never liked selling them to the whorehouse, but a deal was a deal.

"Pardon?" Colby asked, turning his head to look around and not seeing any women.

"Henny's taking care of her business and will be back in a moment. I hope you ain't too picky, seeing's how I only have the one girl. But, then again, you won't have any trouble choosing." John laughed at his own joke. Jack joined in. Colby smiled to be polite, but wondered what could possibly be left over.

Just then, a vision walked out of the trees and came to stand before the four men. Colby resisted the urge to shake his head, because surely the beautiful woman standing before him had to be a hallucination. She was of a medium height, and had a well formed body, all curves in the right places. Her hair was a chestnut brown, that glowed gold in the sunlight and surrounded a heart shaped face with big, brown eyes. Full lips completed the face that were so red and kissable that Colby could feel himself responding to the thought. He was instantly enamored. First he thought, "How could she still be here?" Then he thought, "What the hell is wrong with her?"

His second thought, impolitely, was spoken aloud and put quite a scowl on the young woman's face.

"There's nothing wrong with me," Ginny replied automatically. She could feel the anger building up again, despite the fact that she knew, beyond a shadow of a doubt, that this was her mega-hunk. Her mind was screaming for her to shut-up, but her mouth, as usual, had to say something completely different.

Her mega-hunk was tall, with broad shoulders and muscular arms. His thick, brown hair was cut short, and looked like it would be soft to the touch. His eyes were the color of the sky, azure blue and clear. He had a day's worth of beard growth on his face and beautiful white teeth.

John placed a hand on her shoulder, probably in the hopes of conveying that this was her best chance to stay out of the whorehouse. Ginny stiffened to the warning, but nonetheless took the advice and turned her gaze to her boots. It turns out that she could be taught.

Colby, momentarily stunned by how brilliant she looked angry, turned to John and asked, "She's far too pretty to be the only one left behind. Why wasn't she already picked? Are you telling me that there were more women than men?" Not for one minute would Colby believe that. Finding a wife in this part of the world was harder than finding a talking dog.

"Naw, we had quite a few men leave empty handed. They felt she was too..." John scratched his head under the brim of his hat, trying to think of a nice way to say what he wanted to say. "Well, now, she's a fine woman. She just doesn't know anything about her past is all. I had to give her a name, seeing's how she couldn't remember hers."

Colby turned and looked Tim in the eye. "They have one woman left and she's crazy."

Looking up from her boots, Ginny stared at the man before her. He was a sight to behold. He definitely worked hard and his body showed it. To Ginny, he looked like he walked right out of a western romance novel.

Great looking, yes. Smart, not so far. "I am not crazy. Something happened to me and I can't remember who I am." Ginny felt the need to enunciate each word, just in case he wasn't dealing a full deck.

"Sounds crazy to me. How do I know you're not already married, a pretty girl like yourself?" Colby asked, meeting her eyes and holding his own.

John decided to intervene. "I don't think it matters much, Mr. Miller. I found her alone and desperate, on the streets of St. Louie. If she had a family, no one came forward before we left. I made sure I read the paper to see if any pretty girls went missing."

"I'm so glad that we all think I'm pretty, but it doesn't change the fact that I'm not crazy." Colby lifted an eye to her little speech. He had to admire her spunk.

Reaching over, Colby took her hand. After running his thumb over her palm, he knew without a doubt that this woman had never done an honest day's work. He felt her stiffen at his examination and realized that some other man made the same observation today. That was why she was the only one left.

What did he need with some pampered, rich girl who couldn't even remember her own name. To Colby, it seemed like more trouble than it was worth. Before he could say something really rude, his friend grabbed his arm. Tim pulled him a few feet away and whispered in his ear.

"She's the only one they have and you're pretty desperate. Don't look a gift horse in the mouth, my friend."

"What good will she be to me," Colby whispered back. "She probably can't even cook."

"Dammit, Colby, you got Nizhoni for that. She will be there to tutor your brothers and keep a close eye on your sister. Isn't that what you wanted? Not to mention, she's real pretty. You might want to have a wedding night after all."

"Tim, I don't want a wife. I'm only here because I have no other choices."

"Exactly. So, why haven't you made an offer?" Tim knew it wouldn't be easy for Colby to finally get down to business. After all, he had wanted to be a lawyer. The man couldn't help arguing about every little damn thing.

Heaving a sigh, Colby turned back to the small group. John was looking at him expectantly. The girl stood staring at the horizon, with what could only be described as a pout on her face. She looked so spoiled that Colby knew it wouldn't work out. On the other hand, Tim was right. What choice did he have? He wouldn't be able to come back for some time and by then, his brothers could get themselves in a lot of trouble.

He lumbered back to the group and began to question the girl.

"Are you educated?"

Turning her head slightly, she regarded him for a moment before

19

answering. "Are you speaking to me?"

"Who else would I be asking?" he replied, letting his annoyance known.

"Point taken," she answered. Ginny knew she should take the high road here, considering that her life was on the line. But, somehow, she just couldn't do it.

"Well...?" he asked.

"Well, what?" she replied.

"Are you educated?" he asked again through clenched teeth.

Smiling, she replied, "Yes. I'm very educated."

Smiling in return, although the smile didn't quite reach his eyes, he asked, "How would you know if you have no memory of your past?"

Ginny turned her head to the other side and regarded him again. "You make a good point again, but I know I can read and write. I have knowledge of medicine and some history. I'm pretty good with math, although not as good when you add in letters. Is this sufficient to be considered 'educated'?" Ginny made sure she added the air quotes when she said educated.

Grumbling under his breath, he asked, "Do you know how to cook?"

Scrunching her face up, Ginny replied, "I guess it depends on what you want cooked."

"Can you skin an animal?"

Ewwwww. Ginny wasn't a vegetarian and she definitely enjoyed a good steak, but she never gave much thought to where the meat came from, other than her grocer's refrigerated case. "I suppose I could if I had to, but I have no knowledge of how it's done."

Colby turned to his friend with a look that said: *See what I mean?* Tim kept his face straight. He figured he would have to intervene. Clearing his throat, Tim turned to the girl and asked, "Do you have any objections to living on the frontier? There ain't no shopping and there are many chores. Do you think you could handle that?"

Ginny liked Tim. He was straight forward and kept his cynicism to a minimum. Giving him her full attention, she replied, "I've no experience, but I also have few choices. I would be happy to do my best and do what I know how to do. As for the rest, I would be happy to learn."

Satisfied, Tim turned back to Colby with a look that said: *See, she's not so bad.* Colby rolled his eyes and looked back at John. "Shall we negotiate the price, John?"

"Excellent. Let's walk over to the cart and settle this. I'm sure you three would like to be on your way as soon as possible."

And that was how Ginny was sold for the grand sum of five dollars. A king's ransom for the time, but could one really put a price on a soulmate?

Chapter 4

After paying for his new bride, John performed a wedding ceremony for Colby and Ginny. Colby began to object at first, saying it wasn't necessary, but John wouldn't hear any of it. He said that he couldn't turn over his charge until she was legally married. It wasn't lost on Ginny that he would have no issue turning her over to a whorehouse though.

After the ceremony, Colby loaded her up in the back of the cart, with her one bag and promptly ignored her. He was curious about her but refused to speak to her. Plus, he knew that Tim would jabber on with her, and he would find out everything he wanted to know. He wasn't disappointed.

Not long after leaving John and Jack, Tim began his questioning. He asked her every possible question, only to have her answer that she didn't know. It was useless and tiresome, but Tim never grew tired of talking.

"Maybe you hit your head. I heard once that a man didn't even recognize his wife after a fall."

"It's possible," Ginny replied. "We won't know until my memory returns. How about you, Tim? Are you married?" Colby flinched. Leave it to his new "bride" to bring up such a sore subject. And leave it to Tim to completely ignore Colby's discomfort.

"Yes. Fairly recently. My wife, Eloise, is pregnant with our first. She's a little worried about birthing on the ranch though."

"I know a little about... birthing," Ginny said. "I would be happy to help if I can."

Colby rolled his eyes. How could she know about birthing and not know who she was? It seemed fairly impossible and the more she spoke, the more he felt he was being scammed. Wouldn't be the first time a rancher took on a wife only to find out she was just out for the money. Well Henny would be fairly disappointed with him, since there wasn't much money to speak of.

"I can't wait to introduce you. She's been lonely since moving out here. Not many women her age and all. Of course, Georgia is around," Tim answered, while glancing at Colby.

Ginny turned to stare at her new husband's head. He hadn't spoken a word since they left, and he seemed very tense. Sighing, she decided to throw out the olive branch. "Excuse me, Colby. You have family with you at the ranch?"

It took a full minute before he answered, just not to the question that Ginny asked. "We'll camp here for the night. We lost some time today, so we'll be getting up early tomorrow." With that, he put the brake on the cart and hopped down to attend the horses.

At least he's childish, she thought. Ginny could be pretty childish too at times so she wasn't going to hold it against him. Not to mention, Tim would give her the answers she sought. He was worse than a woman when it came to gossip.

Working together, they set up camp. Colby had brought an extra bed roll for his new wife. Ginny set out to gather firewood, while the men unhooked the horses and led them to the creek to drink. Once the fire was started, Tim made a stew out of provisions they'd brought with them. He told her that this would be the last of their meat, and he and Colby would catch something for tomorrow's dinner.

Sitting around the fire, eating their supper, Tim explained the Miller family dynamic. "Well, Georgia is the oldest girl. She's eighteen now and many a ranch hand has come sniffing around her." Ginny nearly laughed thinking how flattering that must be.

"Then there's Frank and Nate. Thirteen and ten and very... what's the word I'm looking for. Not exactly naughty, but..."

"Precocious?" Ginny asked.

"I don't know that word," Tim replied.

"It means... too smart for their own good."

Snapping his fingers, Tim nodded. "Exactly! Both them boys get themselves into a heap of trouble, but you can't help but admire the smarts behind their schemes."

Ginny laughed. She had a couple nephews who were exactly the same way. The memory brought on the familiar homesickness, which she promptly squashed. Nothing she could do about it anyway.

Turning to Colby, she asked, "Are you the oldest then?"

"No," was his only reply. Colby stood up and walked toward the horses.

Whispering, Tim said, "I'm sorry about Colby. He's just a little upset over being late today."

"You mean, he's upset that he got stuck with me and didn't have more to choose from." Ginny would call a spade, a spade.

"He's not a bad guy. He just hasn't had a lot of luck lately."

Looking over at the solitary form patting down one of the horses, Ginny stood up and walked over to try and make things right. She knew the drill. They would eventually come together, but not before some silly misunderstandings. Maybe she could bypass all that by being civil.

"Excuse me, Colby. May I speak to you?" Ginny used her sweetest voice.

Turning to face her, she looked at him. His face was mostly shadows, caused by the firelight. Ginny had to admit that he was stunningly handsome. He was quintessentially male: buff, built and strong. Not a bad combination.

"I'm not really in the mood for conversation, Henny."

He had brought up the first thing that had to change. "You know, John gave me the name Henny and I never really cared for it. Would you mind calling me Ginny instead?"

His face turned to stone and his eyes took on an angry glint. "Ginny, huh? I thought you didn't know anything about yourself."

It occurred to her that Colby thought she was lying about her amnesia. Why would she lie? Who knows, but she knew she had to put that thought to rest. "It was the name of one of the other girls in our group. I just liked it better than Henny. Sorry if that bothers you." She had to disprove she was lying by lying. Interesting.

"I don't know what your game is... Ginny. But I need someone I can depend on. My brothers need a mother. Did I make the biggest mistake of my life today?" His voice was steady, but twinged with sadness and regret.

Ginny dropped her gaze to the ground. How could she respond to that? Did he make a mistake? Of course not. He would eventually fall in love with her and they would have tremendous, earth moving sex. But then, she couldn't tell him that. Caught between a rock and a hard place, Ginny knew she would have to play the game again. As much as she was loathe to do so, anything else could spell disaster.

Taking a deep breath and trying to determine the best "game" for this story, she answered, "Colby, I will do right by your family. I know you have no intention of honoring this... 'marriage,' so let's make a deal."

Squinting his eyes in uncertainty, he asked, "Deal?"

"Yes, a deal. I will work for you, for a fair wage, until I've paid off the money you spent on purchasing me." The words nearly stuck in her throat. It may have been common then, but dammit, it just wasn't right. "When I've paid off my debt, I'll move back to St. Louis and you can find someone more acceptable to fill the role."

Shaking his head, Colby couldn't believe his ears. "So, you would be a governess to the boys and nothing else?"

"Isn't that what you wanted anyway?" she asked, hardly believing that he wasn't jumping at the plan.

Sputtering a few unintelligible sounds, Colby realized she was right. He had only wanted someone to care for the children, not a wife. If he did bed her, he couldn't very well deny their union. But, if they kept things strictly on a professional basis, and it didn't work out, he could boot her out without feeling guilty. Hell, she had practically given him permission to boot her out if he so desired.

"I suppose we could consider that. But first, I'd have to see you with the boys. If you're no good, I won't be paying ya."

Ginny resisted the urge to roll her eyes. *Yeah, yeah*, she thought to herself. Out loud, she said, "That's certainly fair. I will tutor the boys and keep them out of trouble, and I will make sure that any man sniffing around your sister does so properly."

"It doesn't sound like much of deal for you." Colby worried that there must be something more.

"What do you mean? You just paid five dollars for me. I made an agreement to come out here. I pay my debts, and I don't ask for any free rides."

"It won't be easy, you know. My brothers... they can be a handful."

"You can't imagine how 'not easy' my life has been recently. Now, I think I'll take care of myself by the stream and get to bed. I imagine tomorrow will be a very long day." Ginny turned and walked toward the stream.

Colby watched her back as she strolled away. *She sure is pretty*, he thought. Shaking his head to clear his errant thought, Colby got back to making sure the horses were set for the night. The last thing he needed was to get emotional about a strange girl. And this particular girl smelled of serious trouble.

Kneeling next to the stream, Ginny splashed the cold water on her face. Then, she cupped her hands and began to drink. Surely there wasn't any pollution during this time period, way out in the woods. Not that it mattered. This was the only water to drink, so she would drink it. Nothing like a case of dehydration to really ruin someone's day.

Once satisfied, she walked back to the camp. Tim was already lying on his bed roll, with his hat over his eyes, snoring like there was no tomorrow. Ginny was so tired, she knew it wouldn't matter. Colby was no where to be seen, so she undid her skirt and let it drop to the ground. After removing her shoes, she laid her skirt carefully on the outside of the bedroll, and inched her way inside, hoping to God no snakes or critters had crawled in to warm up. Not feeling anything creepy, Ginny settled herself down and closed her eyes. Exhaustion took hold immediately and Ginny was out to the world.

Colby, having finished with the horses, wandered back to camp and noticed that both his companions were dead to the world. He took his time removing his boots and pants. He would keep his shirt on, just in case of emergency in the night. And of course, he had on his long drawers.

Lying on his bedroll, he watched Ginny sleep. He remembered how indignant she had gotten that afternoon when he questioned her. Her eyes had lit up with an internal fire. She was spirited. It was a good thing since life on a ranch in Wyoming Territory wasn't easy. Although she wouldn't be expected to do any truly back breaking work, she would have to keep an eye on Frank and Nate. That alone might break her fiery spirit.

As he watched her, she sighed deeply in her sleep. The act, so feminine and delicate, made him harden almost instantly. How long had it been since he'd bed a woman? Not since the last time he ventured into Cheyenne for supplies. Cheyenne was a big enough city that a man could partake of a certain female's attention with total anonymity. That had been months ago. Nine long months ago. Perhaps he should make use of a brothel when they passed through on their

26

way back to Sherman.

Exhausted after all the tension of the day, Colby laid his head down on his arm. His mind began to work as it usually did right before sleep. He thought about giving the girl a chance. She might, after all, work out just fine. If she worked hard, she could make back what he had spent on her in less than six months. Then she might decide to stay on. It was important for others to think they were married, so they didn't try to steal her away. That was the problem with too many men, not enough eligible females. Any woman was fair game, even if she might belong to someone else.

He would discuss it with her tomorrow. It was probably time he stopped acting like a child who hadn't gotten his way. Maybe they could forge some kind of friendship. There weren't too many people to socialize with near the ranch. On occasion, Colby would bring the kids into Sherman to do some shopping. With only a general store available, the boys usually got a piece of peppermint, and Georgia sometimes picked up some fabric. That was pretty much the extent of their "socializing."

The last of these thoughts were swirling in his head when he finally succumb to sleep. His last thought was a positive one. Everything would work out for the best.

Chapter 5

Colby's hope that everything would work out for the best was dashed early the next morning as he tried to wake his new "wife." After several tries, and her just rolling away from him, he finally just picked her up and threw her in the back of the cart.

Half naked, wearing only a shirt and slip, Ginny turned and looked at her keeper. Her hair was undoubtedly a mess and her temper was worse. After only sleeping a few hours before the discomfort got to her, Ginny was in a foul mood. Camping was fine, when one had a tent, a cot, and an air mattress. This "roughing it" was for the birds.

"I guess we're getting up," she stated sarcastically.

"So nice of you to finally notice. We have a lot of miles before we get to Cheyenne. If we can get to Cheyenne today." Obviously, Colby was in a big hurry and didn't feel like pampering any princesses.

"May I have a minute before we leave?" Ginny had perfected her faux sweet voice and was using it on her new "husband."

Colby gritted his teeth and said nothing in return. He was now, more than ever, convinced he'd been duped. This woman would want to sleep all day and be catered to. Shaking his head, he went back to cleaning up the camp.

Ginny wandered into the woods and took care of her business. She put her skirt and shoes on, tried to pull all her loose hair back with the clips she had and drank from the stream. It only took her five minutes, but by the time she got back to the cart, Colby was waiting for her. Tim was seated next to him smiling.

"'Bout time!" Colby muttered under his breath.

"Grow up!" Ginny muttered right back at him.

The cart drew forward to what promised to be a fun-filled day.

They only stopped a couple of times for bathroom breaks and to water the horses. There was no cushioning in the back of the cart, so Ginny sat on hard wooden slats. The road was decent, but that didn't make the ride smooth, so by the time they stopped for the night, Ginny's ass would be black and blue. She was sweaty from the hot sun and covered in the dust from the road. Worst of all, she was bored out of her mind. Tim had run out of things to say after the first couple of hours, and she had sat staring at a whole lot of nothing for most of the day. She had to admit that the scenery could be breathtaking, but after a while, it started to look the same.

It was nearly evening as they approached the city of Cheyenne, Wyoming. Ginny hadn't been there in modern times, so she had nothing to compare it to, but it seemed a big town for the time period. For the first time since they set out, Colby finally spoke to her.

"We'll make camp on the outskirts of town. I have some business to attend in town, so you'll stay in camp with Tim." he said with no smile or no emotion at all.

"Okay." What else could she say? It wasn't like she had any money to buy something in the stores. And she didn't know anyone in town so she couldn't claim she had anyone to visit. She would just be happy to not sit in the cart any longer.

Tim noticed how worn out Ginny had gotten. "Maybe Ginny and I could have supper at the Bootleg."

Colby glanced at his friend. He wanted to dump them off at the campsite, then pick up some supplies and head over to a brothel for a few hours of "relief." He didn't want to worry about having to pick them up afterward. He came up with a compromise.

"How about I have them put together a meal for y'all to take to camp? That way, if my business goes long, you won't have to be waiting on me to return."

Ginny watched as Tim gave Colby a sideways glance. Colby turned and stared daggers at his friend in return. Then, they started talking in code.

Tim started with, "What kind of business do you have this late?"

"There are a few people I want to meet with," was Colby's response.

"What about?"

"The ranch, alright?" Colby's voice was low and suggested that Tim drop the topic in front of their guest.

Tim wasn't about to let it go, instead forging on and forgetting that Ginny was in the back of the cart. "Maybe I should go with you. Might need my help."

Colby couldn't believe his ears. He just wanted a couple of hours. It wasn't like Tim would go with him anyway, since he was so in love with his new bride. Struggling for an excuse that wouldn't alert his new "wife" to his plans, Colby said simply, "You won't want to go." Then he whispered, "I doubt Eloise would approve."

Of course, Ginny overheard the comment and figured out the plan. As much as she wanted to torture Colby for his childish behavior, she wasn't going to deny him his only chance to get laid any time soon. If this story went the way they usually did, it would be some time before they were having sex with each other. And, since he was the mega-hunk, she knew he wouldn't have some nasty disease from using what was currently available.

In the spirit of harmony, Ginny said, "I'm really pretty tired guys. I wouldn't mind having dinner brought to the camp, then hitting the sack early. That is, if you wouldn't mind staying with me Tim?"

Turning in his seat, Tim smiled at her. "Of course not, darling. We can dine at our camp and relax."

"Thank you."

Colby felt a little guilty about leaving them. He did need to collect supplies before they journeyed back to his ranch, but his plans to visit the brothel were pretty selfish. "I just need a few supplies. How about we all have supper at the Bootleg? Then I can run out in the morning for the supplies."

Ginny looked perplexed. Was she wrong about his plans? Or was he trying to martyr himself on some "no sex" cause. She figured it was choice number two. Turning her head to roll her eyes, she came back with a compromise of her own.

"I know you want to get back to your ranch as soon as possible, so how about a quick dinner? Then you should still have time to get your... uh... supplies tonight."

Colby turned in his seat and looked at her. She was being awfully sweet by allowing him some time alone. And she was doing it without making himself or Tim feel bad about it. Did she know what he wanted to do? No, impossible. She was most likely an innocent, or at least extremely inexperienced. She might know what men and women did in privacy, but she wouldn't know how crucial it was that he bed a woman or explode.

"That sounds like a good idea. That way I don't have to cook dinner and you can still get your... supplies." Tim smiled at Colby, then turned and shined his smile on Ginny. Ginny could only return his smile.

Once again, Colby was thinking too much. She couldn't know and if she did, what did he care? They had already agreed that their arrangement was to be only professional, so she would have no say in who he slept with anyway. What he couldn't figure out was why he felt so guilty about it.

"Fine." Ginny was realizing that Colby was a man of few words.

The cart stopped outside a nondescript brick building. There were a few other buildings around, but they were clearly outside the main part of Cheyenne. Tim came around and lowered the end of the cart and assisted Ginny to her feet. After sitting so long in the cart, she decided it would be prudent to walk around a bit to get some feeling back in her feet and legs. Colby and Tim watched her as she circled the cart, stretching her back by sticking out her chest. Both men continued to stare as she bent down and touched her toes.

"What are you doing?" Colby asked, sounding his usual perturbed.

"Stretching. I'm a little sore after sitting all that time." Ginny wasn't going to start a fight. She answered nicely and kept a smile on her face.

"Well, don't know about you two, but I'm hungry. Let's go inside." Tim just had a way to keep things even.

They entered the building and sat down at an open table in the front. There were few diners, so the bartender was able to come around quickly and take their orders. Both men, having been there before, knew exactly what they wanted, but without a menu, Ginny had no idea.

Both men ordered a steak dinner, then turned to stare at Ginny. Like a deer in headlights, she just stared at each man in turn, including the bartender. Finally, she relented.

"What's good here?" she asked with a false cheerfulness that she hoped covered her exasperation.

Each man then turned and looked at each other. The bartender decided to take pity on her and answered that his wife made the best damn fried chicken this side of the Mississippi.

"Sounds good to me. I'll take the chicken."

"What'll you drink?" the bartender asked flatly.

The men ordered beers, so Ginny followed suit. When both men stared at her incredulously, she asked, "What do you want me to drink then?"

Colby shook himself and looked at the bartender. "You heard the lady. Three beers, thank you."

With that, the bartender disappeared behind the counter and stuck his head through a hole in the wall to call out their orders.

"You like beer, Ginny?" Tim asked.

"I don't know. I just had no idea what they had and it seemed the safest thing to order."

With that, Colby snickered. "You could have had a sarsaparilla or something like that."

At this point, Ginny had had enough. "Look guys, I'm sorry if I'm so dumb that I don't know what a restaurant serves without a menu, and I don't know the proper beverage for a young woman like myself."

Tim immediately looked contrite. "Nah, Ginny. It's nothing like that. We've been coming here for a long time now and we didn't think that you wouldn't have known what's good. Sorry."

Ginny looked over at Colby to see if he had an apology waiting. She would have to wait since he was busy examining his fingernails for dirt. *Just let it go, Ginny. Just let it go.*

The beers arrived in large, glass mugs. It was warm and a little flat, but it would do. At this point, Ginny was too tired to care. Honestly, she just wanted something to eat and then off to bed, although she admitted that sleeping on the ground again was not her first choice.

Dinner came soon after and Ginny had to agree with the bartender. It was the best damn fried chicken she had ever had, this side of the Mississippi or not. She attacked it like she hadn't eaten in days, not knowing when her next good meal would be. It was served with sliced up, fried potatoes. No other vegetables were to be seen anywhere on the plate. Ginny had the feeling that it wouldn't be long on this diet before she had constipation issues. Maybe she could ask Colby to pick up some apples when he went into town to gather supplies. Unless he couldn't fit it in with his whoring.

The thought actually made Ginny smile. If she were truly the heroine, she should be righteously mad that her man was sleeping with a prostitute. However, he wasn't technically her man yet and she couldn't work up any indignation over someone she didn't even like at the moment. On the other hand, they were, for all intents and purposes, married and he should take their five minute marriage ceremony, vows included, seriously. At this thought, Ginny laughed out loud.

Turning to stare at her, Colby lifted an eyebrow questioningly. Before he could ask the obvious question, his friend got to it first.

"What's so funny, Ginny?" Tim was smiling as well.

"Oh, I just thought of something... humorous, you know."

"And that was...?" Colby asked, the only one not smiling.

Taking a deep breath, trying to decide if she should be truthful, Ginny's smile grew larger. Now she was trying to hold back a major case of the giggles. Tim started to laugh watching her and Colby's frown just got more pronounced.

"Well, I was thinking about our wedding ceremony..." Ginny snickered out the last word, before she burst out laughing. Tim kept laughing, but not because he knew what exactly was so funny. Mostly, he laughed because Ginny was laughing.

"And what was so funny about that?" Colby inquired, keeping a straight face and not seeing any humor whatsoever.

Calming down, mostly because her new husband looked so dire, she replied, "Well, it was just so silly. I seriously doubt that John is a minister of any kind or that it will be recorded anywhere. Seemed kind of superfluous."

"What's that mean, Ginny?" Tim asked, without any reserve.

Before Ginny could answer, Colby chimed in. "It means unnecessary. Although I don't disagree with you Ginny, I don't quite understand why that is so funny."

With all the power of a bucket of cold water being poured on her head, Ginny felt all the silliness dissipate. Taking a steadying breath, she responded as best she could without getting angry. "It's been a long day. I'm tired and more than a little punchy. I just got to thinking about it and it seemed funny at the time. Thank you so much for pointing out how wrong I am."

Colby felt her sarcasm like a slap to his face. Rather than apologize for his being such a stick in the mud, he just nodded his head in acknowledgment. The rest of the meal was eaten in silence.

After the meal was completed and paid for, all three returned to the cart and made it to camp before full nightfall. Ginny had only enough time to find wood for a fire and go to the outdoor outhouse before it was too dark to do much else. Tim completed the camp by laying out the bedrolls, starting the fire and filling his canteen from a nearby stream.

Once all was settled, Colby announced, "I'll take one horse into town tonight and see if I can arrange for some supplies that we'll pick up tomorrow. Don't bother to wait up." With that, he took one of the unhitched horses and left.

Sitting in front of the fire, Ginny still hadn't said a word. Tim sat next to her and offered her his canteen. Smiling, she took the offering and drank deeply.

"Colby just needs to get used to ya. He's been without a woman for a while," Tim offered.

"You make a lot of excuses for your friend, you know that, Tim?"

"Nah, it just ain't like that, ya know. He's a good guy. He pays us well and he's good to everyone. Even the Indians. His housekeeper is Navajo, ya know."

Ginny smirked. After spending over a year in Regency England, as part of the upper class, she was used to such ridiculous and flagrant racism. *Oh, he's a really good gardener... too bad he's Irish.* "No, I didn't know that. Good for him." Ginny came pretty damn close to not sounding sarcastic that time. She really did.

"Now, Ginny, don't be like that," Tim obviously translated her last trenchant statement. "He's a really good guy. I think once you two find some common ground, y'all get along like two peas in a pod."

There just wasn't any way to stay mad at Tim. He was a genuinely nice guy who wanted everyone to be happy. Maybe it had something to do with his new wife or his soon to be daddy status, but whatever the reason, she couldn't stay angry.

Smiling warmly Ginny nodded then bumped into him with her shoulder. Tim smiled in return and bumped her back. "Maybe you should get some sleep Ginny. We've got another long day tomorrow."

"Alright then, good night, Tim. Thanks for making this trip bearable."

"I never could refuse a pretty girl, ya know."

Ginny climbed into her bedroll again leery of creepy crawlies. Once settled, she stared at the fire until she fell asleep. It took a little more time tonight, since Ginny could feel her worn muscles relaxing slowly. She would probably be sore in the morning. Her last thought before falling asleep was wondering if she would ever know who she was and if it would end up being "the" problem.

Chapter 6

Colby rode into the town just as the nightlife started. He had already figured that most of the stores he would need to get supplies from would be long since closed for the evening. It wasn't his primary focus anyway. After passing several saloons and burlesque shows, he found himself in front of Ma Belle's.

Ma Belle, the original owner and operator, died a few years back. In her will, a will drawn up by Colby himself, she left the place to her favorite girl, Naomi. Wanting to profit from Ma Belle's reputation for fairness and cleanliness, Naomi kept the name and continued to operate the business in the same fashion. Colby was always welcome and even given a discount due to their business relationship.

After hitching his horse, Colby walked to the front door and knocked. Naomi herself answered the door with a smile. When she saw who it was she smiled genuinely.

"Well, do my eyes deceive me? Or could it be the one and only Colby Miller." Naomi, although well into her forties, still had the perfect girl next door face. She had big, brown eyes and reddish brown hair not yet marred by gray. Although her figure had filled out in the past few years since not actively working the brothel, she was still a stunner.

"Hi, Naomi. How's business?" Colby already felt himself relaxing. He realized that just being away from his "wife" was enough to help him unwind. He knew his problems weren't Ginny's fault, but she was the personification of those problems. It occurred to him that maybe he would never be able to have a friendly relationship with her.

"Good, good. But, you didn't come all this way to ask me that, did you?" Naomi had a soothing voice which had added to her popularity when she was a working girl.

"No. I was wondering if you were busy tonight?" Colby had always had a sweet spot for Naomi. Although much older, she never rushed him to finish the job and move onto the next. Besides, she didn't take too many clients anymore, so a guy didn't have to feel like he was just another lay.

Smiling seductively, she gave him her full attention. "Well, now darling, you know I don't really work that side of the business anymore. But for you, I will definitely make an exception."

Calling to another girl to watch the door for the evening, Naomi brought Colby up to her rooms. She kept a large room on the third floor for her private use. Not many men had ever ventured beyond its door, and Colby couldn't help but feel honored.

"Have a seat, darling. Can I get you a drink?" she asked, walking to a sidebar and holding up a whiskey bottle.

"Thank you, Naomi." Colby took a seat in a small sitting area on the side of the room. The bed, a big, four poster, was located on the other side of the room, behind a curtain that was currently open. First thing Colby did was remove his boots and hat. Propping his feet up on a small ottoman, he felt himself relax for the first time in days.

Handing him his drink, Naomi began to massage his shoulders. "Oh my Colby, you have a lot of tension in your shoulders. What have you been up to that is causing you to be so uptight?" The other thing about Naomi, she sounded like she cared.

Taking a long sip from his glass, Colby answered. "Got myself a wife."

The massage ended, and Naomi came around and sat in the chair opposite him. Concern marred her eyes, showing off the crow's feet. "Maybe we should talk first."

"Nothing to talk about really. I needed someone to take care of my brothers, and so I traveled all the way to Denver to buy a wife." Colby took another sip of the whiskey and continued to regard her. A stray thought occurred to him that this woman should be someone's mother. He quickly quashed the thought as it would have destroyed his purpose for being there.

Bending her head to the side, she stared at him for another moment before responding. "And this woman... she's not pretty?"

Colby could see she was trying to sort out why he would be here and not with her. Smiling, he said, "No, she's real pretty."

"Are you afraid you might hurt her because it's been awhile?" Naomi looked even more perplexed now.

"No. I just don't like her, is all." Now, he could feel himself chuckling. Colby could be sour, but after some whiskey, he loosened up a bit.

"Colby Miller, what a thing to say! If she's pretty, then what difference does it make to you what she has to say." Naomi had been around the block more than once, and she knew men. They were interested in few things. Top of the list was sex. Didn't matter what the girl looked like if she was willing to fulfill that top item on the list.

Colby proceeded to explain the tale of his new wife. Naomi listened with rapt attention through the tale, not stopping to ask any questions, although it was obvious that she had many. When Colby was done, she took his glass and refilled it and filled one for herself. Handing him his glass, she sat across from him once again and appeared pensive. Colby wasn't fooled.

"Seems like it wasn't her fault... this mess you're in. Maybe you should be a little nicer to her."

"I know that, Naomi." Colby looked down to hide his shame. "I know that she didn't ask for any of this. But I just can't help thinking that she's deceiving me. I just got this gut feeling that she's gonna be more trouble than she's worth."

"Darling, I haven't met a man yet who didn't think a woman was more trouble than she's worth. It's why Ma Belle was in business for so long." Arching her eyebrow, she knew she'd made her point.

"Very well. I'll try to be nicer to her." Colby answered more to his glass of whiskey, than to his companion.

Naomi put her glass on the floor and knelt in front of him. Catching his eye, he was forced to give her his attention. First, she removed the half drank glass from his hands. Then, she slowly unbuttoned his shirt. "I don't have any answers for you darling, but I think I can take your mind off your problems for a while." Her mouth turned into a sweet smile, seductive and alluring.

Smiling in return, Colby relished the feel of her hands on his chest. Closing his eyes, he pictured his wife's face and that was all he needed to prepare himself for his night out.

Chapter 7

Early the next morning, Ginny surprised herself by being the first one awake. The sun was just cracking over the horizon and the morning smelled of fresh dew and flowers. After stretching her sore muscles, she looked over at the men. Tim, once again, laid on top of his bedroll, with his hat over his eyes, snoring. Colby was on his side, facing away from the fire. Staring at her husband for a moment, she wondered if his position was caused by guilt over already stepping on their wedding vows. Before the giggles could beset her again, she wandered over to the wagon to look for a towel to wash up at the stream.

She was in luck, finding not only a towel, but a bar of soap and a metal pan to hold some water. The stream was a few hundred yards from their campsite and seemed isolated. There was still a chill to the air this early, but Ginny didn't think her chances of washing up would wait until it warmed up. So she removed as much clothing as possible without revealing all her charms, filled the basin with water, and began to wash the more crucial areas of her body.

She started with her feet, which were not only dirty, but smelled of sweat. Working her way up her body, she was happy to remove the grit that had accumulated under her breasts and in her armpits. The face and neck were next. When her body was as clean as it would get without an actual bathtub or shower, she bent over the stream and got her hair wet.

Few things in life creeped Ginny out more than dirty, stringy hair. As she scrubbed the hard soap enough to get a lather, she thought back to her first adventure. After being kidnapped by the dirty lowlanders, she could still picture the filth, the hair so dirty it looked like dreadlocks. The smell of so many unwashed bodies that one could hardly draw breath. Although she admitted that sometimes she missed the warmth of Ian's body, she definitely did not miss the poverty and desperation.

After rinsing the soap off, Ginny got out her brush, which was one of the few items in her bag, along with a change of undergarments and one other skirt and shirt. Ginny had every intention of wearing the new clothing today, in order to appear somewhat clean when she met Colby's family.

With the rhythmic brushing of her long locks, Ginny began thinking about Colin. Her previous husband, in Regency England, was still a bit of a sore point. No, she hadn't fallen in love with him yet, but she knew she was close. He was a very good match for her personality, although her temperament was ill-suited for the time period. Regardless of the level of society she got to enjoy, being a second class citizen would have worn thin after a while.

Still, they had just reached an understanding in their relationship that would have led to happiness for them both. Sighing quietly, she stared at the running stream, wondering "what if." As is often the case, "what if" always led to a sense of depression, which, although she had no control, Ginny felt that she could have done something more or different.

She lost track of time sitting there, watching the stream. So deep in her thoughts, she didn't hear her husband walk up beside her.

Colby woke with a start. It took him a moment to realize that it was Tim's snoring that startled him awake. Moving to lie on his back, putting his arm behind his head, he stared for a moment at the lightening sky. He was surprised that he woke so early, since he'd only returned to the campsite a few hours earlier.

He and Naomi had spent a few hours together, before she told him that she really did have work to do. It was nice, but Colby had to admit that he was picturing his wife's face most of the time. After leaving Ma Belle's he rode his horse through town for another couple of hours. He used the time to analyze the strange feelings he was having.

Colby couldn't be feeling guilty. After all, he hadn't truly married Ginny. Not to mention, they had made a bargain to keep things professional and not get tangled up together. So, what was it? He could be feeling guilty about being selfish and leaving her and Tim alone for the evening. He quickly squashed that idea. It had been months since he was with a woman and denying his needs would have made him even more ornery.

He thought about his conversation with Naomi. She had suggested that he be nicer to his "wife." Although he knew he should, he wondered how long before she said or did something to irritate him again. He was never the most understanding person. His mother used to tease him about his self-righteousness, always reminding him to walk a few steps in the another man's shoes.

Colby got himself up, not resolving anything except his need to empty his bladder. Once standing, he realized that Ginny wasn't in her bed roll. Scrunching his eyes together in confusion, he wondered if she had taken off. They were only a few miles from a city that she could effectively hide in. Walking over to the cart, he noticed that her bag was gone. Cursing softly, he wandered to the trees to pee. Then he would saddle his horse and go off looking for her.

Dammit, he thought to himself at the trouble she was putting him through. Didn't he just say to Naomi how she would be more trouble than she was worth. He might have just let her go, but he was five dollars poorer because of her, and he wasn't about to let that go. As he walked quickly to the stream to get a drink and wash up, he saw her sitting by the shore running her brush through her hair, but not paying it any attention. She was staring at the water looking so lost in thought that he wondered if she would even hear him approach.

He was practically standing on top of her, and she still didn't notice him. *What could she be thinking about?*, he wondered. She claimed to know nothing about herself, a victim of some amnesia. And yet, she was clearly working through something in her head.

Then, Colby noticed her expression. She looked so sad, so lost, that it nearly broke his heart. Her face looked like a small child, despairing over some loss. He was about to ask her what was wrong when he noticed that she was only wearing her slip, and it was practically see-through. Even after spending the evening with a beautiful and experienced woman, he felt himself harden at the sight of her full, plump breasts pushing against the taut fabric.

He stooped quickly next to her, alerting her finally to his presence. She didn't realize her state of undress, because she turned toward him, giving him a better view of her breasts. Raised to be a gentleman, he turned his head and stared at the stream.

"You're up pretty early, Ginny," he said, continuing his stare anywhere but her chest.

"I wanted to get cleaned up. Tim said we should be able to reach the ranch today. I didn't want to look filthy." Ginny's voice was robotic and flat. After so much introspection, she didn't have it in her to spar with him.

Colby considered admitting that he thought she had taken off on him, but decided against it. He was vulnerable enough around her without calling attention to it. Coughing against his discomfort, he said, "Well, we should get going soon. I was just going to clean up a bit myself then start loading the cart. We still have to stop in Cheyenne for supplies, then we'll be on our way. I don't expect to reach the ranch until after nightfall, so you may not meet my family 'til tomorrow." Colby forced himself to stop babbling.

Ginny noticed his discomfort and dismissed it. As far as she was concerned, it meant little. She stood up, grabbed her things and walked toward the woods to change. She turned and caught him staring at her as she departed. Perplexed, she entered the woods with her supplies and pulled out her clean clothing. As she began to change, she noticed her near nakedness. A smile crossed her face as she realized why he was uncomfortable. It wasn't because he had slept with a whore last night, but because he noticed her. She began laughing, finally breaking her from her funk. As silly as it was, it was exactly what she needed to keep going.

Returning to camp, Ginny saw that Tim was up and making a pot of what looked like oatmeal. Colby was busy preparing the horses and wouldn't look in her direction. Smiling, she said her good mornings to Tim.

"Good morning to you too, Ginny, " Tim smiled and continued his cooking. After packing her bag on the cart, Ginny went about rolling up the bed rolls and filling the canteens.

After breakfast, they were off once again for a seemingly never-ending ride. Ginny just didn't have the patience for this kind of slow going. Living in the 21st century spoiled a person. She liked that she could get anywhere in the world within a day. She could drive across the valley in an hour (obviously not during rush hour). She liked that she could go to one of the seven grocery stores within five miles of her house and get anything she wanted for dinner. Spoiled.

They picked up their supplies, and now Ginny was crammed into the back of the cart with crates of tools, fabrics, and household goods.

At least she could sit on one of the crates, which was just slightly more comfortable than sitting on the floor of the wagon.

Morning turned into afternoon, and Colby once again kept his thoughts to himself. Tim would point out landmarks and views of interest to Ginny, trying to keep her from falling asleep sitting up and falling over the side of the wagon. They stopped only a handful of times for bathroom breaks and to eat lunch. Each time, Colby would disappear into the woods and not return until it was time to move on.

As the sun was setting, Tim and Colby discussed whether they should push on or camp one more night.

"We made great time from Denver to Cheyenne. Nobody would expect us home tonight anyway," Colby said.

Tim looked uncomfortable. "Colby, nobody knows the pass like you do. We could press on and make it tonight. I miss Eloise something fierce."

"We have a loaded cart. It could be dangerous in the dark," Colby was hedging. He knew he could make it, but didn't want to get home yet. With something close to embarrassment, he didn't want to admit that he wasn't ready to show his family the real reason he left them several days earlier. Only Tim and Eloise knew that he had planned on buying a wife.

"Please, Colby. With Eloise expecting, I just want to get home as soon as possible." Tim's face was forlorn and Colby didn't want to cause him more pain.

"Alright Tim, we'll press on. But if I think it's too unsafe, we stop. Agreed?"

"Agreed. What do you think, Ginny?" Tim turned in the seat at the front of the cart and looked at her.

"I'm fine either way, guys. I wouldn't mind getting out of this cart, but am willing to put up with it for a little while longer in the hopes of more comfortable accommodations tonight." Ginny smiled when she said it, but since Colby wouldn't turn around, he missed it.

"What makes you think your accommodations at my home will be so much more comfortable?" he asked, sounding surly.

Tim immediately came to the rescue. "I don't think that's what Ginny meant, Colby. I don't think she expects a palace or anything." Tim chuckled, trying valiantly to stop the coming storm that he saw on his friend's face.

Ginny remained quiet. She was interested in how this would play out. Colby was ready to fight and after sitting in the back of the cart all day, so was she.

Colby stirred the pot a little more by saying, "How do you know what she expects, Tim. You know her as well as I do."

"How do you expect to know anything about me when you act like a child and refuse to talk to me?" Ginny kept her voice even, but it was obvious that she had every intention of shaking the bee hive.

Colby stopped the cart and turned fully in his seat to look at her. His face showed fury, pent up and boiling over. Apparently, he had been seething all day and this was just the type of conversation to let his anger loose on. "How would I get to know you? According to you, you don't even know yourself. Why would I waste my time talking to you when you couldn't answer a damn question anyway?"

Ginny's eyes narrowed, and she responded through clenched teeth. "I know enough to answer any question your simple mind could come up with. No, I don't remember my past, but I do remember how to treat people and act like a civilized person. I also remember telling you that I didn't expect anything from you except a fair chance to pay back my debt and get the hell away from you!" Ginny couldn't believe how upset she was getting. How could she get so caught up in these lives every time? Why couldn't she just lay back and enjoy the ride?

The look on Colby's face spoke of physical violence. Ginny flinched, as much as she hated herself for doing so. Colby noticed and was suddenly appalled with his behavior. He may be a simple rancher, but he was also a gentleman. He would never hit a woman out of anger or for any reason for that matter. Embarrassed, he got out the wagon and walked ahead a few dozen yards. He let his anger dissipate and waited a few minutes until he could trust himself again. He could hear Tim apologizing for him, again. After a few minutes, he walked back, climbed into the cart and drove off without another word. Even Tim was smart enough to keep his thoughts to himself, allowing Colby his time to settle down and get them all home.

It won't be too bad, Tim thought to himself. *After a couple of months, they'll get along just fine.* Tim hoped he was right, or he was probably going to be stuck in the middle until Ginny either left or killed Colby.

Chapter 8

Ginny sat quietly in the back of the cart as they made their way through a small trail between tall trees. In the fading light, Ginny got her first glimpse of the valley where they were headed. Surrounded by mountains to the north and west, the valley seemed to go on forever to the east.

They were coming south, through a mountain pass that could only accommodate one vehicle, but Colby seemed to be very familiar with it. Even in the limited light, he adjusted the cart perfectly, anticipating turns and drops in the road. He had the sure hand of someone who had taken this path many times before.

Once they had made their way into the valley, it was a straight shot to the only lights to be seen for miles. The moon was not full, so Ginny had little light to get a sense of the surroundings, but she could see several buildings, only a few of which were lit.

As if anticipating her, Tim explained, "That's Sherman. Small town, needless to say. We've got a mercantile, a top notch livery and feed store, and even a dress shop. There's the saloon, too. Some of the supplies in the back are for the folks in town. Then there's a bank that also doubles as a post office. Oh, and of course the sheriff's office and jail. We don't have much use for them too often."

"Are the other buildings homes then?" Ginny asked, liking the break in silence as they made their way across the valley.

"That's right. Well, except for the church. You go to church, Ginny?"

Did she? She didn't know, but figured she'd better. God knew she could use all the help she could get. "I haven't in a while, but I would like to. Is the minister nice?"

Tim chuckled a bit. "Well, he's very... what would you call it, Colby?"

"Pious." Colby was a man of few words, but at least he answered.

"Yeah, pious. He figures he knows how everyone should live and doesn't hesitate to let you know how that should be."

Ginny was about to tell a story, but knew that it would only make Colby more suspicious. It had been Ginny's experience that when someone is so sure he's right about something, especially religion, it usually meant he wasn't walking the walk himself. How many ministers in the 21st century had to confess to adultery, drugs, or general bad behavior? Ginny had to wonder what the minister of Sherman was up to.

The dirt road entered the town, and Colby turned east toward the livery. As they approached, Colby finally spoke to Ginny. "I want you to stay in the cart. I have to drop off some supplies to Noah and I don't want to do any introductions tonight."

Ginny closed her eyes and prayed for patience. Why did he have to sound so obnoxious? "Sure," was her only reply. If Colby could keep to one word answers, so could she.

Stopping the cart, Tim and Colby got out and picked up several crates. Ginny watched from the cart as they stacked the crates outside a set of barn doors, then walked up to the door of a home next door. She couldn't make out the conversation, but heard some laughter. Then Colby and Tim disappeared inside the home, leaving her alone in the dark.

Nice, she thought as she sat, not necessarily scared, but not precisely comfortable either. Even as she thought to get out and stretch her legs, a man walked out of the darkness and approached the cart.

"Hey, there, mishy. What's a lady doing all by hershelf in the dark?"

Ginny's heart caught in her throat for a moment, having been shocked by his appearance. Then she realized by the little light coming from the livery, that he was a little old man, who was extremely drunk.

Ginny smiled, no longer feeling any threat. "How do you do?" she asked.

"I'm fine. Do you have anyshing we can drink?"

"I only have water in my canteen, but I doubt that's what you meant."

"Nah. Do you have any money for a poor, lost shoul in need of a drink? That awful Mr. Pratt kicked me out of his est... estab... shaloon."

Ginny was trying hard not to laugh. This man was a perfect caricature of a town drunk. The slurring of words, the clothing, the smell all seemed too spot on to be realistic. It was characters like this one that let Ginny know she was definitely living in a novel.

"I'm sorry, but I don't have any money. I'm Ginny, by the way. And you are?" Ginny prompted.

"I'm Henry. I've lived here my whole life." Henry made a sweeping gesture that nearly knocked him on his knees.

"I'm pleased to meet you, Henry. Are you hungry? We have some leftovers from lunch. You look like you could use some food." Ginny wasn't kidding. Henry's face was cadaverous, and his clothing seemed to hang from his bones. Ginny didn't doubt that he had cirrhosis. If the light were better, she'd bet he'd be yellow skinned.

"Nah. Just need a drink, is all." Henry looked disappointed. He leaned heavily against the cart, as if he no longer had any will to stand on his own.

"I'm sorry, Henry. Maybe by the next time we meet, I'll have some money."

"Don't give him any money!" Colby nearly shouted. Ginny, for the second time in a few minutes, felt her heart stop.

Whipping around to see that he was next to the cart, she glared at him. "You move like a freakin' cat, Colby. Geez, I didn't even hear you walk over."

The damn man had the nerve to smile at her. It was gone as quickly as it had come. Colby then turned his attention to Henry, still leaning against the cart. "Get a move on, Henry. You'll get nothing from us."

Henry lifted his body, with a great deal of effort, snorted something unintelligible and wandered off in the dark. Ginny would have liked to do something for the old man, but what could she do? Liver transplant, no. Get him to stop drinking, unlikely. Even if he did, it was obvious that the damage was done and his days were numbered. Heaving a sigh, she turned back to Colby.

"Are you ready to leave?" Ginny asked, still remembering how they left her alone in the dark.

Picking up on her tone, Colby climbed back in the cart and kept his retort to himself. They were close to his home and he didn't want to start up the fight from the ridge again. He was tired and soul weary. Tomorrow would be soon enough to pick up where they had left off.

Tim rushed out of the house, calling a goodbye as he ran to the side of the wagon. Turning to Ginny, he said, "We're so close, now. Can't wait to see Eloise."

Ginny smelled liquor on his breath and made an incredulous look back to him. Part of her wanted to say something, but another part just wanted to get out of the cart and lay down in real bed. Not that she was sure she would be getting a real bed tonight or ever.

Seeing her look, Tim scrunched his eyebrows. "You seem kind of surprised that I would want to see my wife, Ginny." His voice was genuinely perplexed.

Shaking herself out of her mood, she said, "No, I'm sure you miss her."

Colby started the horses again, heading east toward who knew what. It was so dark, she couldn't see any road, but Colby seemed to know where he was going. Sitting on her crate, Ginny waited to see what would be next.

After a half hour of riding, Tim informed her that they were now on Miller land. Looking around, Ginny was hard pressed to determine how he could know that, with nothing much to see, but she would have to take his word for it. Colby certainly didn't object.

"See those lights there," Tim asked while pointing to the right. "That's my house. Eloise must have kept a lantern on in case we got home."

"Damn waste of oil," Colby muttered.

"Now, Colby, ya know that Eloise doesn't like being alone. If it makes her feel better having the light, I won't begrudge her that."

Colby smartly kept his next thought to himself. Ginny rolled her eyes behind him. He was so sullen that it hurt to be around him. Hopefully it wouldn't take that much longer to get to his house and away from him, however temporarily.

Stopping in front of the small log cabin, Tim jumped down just as the door opened. Ginny felt herself smiling as she watched the family reunion unfold. A petite woman, barely taller than the cart, walked out on the porch smiling.

"Hey there, missus. What's a beautiful woman like you doing all alone?" Tim asked.

"Well, I'm not alone now, am I?" she replied. It was hard to see her features, but she seemed very pretty.

Ginny heard Colby groan quietly in response to the couple. Although Ginny had to admit that it was a little too lovey-dovey for her taste, she was happy for Tim to be home. Whatever lay ahead for her at the Miller house, she knew that Tim would be a friend to her.

Walking together hand-in-hand, Tim introduced his wife to Ginny.

"Ginny, this here is my Eloise. Eloise, this is Ginny, formerly of St. Louie."

"It is a pleasure to meet you, Ginny. I hope you join me sometime this week for luncheon. I would love to get to know you." Up close, Ginny saw that Eloise had the look of a governess: prim, proper and very ladylike.

Colby couldn't resist when he said, "Well, Eloise, that might be a problem. See, Ginny doesn't remember anything about herself." His voice was filled with mockery, which wasn't missed by anyone.

Stunned, Eloise looked again at Ginny. "You don't?"

"No, I have lost certain memories. I only remember the man who made me the deal to come out here to be someone's wife. And the trip afterwards, obviously."

"Whatever happened to you? Oh, I suppose you don't know that." Eloise looked both shocked and embarrassed.

"No. I suppose I had some accident. I couldn't really say."

"Well, then we shall make all your future memories pleasant ones. I will stop by your house tomorrow and we can discuss where the children are in their studies." Eloise seemed to hedge a bit and added, "I hope I can also give you some tips on working with the two youngest boys."

Ginny had never heard anything more diplomatic in her life. From what Tim had mentioned, the two youngest boys excelled in getting into trouble whenever possible. She found she looked forward to meeting them. She would probably learn to regret it later.

"Well, we better get on our way," Colby grumbled.

"It was nice to meet you, Eloise. I look forward to seeing you tomorrow."

With that, Colby started the horses again and was heading off toward some distant lights on the horizon. Ginny leaned back on the crates, thinking about how good it would feel to be off the cart. Her head fell back and she looked at the stars. One of the things she liked about living in the past was being able to see so many stars in the sky. There was virtually no surface light to mar the scenery. What little she knew about astronomy didn't take from the joy she felt at a night sky filled with millions of stars.

So lost in her thoughts, she didn't hear his comment.

"What? Sorry. Did you say something, Colby?"

Sighing like she had suggested he be castrated, he replied, "I asked if you wanted to sit up front with me. I doubt it's very comfortable back there for you."

Ginny was stunned. Was he being nice? Was he extending an olive branch because they would now be living together? Best she take it, because it didn't look like she would leaving this world for a while.

"That would be great. Can you stop for a moment? In the dark, I'm afraid I'll fall off." Ginny kept her tone light, hoping that he would realize that she appreciated the offer.

Without a word, Colby stopped the cart and stood up to lend her his hand. Ginny lifted up her skirts, and scampered over the bench to sit next to him. She could smell him and it made her smile. Romance novel heroes always had the best smell. No sweat or body odor. Just a rugged maleness that's hard to describe. In this case, Colby smelled of woodsmoke, musk and some kind of liquor.

The rocking of the cart was making her sleepy. Between the darkness and her weariness, Ginny was having a hard time keeping her eyes open. Maybe she shouldn't have climbed into the front after all. She shook herself slightly to try to wake up. Colby misunderstood her action.

"Are you cold, Ginny?" he asked, in a voice that, for once, didn't sound angry.

"Huh? Oh, no. The movement of the cart is lulling me to sleep. I'm trying to stay awake so I don't fall off." Her voice was filled with laughter.

"Move toward me," he said, grabbing her shoulder and pulling her closer. "Put your head on my shoulder. I promise I won't let you fall."

Ginny did as she was instructed and felt that she had finally met the man she was to fall in love with. Only a few hours earlier it felt like Colby would have pushed her and now, he was being so sweet. It was a strange experience, when you first feel some kind of attraction toward someone. Love? Hell no. Lust? Not yet, but definitely some potential. Friendship? Hopefully.

Ginny felt her eyes closing to the roll of the cart and sound of the horses hooves. She'd never been one to fall asleep anywhere, usually having to rely on medication to help her out. In this case, the combination of a warm, nice smelling body, rocking movement and steady beating sound was just too much to ignore. Ginny fell asleep.

Ginny awoke the second the cart stopped. She thought it might have been because her body had longed to get out of the cart for so long, it wouldn't miss its chance. Still, she had to fight some disorientation before realizing that they had stopped in front of a large, wood sided house.

"I'll get you settled, then I can take care of the horses."

Hmmm, still being sweet. "No, I'll help you. I'm awake." To prove her point, she hopped down out of the cart without assistance. To not prove her point, her knees buckled and she had to grab the cart to keep from falling on her face.

"You can barely stand," he said with noticeable exasperation.

"I've been sitting for a while. I just need to walk around a bit. Please. I really do want to help." Ginny meant every word. She didn't like being a burden, and Colby had to be as tired as she was. The least she could do was repay his recent kindness.

"Alright, I have a few crates to unload for the house. The rest will go in the barn." He went to the back of the cart and started grabbing crates. Ginny grabbed one as well, and gingerly placed it on the porch. Going back to the cart, Ginny grabbed her bag and placed it on the porch next to the crate. Colby stared at her as she returned to the cart. *Not as spoiled as I thought.*

"Let's get back in the wagon and head to the barn." His voice sounded funny. Colby was rarely surprised.

"If you don't mind, I'll walk behind it. I really need to stretch my legs."

"Fine." Colby climbed back into the cart and drove the horses toward the barn. He arrived a minute before Ginny did and took the time to watch her silhouette as she approached. She was neither tall, nor short. She walked as if she hadn't a care in the world. He could see her head turn this way and that, looking around as if she could see in the dark. He remembered how pretty she was and knew he needed to shield his feelings. This woman could very well be the end of him.

"Sorry to keep you waiting. I was making sure I didn't trip over anything. What can I do to help?"

Again, Colby got that uncomfortable feeling like he'd been too much of an ass over the last couple of days. "How about you start unloading the crates and put them against the wall over there." Colby pointed to the spot he wanted his supplies. "I'll unhitch the horses and get them settled."

"Okay." Ginny went about her duty as quickly as possible. Some of the crates were heavy, but nothing she couldn't manage. When complete, she walked to Colby who was brushing one of the horses.

"Would you like me to do that?"

"Nah. I'm done. Let's head back to the house and call it a night."

Colby smiled and Ginny's heart skipped a beat. Oh yeah, lust could play a major part of this relationship. His two day old beard and his handsome features were playing heavily with her. Maybe she wouldn't have to wait too long for this romance thing to blossom. But if that were the case, it wouldn't be Ginny playing this part. Her experience told her that she was boned.

Walking side by side, Colby remained silent. He didn't know where this newfound acceptance had come from, and it scared the hell out of him. Hadn't he been thinking about all the trouble she would cause?

As they approached the house, Ginny tripped over some invisible obstacle. Colby grabbed her arm and pulled her against him before she could face plant. Before he could think better of it, he turned her towards him and stared at her eyes. There was little light, but he could see her expression. She looked embarrassed and of wanting to be anywhere else at that moment.

"I'm sorry. I'm not usually that clumsy." Ginny was shocked at how quickly Colby had caught her. His face looked amused, which only made her madder. *Yeah, like you never tripped before, asshole.*

Seeing her expression change from embarrassment to anger, Colby figured he should get her to bed quickly before they were arguing in his front yard. The last thing he wanted was to wake up his family and introduce his wife this late.

Clearing his throat, he spoke quickly, "I think we should get to bed. It's late and we're both pretty tired. Let me show you your room." With that, he let go of her arm and walked toward the steps to his home.

The Miller family home had changed drastically over the years.

When his parents had first settled in this valley, there were only a handful of families. Most of the settlers were ranchers, like the Millers, but some had tried their hand at farming too. Colby's earliest memories were of a small, two room log cabin that his father made when he wasn't caring for their stock.

As his parents became more successful, and after a few years of good beef prices, his father decided to add on to their home. Now, the house had two stories, five small bedrooms, a parlor, a dining room, a kitchen and a bathroom. They even had an inside toilet, since walking across the yard with a few feet of snow on the ground had become very tiresome, especially with small children.

Colby loved the house but had no qualms about leaving it. He still would, if he could.

He walked Ginny up the stairs and opened a door at the top of the stairs. Walking inside, he lit a candle and turned to watch her expression. He expected to see disappointment, but was surprised.

Once Ginny saw the small bed, her eyes lit up with excitement. *Praise the gods*, she thought merrily as she dropped her bag that she'd left with the crates for the house. Smiling at Colby, she said, "Thank you. I can't wait to get some rest. Good night." Ginny knew she wasn't being very subtle but didn't care. She had a date with a bed!

"Well then, good night." Colby felt put off by her attitude. It seemed that no matter what she gave him, he wanted something different. He expected her to be disappointed, and when she wasn't, he was bothered by it. *I used to be able to read people so well*, he thought as he left the room and closed the door behind him.

Ginny changed into her nightgown, but since there wasn't any water in her room to wash up, she just went to bed. She could wash up tomorrow, she figured as she climbed between the sheets. The linens smelled a little stale, as if they'd been waiting for someone to use them for a long time. The bed wasn't her pillow top at home, but it was not sleeping on the ground either. Moving this way and that, Ginny finally found a comfortable position and fell fast asleep. Any worries she had would wait for morning, where she could confront them in the light of day.

Chapter 9

The next morning, Ginny awoke to screams of joy. *Apparently*, she thought to herself, *the boys get up pretty early.* Her one window showed that the sun had barely risen in the east. Fighting the urge to roll back over, Ginny pulled herself from the bed and went about getting dressed. Lamenting her lack of water, Ginny did the best she could with her body and hair. She put on her same traveling clothes that had seen better days, even before her traveling.

Ginny walked down the same steps she came up the night before, following the sounds of laughter coming from another part of the house. Entering a small doorway, Ginny peered into a kitchen, where a boy and a girl sat around an old wooden table eating breakfast. The smell of eggs and ham made Ginny's stomach gurgle so loudly that they turned suddenly and stared at her.

No one said a word for a full minute. The girl finally found her voice and said, "Oh, my. Please come, sit down and join us."

Afterwards, the little boy couldn't contain himself. As Ginny sat at the table, he began his inquiry. "Who are you? Did my brother find you and bring you home? Are you my new teacher?"

The girl, suddenly remembering her manners, put a hand on the boy's arm to stop him from asking any more questions. Smiling at Ginny, she apologized. "We weren't expecting guests. Colby didn't mention he'd brought anyone home with him. My name is Georgia, and this is my youngest brother, Nate."

Returning the smile, Ginny replied, "It's a pleasure to meet you both. My name is Ginny." Ginny wondered how Colby wanted to play this. They agreed not to be married, but she didn't know how he would handle any questions from his siblings. She decided to wait until he was around to answer too many personal inquiries.

"Where is your brother now? Is he going to have breakfast with us?"

"Nah, Colby already left to check the stock. He won't be around until this afternoon." Nate continued to shovel food into his mouth during his explanation.

Georgia, who had stood up to retrieve a plate for Ginny, began to dish out from a platter of eggs and ham. Handing her the plate, she offered, "Colby's been gone for a few days and needs to make sure everything went well in his absence."

Something about the way Georgia spoke reminded Ginny of all the ladies from her Regency England novel. Perhaps it was Eloise's influence, but it seemed that Georgia was striving to be extremely ladylike.

"Oh, and he didn't mention me at all, huh?" Ginny couldn't say she was surprised, just annoyed.

"No, he didn't. May I ask why you've come to visit us?" Georgia looked pained to ask, as though she was stomping on some piece of etiquette she'd practiced so hard to perfect.

"I'm... uh..." Ginny didn't want to say the wrong thing. After a moment, she decided to be as honest as she could. "I'm your new governess. I'm to teach the boys, and I suppose be a chaperone for you." Ginny addressed Georgia, since Nate had obviously grown bored with her when compared to his breakfast.

Georgia's eyes lit up with excitement. "That's wonderful. Since Eloise married, the boys schooling has been lacking."

"There's another brother, right? Frank?"

"Yeah, Frank left with my brother to check on the cattle. He thinks he's bigger than he is." With that, Nate shoveled one last bite in and left the table in such a hurry that he nearly knocked his chair over.

Looking embarrassed, Georgia said, "Don't mind, Nate. He's a little jealous because Colby started showing Frank how things are done around here. In a few years, he'll do the same with Nate."

"Of course," Ginny didn't know what else to say. All her siblings in her real life were much older. She had to live through a lot of "why does he get to do that and I can't" conversations with her mother.

"After breakfast, I can show you around." Georgia smiled again. She had a beautiful smile, with perfect white teeth. She was also stunning. Her hair was golden blond and wavy, coming out of a loose ponytail in the back of her head. Her eyes were sky blue, and she had a very flattering figure. Not that it mattered, but in this part of the world, a pretty and available girl were very sought after.

"That would be great. Should we collect Nate as well. From what I hear from Tim, he can get himself into trouble very quickly."

With a laugh that sounded almost musical, Georgia said, "Tim would know. He's always caught in the middle of one of their schemes."

Ginny was impressed with how mature Georgia seemed. At eighteen, she should be silly and frivolous. It was probably difficult to be either when living in the frontier.

"So, do you have any boyfriends?" Might as well cut to the chase.

Looking down into her lap, Georgia took on a bright, embarrassed hue. "No. I suspect that Colby would like to marry me off as soon as possible, though. No one has captured my heart as of yet."

Ewwww, she thought. Sounded like too much romantic drivel. It *was probably one of the things I'm supposed to do here anyway.*

"Well, you're still pretty young. There's plenty of time for marriage and babies." Ginny finished her breakfast and asked if there was anywhere to wash up.

"The bathroom is right behind that door," Georgia said while pointing to a door in the back of the kitchen. Walking her over, she opened the door to reveal a wash basin, toilet and tub. "The water is connected to the stove and should be very warm now. We usually wait until evenings to use the tub, since the hot water is more plentiful, but there you could fill the sink and clean yourself up if you wish."

Ginny stared at the toilet. It had been a long time since she'd seen one and wondered if it flushed. She couldn't imagine it did, since there was no sewer system around here.

"There are clean towels in the cupboard," Georgia stated as she pointed to a cabinet in the corner. "Why don't you clean up, and I'll go collect Nate for our tour. Will ten minutes be sufficient?"

Staring at the bathroom as if it were plated in gold, Ginny murmured her affirmation. She entered the bathroom and closed the door. There was no lock, so she would just have to take her chances. Opening the lid to the box like toilet, she saw that she was right. It was essentially a deep hole. Ginny wondered if there was something that was emptied occasionally or if they had made an extremely large hole. She didn't care, since it was clean and she didn't have to use the woods.

After using the lukewarm water from the water pump, Ginny left the bathroom feeling much better than she did before hand. She found Georgia and Nate in the parlor, waiting for her. Georgia smiled and Nate looked somewhere between pissed and annoyed.

"I don't see why I have to go and all. It's not like I don't know where everything is myself." Nate's statement confirmed Ginny's impression of his mood.

Before Georgia could say something, Ginny replied, "It's because you are so knowledgeable of the ranch that I need you to show me around. You undoubtedly know where all the most interesting sights are." Ginny smiled and batted her eyelashes at the boy.

Nate took the bait. "Oh, yeah. I can show you the special fishing spot at the stream, and where Frank and I like to hide our treasure, and where Nicki and Joey hide when there's thunder..."

"That sounds great," Ginny responded before he could continue. At that rate, their tour would take all day just waiting for Nate to finish his commentary.

The group set out, and Nate narrated the entire tour. He offered little tidbits of information that, at times, Ginny didn't even think Georgia knew about. Although she grew up on the same land, she grew up a girl, with different priorities and imaginings. The water hole to her was a moat around a fairy tale castle. Where to Nate and Frank, it was a vast sea where pirates ruled.

Ginny met their horses, their dogs and even their barn cat, Reggie. After seeing everything there was to see of the ranch, Nate offered to take her out on horseback to see the rest of the land.

"Maybe another day, Nate. I just got here and I believe Eloise is coming by soon to visit."

"You met Eloise?" he asked. The look on his face spoke of pure, unadulterated, puppy love.

Smiling, thinking about her early crushes, she answered, "Yes. I met her last night when we dropped off Tim at home. I only got to speak to her for a few minutes before we left to come here."

Slightly dazed looking, Nate said, "She is so pretty, isn't she?"

"Yes, she is. She wanted to discuss where she left off with your lessons. I hope that I can teach you as well as she did."

Georgia snorted at this, and Nate shot her a dirty look. Ginny decided that she didn't want to get caught up in whatever scandal was brewing, so instead suggested they get some water.

"Nizhoni probably made some lemonade. If Colby went through Cheyenne, he would have picked us up some lemons." And with that, Nate ran towards the house.

Ginny and Georgia turned to walk toward the house. Georgia wanted to say something, but looked as though she struggled on how to put it. Ginny, taking pity on her, just asked her what was on her mind.

"Eloise didn't really control the boys very well. They can really be a handful, Ginny. Eloise expected them to behave. When they didn't, she just... well, she just gave up. I hope you won't. Colby isn't around enough to discipline them, and Nizhoni has too many other things to do."

"I'll do my best. I'm not afraid to get my hands dirty. I'll figure out how to get through to them, you'll see." Ginny smiled to reassure Georgia, who in turn smiled back.

They entered the kitchen to find Nate already sucking down a glass of lemonade. By the stove, stirring a large pot of something that smelled like heaven, was a short, older woman. She had long, black hair, styled in one braid down her back. Her face was heavily lined showing both her age and life experience. Her coloring and features were Native American. She was the Navajo that Tim spoke of. From what Tim told her, Nizhoni refused to speak English, although she could understand it just fine. She mumbled something to Georgia, who retrieved two glasses from the cupboard. Nizhoni filled the glasses with lemonade and turned back to her pot. Georgia handed one of the glasses to Ginny, who walked over to the woman and said, "Thank you, Nizhoni. My name is Ginny and it is a great pleasure to meet you." She smiled as the old woman stared up at her face.

Grabbing Ginny's face with both hands, she mumbled something unintelligible, but kept eye contact with Ginny. Georgia translated.

"She says she welcomes you to her family, Ginny." Georgia's smile beamed.

"I know you don't like to speak English. I'm sorry that I don't know any Navajo." From what Ginny understood, during World War II, the Americans used the Navajo language as the only code that the Japanese were not able to break. If it was that difficult, she couldn't see how she could learn it proficiently.

"Too bad you don't speak Spanish, Ginny. She seems to like that language better than English."

Did Nate say Spanish? Ginny thought. You couldn't be a health professional in the Southwest without being able to speak some

Spanish. After a few years in a busy downtown ER, Ginny was more than proficient.

"Hablo español." Ginny saw the woman's face light up. She had to wonder why she would speak Spanish over English, so she decided to ask her. The woman went into a long story about her dead husband being Mexican, so they taught their only son both languages. It was the Miller family that taught him English as well.

Georgia expounded on Nizhoni's son. "His name is Antonio Vasquez. He's traveling at the moment, but he said he would be back soon to help with the ranching." There was something in her voice which Ginny assumed was admiration. Perhaps Georgia considered Nizhoni's son like a brother, to be loved like the rest of the family.

Ginny spoke to the old woman, asking in Spanish what she was cooking. The woman responded in kind, describing the stew, and the homemade bread cooking in the oven. The two women continued their chatter when Nate heard a knock at the door and went to answer it.

A few moments later, Eloise entered the kitchen carrying a few books in her arms. As soon as Nizhoni saw her, she turned back to her stew and ignored Tim's wife like she wasn't there. Ginny was momentarily stunned, not realizing the dynamic. Turning toward Eloise, she said hello.

"How are you doing, Mrs. Miller?" Eloise asked, her back ramrod straight and her expression neutral.

At the mention of "Mrs. Miller," Georgia, Nate and Nizhoni all turned and stared at her. *Crap*, she thought, realizing what a precarious position the former governess had just put her in. Thinking on her feet was a specialty, so this was not the disaster it could have been.

"Eloise, please call me Ginny. I'm not really Colby's wife." Ginny knew she had to fix this before Colby got home. She didn't need him being mad at her for yet another thing.

"Tim mentioned that you two were married. He bought you from a wife dealer." Eloise may be prim and proper, but she had no clue.

"Yes, he did. He saved me from what could have been a much harder life. But Colby and I agreed that I would be an employee only, not a wife. I would work for him to pay off the debt of buying me, then I would decide if I wanted to stay on with the children."

During this exchange, the three other occupants were turning their heads back and forth, like watching a tennis match. Nate's mouth was open, Georgia looked very surprised, and Nizhoni kept making strange tsking sounds.

"Oh my, I do apologize. So, the two of you... you aren't... there's no..." Poor Eloise. The harder she tried, the more frustrated she became. It was actually pretty funny. Nizhoni thought so as well, as she began laughing a deep laugh that Ginny always associated with heavy smokers.

"Eloise, why don't we sit in the parlor together. You can give me your information."

Georgia, being her most diplomatic, asked Eloise to stay for lunch. One look at Nizhoni suggested she might want to think better of it. Eloise, however, wasn't the quickest on the draw, so to speak.

"That would be delightful, Georgia. Thank you."

Turning her back on the group, Eloise led the way to the parlor. Ginny smiled at her new family and followed closely behind.

Reaching the parlor, Eloise chose to sit on the settee and motioned Ginny to join her. She went about fixing her skirts, waiting for Ginny to get settled, before picking up the books she placed on the table next to the couch.

"I brought over the books I've been using for the boys." Eloise handed Ginny the books.

Taking them, Ginny paged through the first few pages of the top book. "Why do you have these? Shouldn't the boys keep them here to do homework and such?" Ginny saw that the first book was a history book. She thought it would be interesting to see historical perspective in this time period.

"The boys would destroy the books, rather than read them."

Looking up from the book, Ginny could see that Eloise was not pleased with her teaching position on the Miller ranch. Hoping for honesty, Ginny decided she would hold off on the subtle and just jump into her questioning.

"Were the boys difficult to teach?" *Well, I wouldn't call that subtle.*

Smiling like she'd just eaten a lemon, Eloise expounded for a full twenty minutes on all that was wrong with Frank and Nate Miller. They were rude, obnoxious and dirty boys. Frank would constantly use profanity in his regular language, and Nate seemed to have an affinity toward mud.

"What sort of teaching position did you have before coming here, Eloise?"

"I worked for Mrs. Hopewell's School for Affluent Young Women. It was a lovely place, but I found myself needing to leave."

Not wanting to change her "lack of subtlety" tack, Ginny asked why.

Looking down, Eloise blushed. Clearing her throat, she said, "I don't really like to discuss the particulars. I came with the best of intentions, but it just wasn't an appropriate position for me. I worked well with Georgia, but I find that working with boys just doesn't suit my skills."

"Okay. Well, I appreciate the books, and I will keep in mind that the boys can be... boisterous. Thank you." Ginny smiled. Eloise was wound tighter than twine. Everything she described to Ginny sounded like "boys being boys." There didn't seem to be anything wrong with them other than their being young and male.

"Perhaps you would like to take a turn around the house with me. It is such a pleasant day, is it not?"

"Yes, great. I'll just go ask Georgia if she would like to join us." As Ginny was leaving the room, she felt relief. There was something about Eloise that just felt wrong. She struck Ginny like a ticking time bomb, that someone would eventually set off. Ginny wasn't sure if she wanted to be around for that or not.

Georgia was still in the kitchen with Nate. Nizhoni was off in the garden, picking some vegetables for dinner.

"Georgia, would you like to take a walk with Eloise and me?" Ginny was still holding the books in her hands, so she figured she'd put Nate to work on something productive. Taking the history book out and opening it to the section on the Louisiana Purchase, she placed the book in front of Nate at the table.

"Nate, while we're gone, I want you to read this section and be prepared to answer questions when I return."

"What?" Nate cried, turning a shade of red.

"Oh, did I speak in something other than English?" Ginny needed to take the upper hand immediately if she hoped to survive the Miller boys.

"Why do I have to do schoolwork and Frank doesn't?"

Ginny made a production of looking over both her shoulders. "Am

I missing Frank? Is he here?"

"No! He got to go with Colby."

"Well, then. I guess you answered your own question."

"What if I don't?" Nate's expression was precious to Ginny. She had nephews, and she had babysat them from the time she was twelve. Ginny was not afraid to put her words into action.

Knowing, by his own admission, that being outside was what made Nate happiest, Ginny replied, "I will lock you in your room until you read it."

"You... wouldn't... dare!" Nate dragged out each word, squinting his eyes like a gunslinger.

Ginny put both her hands on the table, put on her most cross expression, and stared right back at the young, indignant face. "Try me."

Nate, who clearly wasn't used to anyone standing up to him, backed down immediately. He made some sputtering noises but otherwise looked close to tears.

"Look Nate, if it will help, why don't you go outside and read. You could pick a nice spot in the meadow or the barn. I don't care where you read, just that you read it." Ginny felt like she was playing both good cop and bad cop. She had to gain his trust and make him realize that she was not the enemy.

Somewhat placated, Nate took the book and left through the back door. Turning toward Georgia, who had an expression of shock, she said, "Shall we?"

"Of course, Ginny. Let's."

"I can't believe how easily you got him to do an assignment Ginny." Georgia was going on and on. Judging by the look on Eloise's face, she was not just surprised, but also upset. It was clear that Eloise had never had such an easy time of it.

"I applaud your ability, but do you think it's appropriate for the child to do schoolwork outside? It could be a distraction."

Ginny wasn't in the mood for this. She was still tired from the journey and from sparring with Colby. What she really wanted was to sit down, put her feet up and relax for a few days before having to play this new part. Her frustration was already high from not knowing who she was or why she ended up here. As well as not being in her own world with her own friends and family.

"What difference does it make, Eloise? If he doesn't complete the assignment, then I'll make good on my promise to lock him in his room until he does. If it makes him more comfortable being outside, why would I care?" Ginny was trying to control her voice, but she didn't think she was doing such a great job.

Eloise seemed oblivious to her discomfort. "Yes, of course. But, in the end he will not learn how to sit still and take direction."

"He's ten years old. Short of tying him down, he is incapable of sitting still."

At this, Georgia started laughing. "After only a few hours, you know my brother so well Ginny."

"Your brother is nothing extraordinary, Georgia. He's just a boy."

After a few turns around the yard, Ginny had had it. Eloise, the lady she was, felt that the sun was too much today, and that she really should have thought to bring her parasol. So back into the house they went. Sitting in the parlor, discussing nothing in particular.

After a couple of minutes of meaningless chatter, Nate came flying back into the room with the history book.

"I'm done, Miss Ginny." He looked very proud of himself.

Jumping at the chance to leave the stimulating conversation of Eloise, Ginny jumped up and walked to the doorway. "Let's go and discuss it in the kitchen."

"Awww, Miss Ginny. Can't we go outside again?"

"Sure." Ginny caught the look on Eloise's face. Damn, wasn't it precious.

They walked to the barn and found some bales of hay to sit on. Ginny took the book and read a few lines in order to form a question. Nate answered every question correctly, demonstrating a photogenic mind.

"Very good, Nate. You are a smart, young man. Have you given any thought to what you might want to be when you grow up?"

"I dunno, Miss Ginny. I guess I figured I would work the ranch like Colby."

"Is there anything wrong with that?"

"No! I love this place. I don't think I would ever want to leave here."

Ginny smiled at her young charge. He had no idea what he was in for with puberty and wanderlust. Still, he was smart and strong willed. He would make a great ranch owner.

Not a moment later, Frank walked into the barn with his horse. Spotting his older brother and knowing for once he had the advantage, Nate took it.

"Frank, this here is Miss Ginny. She's our new teacher." Nate grabbed Ginny's hand and led her over to his older brother. Frank was nearly as tall as Ginny with chocolate brown hair and the same sky blue eyes as his sister.

Frank glanced at Nate, then turned his attention to Ginny. "Why the hell do I need a teacher. I know all I need to know to run this ranch. I bet this bitch knows nothing important anyway."

Ginny laughed. Loud. She couldn't help it. Eloise had warned her of Frank's propensity toward profanity. It was obvious that he used curse words to elicit some sort of negative response. It was comical.

"What the hell are you laughing at, whore?" Frank looked insulted.

Stopping her laugher long enough to answer, she stated, "Why do you talk like that?"

Frank was turning an amusing shade of pink. "Men curse. Women obey."

That was it. Ginny was doubled over, laughing so hard she had tears in her eyes. When she was finally able to collect herself, Frank looked close to murder. He was sputtering and now beet red.

"I'm sorry. I didn't mean to laugh. That was rude. I only laughed because I've heard babies curse better than you." With that, Ginny stopped laughing and looked him directly in the eye. "My grandmother cursed better than you."

"You bitch! I can curse plenty good. Why don't you fucking go cook me something."

Rolling her eyes, she saw her opportunity to make nice with Frank. "Listen, you little cocksucker. If you think I'm going to fucking stand here and listen to your shit, you've got it all wrong. Your life is worth less than piss and your education is worse. I can teach you how to curse, dickhead. But what's in it for me?"

Frank couldn't believe his ears. Eloise would have rolled over and died by now. Licking his lips, Frank considered his options. This woman had already used words he'd never heard before. She might be able to add to his vocabulary of swears. What could she want in return?

"What do you want?" Frank kept the indignation in his voice, but he clearly sounded desperate. Ginny smiled. She liked her men desperate.

"If you listen to me, do your lessons and complete your chores, I'll teach you new curse words. But, at the same time, you will learn a more effective way to communicate. Do we have a deal?"

Frank mulled over the deal. He'd have to do his lessons anyway, or Colby might take a switch to him. He figured he had nothing to lose, and he might learn more swears to boot.

"You have a deal, Miss Ginny," he said holding out his hand.

Shaking his hand and keeping it firm, she replied, "Thank you, Frank. You won't be sorry." Then she smiled. This might be easier than she thought.

Chapter 10

The two boys walked Ginny back to the house after Frank stabled his horse. She was asking them questions about how far along they were in their lessons. Surprisingly, or maybe not so, they were very close to the same level. Frank explained that after their parents were killed, he hadn't bothered much with his schooling. Nate, on the other hand, used what books he could find to escape the pain. Curiosity got the better of Ginny.

"What happened to your parents?" she asked in a quiet voice as they sat on the front steps of the house.

Frank looked away, while Nate looked her in the eye. "Flash flood," was his only response.

Ginny was from the southwest, so she knew all about flash floods. How a trickle can turn into a torrent in minutes. How people thought their truck could get through the water, only to find themselves clinging to the roof of the car, waiting for rescue.

She said the only thing she could say. "I'm sorry."

Nate looked away, but not before Ginny saw the tears in his eyes. He was only ten. He still needed his mother. Was this what Colby had wanted? Did he think she would make a good replacement? Ginny didn't have kids. Although she would admit to certain pangs at times, she knew she didn't want kids unless she was in a stable, committed relationship. She knew women who were so desperate to be mothers that they forgot all about the father part. Raising kids was hard enough that she could never understand willingly doing it alone.

Changing the subject, Ginny stated, "Well, it will be easy to teach you if you're both on the same level. We'll get started tomorrow after breakfast."

Frank turned back to her. "Sorry can't. I'll be going out with Colby again."

Ginny smirked. "Well, I guess we'll just have to talk to your brother at dinner. I'm here to teach you two, and that's exactly what I plan to do."

At this, Nate smiled. Frank, on the other hand, looked pretty peeved. The sputtering started again, and Ginny waited.

"Bitch!" was all he could come up with.

"Bastard!" was Ginny's not so clever response.

"Dammit!" Nate said just to join in the fun.

It was after this productive exchange that all three of them turned to see Eloise and Georgia standing by the open door, behind the screen. It was Eloise's gasp that alerted them to their presence.

"Ginny, may I please speak to you inside the house?" Eloise looked appalled. Georgia was surprised, but her eyes spoke of laughter.

"Of course, Eloise. Excuse me, gentlemen. I'll put together some lessons for tomorrow, but for now, I want the both of you to figure out the easiest way to retrieve one bale of hay from the barn and place it at the bottom of these steps." With that, Ginny stood up, brushed off her bottom and entered the house.

As she walked away, she could hear the two brothers arguing over what would be the easiest way. The last thing she heard Frank say made her smile. He asked what Ginny meant by easy. It showed a quiet intelligence that Ginny could work with. And it would make her job so much easier.

"What do you think you're doing?" Eloise asked, shocked to the core.

"What do you mean, Eloise?" Ginny responded, knowing full well what the former governess meant.

"You cursed to those two young boys."

"Yes, I did."

"You don't find that behavior improper?" Eloise had a superior look upon her face, and it made Ginny want to wipe it off all the more.

"Eloise, did you have an easy time getting through to those two?"

"We were making progress. I feel, that with time, I could have gotten both of them to behave more like gentlemen than wild savages."

"They're boys, Eloise. Part of them are wild savages. They can't help themselves, especially Frank. He's growing up and wants to be a man so bad, he's invented this theory that cursing will help him achieve it quicker. If I tell him not to, he'll just do it more. If I get on his level, he's bound to listen to me. And if he listens to me, I can get some knowledge crammed into his head."

"But what of books? You have them doing something fun and trivial."

"I beg to differ. It may be fun, but it's certainly not trivial. It's teaching them how to think, work out a problem, solve a riddle. It's developing their brains and making them work as a team. These are skills that will be valuable to them as they grow up and later in life."

"Frank needs to work on his reading skills..."

"I know, Eloise. But if I can reach him on his level, he'll respond to other things as well."

"It is highly unorthodox, Ginny." The pious sound to Eloise's voice was wearing very thin.

"I guess we'll just have to wait and see if it works. But, you gave up this job, so it's my turn to give it a try. I'll do it as I see fit." Ginny tried to keep her voice kind, but she was never one to listen to such condescension.

The look of hurt on Eloise's face was obvious. It would never occur to her that she was being anything but helpful. "I'm sorry to intrude on your domain, Ginny. I was just trying to be helpful."

Realizing that she might need Tim's help someday, Ginny knew she had to make this right. "No, I'm sorry, Eloise. It was a long journey here, and I'm still very tired. I don't mean to snipe at you. I just want to give my way a try first. If it doesn't work, Colby's vowed not to pay me." With that, Ginny smiled to reassure Eloise that she wasn't mad.

Seeing an area where she can show off her superiority, Eloise stated, "Well, I wouldn't put up with anything from him, Ginny. After all, you are not really married, and although he may be your employer, you still deserve respect. Believe me when I say that this job is hard enough without him threatening you."

"Too true, Eloise. I thank you for all your help." Ginny was proud that she didn't sound the least bit sarcastic.

A moment later, Colby walked in the front door, holding his younger brothers by the scruff of their necks. Before Ginny could say anything, Colby asked, "My brothers told me that you told them to move a bale of hay from the barn to the front door. Is that true?" Colby looked as though experience had taught him to be skeptical of anything his brothers might tell him.

"Please let them go, Colby." Ginny recognized the look on Colby's face. It was his impatient look. One she'd seen many times in the two days it took them to get back to the ranch. Placating him, she said, "Yes, I asked them to move a bale of hay."

"You best not be protecting them, Ginny. These two have gotten into enough trouble. I need someone who can handle them, not baby them."

Now, that made Ginny mad. "Let them go, and I'll explain."

Colby released his two brothers and folded his arms over his chest. (His muscular, well-formed chest.) It was clear he expected an explanation.

Turning to the boys, Ginny asked, "Well, gentlemen, what did you come up with?"

Frank spoke up first. "We decided that the easiest way to move the bale would be to use a cart. But, we couldn't find one."

Nate, not wanting to be left out of the explanation, chimed in, "Then, we thought we could carry it between us. But, it was too awkward and we kept dropping it."

"You kept dropping it, ya mean. Then, we figured we could roll it. We've seen some of the ranch hands do that. So, between the two of us, we rolled it all the way to the front steps."

"Very good, gentlemen. You've done a fine job. What did you learn?"

Frank and Nate looked at each other, then Frank ventured, "Well, we had to talk about what we wanted to do."

"Yeah, and we had to work together because rolling it over takes a lot of strength, even for the ranch hands," Nate added.

"Yeah, yeah, and we had to figure out what we could do with what we had available."

"Very good. Now, please return the bale back to the barn and get cleaned up for lunch," Ginny grinned at the two boys as they ran out the door.

Turning to see Colby's expression, she knew he was not impressed. Incredulous, maybe, but definitely not impressed. He took a deep breath and turned to Eloise.

"Are you planning to stay for luncheon, Eloise?" His voice was polite, but carried some strain to it.

Not noticing his restraint, Eloise smiled and said, "Why, thank you Colby. Is Tim around?"

"Yes, he's in the barn. Could you let him know that he's welcome to join us as well?"

"Certainly." With that, Eloise left through the front door.

Georgia, who had witnessed the entire exchange, followed Eloise out the door. *Smart girl. I would rather be somewhere else as well,* Ginny thought.

Deciding to be nice, Ginny suggested they sit down in the parlor. His expression still bleak, he extended his hand to suggest she go first. Of course, Ginny thought, he might be acting the gentleman. On the other hand, he might be waiting for her to turn her back so he can do something awful. Smiling, Ginny accepted his invitation and walked to the nearest chair.

Sitting down, she adjusted her skirts and waited. Colby was pacing the floor. She considered speaking first, but then decided to let him get to his issues in his own time.

Clearing his throat, he said in a deceptively quiet tone, "I believe I am to pay you for teaching the boys. Not inventing silly games for them to play." Colby stopped his pacing and faced her dead on.

"Actually, Colby, we've never really discussed what my duties are to be. Tim mentioned that the boys needed a new teacher, and you alluded that they needed a maternal figure. But other than that, we've discussed nothing."

"I guess I thought it was pretty obvious."

"I'm sure you did think that, but that doesn't make it true." Between two days on the road with Colby and then a few hours of Eloise, Ginny was done.

Colby's eyes narrowed as he considered his next words. Ginny was no pushover, much like Eloise. As a matter of fact, if Tim hadn't fought so hard for Eloise, she would probably be in the same position, miserable from the boy's torture. Ginny, on the other hand, was a whole different animal.

"I want the boys to learn the basics. Reading, writing, math, and whatever science you can offer. Is that clear enough?"

"Perfectly. However, I wish to teach them the way I see fit. Even if that means using silly games to do it."

"It's a damn waste of time. I should have returned today to see them in the classroom we set up in the dining room, learning something productive."

70

Ginny bowed her head and took a deep breath. It was time to show this arrogant jackass what's what.

"You leave this morning before I get up and take one of my students with you. You give me no instructions. You didn't even warn your family of my being here. I walk into breakfast, with your siblings staring at me like I had two heads. So, I have to introduce myself. You never showed me the classroom or the books. So, how exactly was I to do what you expected me to do?"

Colby was prepared to give his answer when he stopped and really considered what she'd just said. How could she have known? He left before dawn, he did agree to let Frank come with him, and he never left any instructions for her. Instead of apologizing, he asked, "So what did you do all morning?"

Ginny's jaw dropped. *He has to be kidding*, she thought. The man was perplexing, to say the least. He obviously couldn't say sorry if his life depended on it.

"Well, I got up and had breakfast. Then, Nate and Georgia took me on a tour of the ranch. I met Nizhoni, and then Eloise came by. We talked for a while about the boys. I gave Nate an assignment, which, by the way, he did brilliantly on. Then I met Frank and got to talking to both boys to assess their skill level. Eloise wanted to talk to me again, so I gave both boys another assignment to do. Then you came home and acted like a big jerk. And, now, here we are." Ginny made sure to keep her voice light and her expression pleasant.

Colby was not amused. His arms were still crossed over his chest. His expression was still angry. His body language gave the overall impression that this would not turn out well. Two stubborn, pig-headed people trying to deal with one another never turned out well. Would this be the one exception? Ginny seriously doubted it.

"Do you expect me to pay you for today?" His voice was no longer very calm.

Standing up, Ginny stood right in front of him. If he was going to hit her, she might as well make it easy for him. "I don't care what you do, Colby. Just back off of me, before this gets ugly."

Clearly stunned, Colby took a few steps backwards. Ginny had to admit that it felt good to scare him for once. Realizing his position, Colby turned and left the room, going out the front door.

Ginny took a deep, calming breath and went to the kitchen where

71

she assumed lunch would be served. If she couldn't have peace with the head of the household, she might as well get really fat on Nizhoni's fine cooking.

Walking from the house, Colby went straight to the barn. He took his horse, which he hadn't bothered to unsaddle, and rode hard out toward the southern plain. All he wanted to do was put some distance between himself and his... his what? Not his wife, not his intended. His brother's governess... teacher? He didn't know what to call her.

It would have been easier to assess if the last ten minutes of their conversation hadn't turned him on so much. When she stood up and stared him in the eye and told him to back off, he just about split his pants.

Ginny was a brave woman. He hadn't met too many women willing to stand up to him. Of course, he hadn't been in any situations where a woman would have to stand up to him.

Many of the conversations he'd had with Eloise had ended with her backing down almost immediately. The few times she found the courage to speak to him about his brother's behavior, he had managed to quash any suggestion that he handle the situation. After all, he wasn't paying her to do her job for her, was he?

He knew that Frank and Nate were a handful. But what was he paying a teacher for if she couldn't handle them? Colby had too much else to worry about without having to deal with that as well.

He'd always admired strong women. His mother was strong, as any woman would have to be to live on the frontier. She helped his father build their home, gave birth to seven children, five of which lived, and took care of all the household duties herself. His father would often be riding his cattle down south for market, leaving his spouse for a month at a time to care for all his children and his home.

Naomi was a strong woman too. Over twenty years earlier, she came out west to avoid her preacher father's influence. When things got tough, she hooked up with Ma Belle and made a name for herself as a whore. Not an easy life for anyone, but she was smart and saved her money. She helped Ma Belle run her business and which became one of the most successful brothels in all of Wyoming Territory. In the end, it paid off, with her taking over the business and continuing its success.

And now, there was Ginny. Strong, independent and as far as he could tell, smart. When she told the boys to return the bale to the barn, they didn't hem and haw, but jumped to it. And that after only knowing them a few hours. What did she do to inspire that kind of obedience?

Reaching his destination, a small watering hole, Colby climbed off his horse and allowed the animal to drink. Picking at a cattail near the edge of the water, he started swinging it around like a sword, just as he did when he was a kid. He and his older brother, Robert Jr., would spend hours pretending to be pirates or knights of England.

It was days like this that he missed RJ the most. At eighteen, RJ announced that he was off to make his way in the world. He needed to prove to himself that he was a man, despite his mother's begging and his father's pleas.

Colby thought about all the letters they'd received in the ten years since RJ had left. They came from all over the world: Europe, Africa, the far East. Each letter that his father would read, would only make Colby wish more to be away, doing his own thing as well.

So, when Colby turned twenty-three, he too left the ranch to make his way in the world. He moved to Denver and became an apprentice to an attorney. It was his hope to save up his money and move east to go to a university and study the law formally. Then, after gaining an acceptance to Columbia University in New York City, he had received word that his parents had been killed by a flash flood, not far from their ranch. The blow had been devastating, and he returned immediately.

His younger siblings were in no position to run the ranch, and his closest friend, Antonio was no where to be found. It was up to Colby to take over and give up his dreams of practicing law.

The last nine months had been a living hell. Not only had he lost the two most important people in his life, the two people who believed in him more than anyone else, but he had to give up his dreams as well. That and being saddled with caring for his family, instantly the patriarch, some days it took every ounce of Colby's will just to get out of bed.

In the end, Colby should be thankful that Ginny was so strong. Maybe she would stick it out longer than Eloise had. Maybe she could get through to his brothers. And maybe, she would just end up driving him mad, with anger, exasperation, and worst of all, lust.

Chapter 11

Ginny sat in the Miller kitchen, talking to Nizhoni about her cooking. The old woman was quite the gossip, providing small details about the Miller family that Ginny doubted she would have ever found out on her own. For instance, Nizhoni loved telling Ginny the story of how Colby and her son Antonio stole a couple of horses so they could ride to Cheyenne to visit a brothel. They were discovered the next day, lost in the wooded area just north of the ranch. They were thirteen at the time.

Ginny wished she could share some stories with the old woman. So far, it was the only relationship that made much sense. But without any memories from the body she inhabited, she was out of luck. It wouldn't be very appropriate to tell her stories from the future, no matter how amusing the look on the old lady's face would be.

It didn't take long before the rest of the clan joined them in the kitchen for lunch, everyone except Colby. As Ginny ate her cold meat and bread, she wondered where she'd driven him off to. Surely she hadn't intimidated him that much. No one else seemed surprised that he wasn't joining them, so she kept her thoughts to herself.

After lunch, Ginny made the boys help Nizhoni clean the kitchen. The old woman was delighted for the help, especially from the two youngest Millers. After the kitchen was clean, Ginny took the two boys into the dining room to look over the books.

Ginny had a lot of work ahead of her. She had never taught children before. She'd helped train new physician assistants, but that was adults only. Her nieces and nephews had told her about their time at school, but she wasn't sure that was enough information to provide a formal education to two errant boys. She knew the information, but did she know how to teach it?

As she sat rifling through the books, Colby walked into the dining room. His face was passive, but it was only a matter of time before that changed. Ginny was beginning to think he was moodier than a teenage girl with her period.

"Nate, Frank, could you please excuse us for a moment?" Well, at least he sounded pleasant.

Nate and Frank turned to Ginny for confirmation. Ginny gave the slightest flick of her head and off the boys went. Before they got out of earshot, she yelled, "Keep reading, boys. There will be a quiz."

She could hear them hem and haw as they left the house to presumably read outside. It occurred to Ginny that she shouldn't leave those two alone for long. It would lead to trouble.

"What can I do for you, Colby? Sorry you missed lunch. We had lots of fun chatting it up." Ginny kept it neutral, but part of her was dying to bait him.

"Yeah, uh, I had something to take care of... in the fields, ya know." Ginny didn't know, but took him at his word.

She waited patiently for him to get to whatever it was he wanted to talk about. Keeping her eyes on him the whole time, she saw that he paced nervously. He would stop and look back at her, but before he would utter a word, he'd begin pacing again.

What the hell, she thought as she watched him burn a hole in the carpet.

Finally, after a few minutes of pacing, Colby sat on one of the available chairs. "I wanted to get some things straight between us."

Finally, Ginny thought that this would be the apology for his behavior earlier.

"I would like to get a plan from you on how you will go about teaching the children. Maybe you could put something together before dinner, and we can discuss it afterwards."

Before dinner? "Colby, I've never taught children before." *Wait, I might have.* "As far as I can remember, I've never taught anyone before." *Good save!* "I'm only now going through their books, trying to decide what do with them."

His stare turned cold and Ginny realized it was time for yet another fight. A person could only walk on so many pins and needles before they bled to death.

"How long do you need?" Ginny would have thought he was being reasonable, except for the exasperated sound in his voice.

"Give me a few days. I will be able to assess where the boys are in their books by then. I will have a chance to see what materials I have and get a better idea of a lesson plan."

"I'll give you until tomorrow after dinner."

All sorts of colorful phrases came to Ginny's mind, but she knew that it would not help the situation. So, in keeping with her own personable, pleasant personality, she said, "Or what?" Ginny could be a diplomat when she wanted to be.

"Or what?" he hissed. "Or you will be out of a job."

"And you will have no one to rein in the boys, and you will be out five dollars. So, instead of taking it to that extreme, shall we see where I am tomorrow night and reassess?"

Colby was in trouble again. He could feel himself responding to her. Felt his insides begin the slow burn of passion. Along with the passion, though, was also anger. How dare she speak to him like that? He was the head of this family and he deserved respect. Colby focused on the anger, trying to keep the passion at bay.

"Ginny, I don't think you realize your position here," he muttered, through clenched teeth. "I'm the employer, you the employee. What I say, goes. Got it?"

"Colby, I am happy to listen, but I won't blindly obey. I also would be happy for your suggestions, since you know your brothers a lot better than I do. But if you are going to come to me every day, in a pissy mood, and try to bully me, then you're right. It's time for me to leave."

Colby realized he had no where to go, in his reasoning anyway. So instead, he muttered something about seeing her at dinner, and left the room. Would he ever win an argument or hear a sorry from her? He was beginning to see that he probably never would.

Chapter 12

A few days later, Ginny had begun to settle into her routine. The boys were both intelligent and creative. She had come to see both qualities when witnessing some of their stunts, each more interesting than the last.

Nate was a brilliant planner and strategist. Ginny realized it was usually his idea that the two executed. Frank, on the other hand, could build anything from the simplest materials. In her head, she began to call him MacGyver. Frank could make a bomb from a toothpick, a rubberband, and a paperclip.

She had to admit that she was really starting to like the two kids. Sure, she had to sit through Frank's feeble attempts at cursing. Never in her life, either before she started living romance novel lives or after, did she ever think she would be correcting a thirteen year old boy's use of swear words. Just that morning, Ginny found herself saying, "Frank, you might want to consider using jackass, instead of cow shit. I think it flows better."

Nate had a quiet strength about him. He was the observer, taking everything in and seeing what he could use. He didn't speak much, and almost exclusively to Frank, but Ginny felt him coming out of his shell.

They decided that afternoon that the weather was too fine to sit inside and do their lessons. So the three set out for the meadow with a picnic basket prepared by Nizhoni and sat on the blanket doing their math. Ginny had some math skills to her credit. She could calculate a tip in record time and figure out how much something cost after the percentage discount. But when you added letters with the numbers, she was lost. Thankfully, the books they had were still basic, concentrating mostly on fractions and percentages, and the usual adding, subtracting, multiplying and dividing. All things that even Ginny could handle.

After going over their lesson sheets, the cheerful group got to talking about the neighbors and the townsfolk. It was Saturday, and they would all be attending church the next day. So Ginny decided to ask about the minister.

"Oh he's real mean, if you ask me," Frank replied.

"What does he do to make you think that?" Ginny asked, hoping that the two tight-lipped boys might expound a little.

Nate scratched his head and replied, "Well, for one thing, he calls Nizhoni a heathen. Just 'cause she ain't the same religion."

"She isn't, not ain't." Ginny said automatically. "I find that some religious people are not very open-minded."

Frank liked this idea. "Yeah, all the stories the preacher's wife told us during Sunday school said that Jesus liked everyone."

Smiling, Ginny asked, "Do you still go to Sunday school?"

"Nah, we sit with the regular service now." Nate sounded as though it wasn't by their choice.

"Are you too old," Ginny asked, suspecting that the two had gotten into some trouble to cause themselves being kicked out of Sunday school.

Both boys looked in any direction but Ginny's. Neither had a chance to respond when Colby walked up.

"Why are you out here when you should be in the classroom?" It came as no surprise to hear him being surly. Ginny had grown accustom to it.

"It was such a beautiful day that we decided to do our math lessons outdoors," Ginny had also perfected her "cheerful despite his anger" voice.

"Boys, go back to the house. Take all this..." Colby waved around at their picnic. "with you," he concluded when the right word wouldn't come to him.

Ginny stood up and helped the boys pack up their basket. Not a moment later, both boys were off toward the house. Before they were out of earshot, Ginny called, "You both have to read two chapters from your readers this afternoon." Their reply was more hemming and hawing. They were always amazed that Ginny could remind them of their duties, even before being chewed out by their big brother.

Turning toward Colby, Ginny prepared to listen to his complaints. That's all she'd heard since her arrival. She never gave him a lesson plan, she didn't teach the boys the way he thought they should be taught, she didn't help out enough. Every accusation she was able to defend which only made Colby madder.

"This is a damn waste of time."

That's the best he's got, Ginny thought. *Weak, truly weak.*

"I beg to differ. The boys are excelling in their math, especially Nate. I was going to ask if I could order some higher level math books from Cheyenne." The trick was to not get mad in return. Something that wasn't going to work much longer, because Ginny was reaching her end.

"We've discussed this, Ginny. Eloise always kept the boys in the classroom, and she's a professional teacher. Maybe you should go and talk to her about lesson plans."

Well, that was the end. "And what did the boys learn from her? From what I hear, they got in even more trouble because she never got through to them. The boys and I have connected. Have they gotten themselves in any real trouble since I came? Have I complained even once about their behavior to you? No, I haven't. If it ain't broke, don't fix it!" Ginny's voice became more elevated during her speech. Colby's eyes got even wider.

Moving forward and standing right in front of her, Colby looked down into her eyes. Keeping is voice low, hissing at times, he said, "I will decide what is appropriate. I will decide what is best for *my* brothers. You are, at best, a short term guest in my home. Don't push me on this, Ginny. You would do best to heed this warning." With that, Colby turned and walked back toward the ranch at a fast clip.

Ginny stood and watched his retreat, feeling her heart pounding in her chest. *Damn him, damn him to hell.*

She hadn't done anything wrong. As a matter-of-fact, she was doing everything right. Perhaps it was unorthodox but still highly effective. He didn't want the job himself, but couldn't resist telling her she was wrong. Ginny was so mad, she knew she couldn't return yet. So she walked slowly toward the barn and corral. Maybe she could walk off some of her anger.

As she wandered back to the house, taking the longest route she could, she became lost in her thoughts. How was she ever to come to an understanding with Colby, the arrogant jackass? Yes, he was just this side of gorgeous, and he had a body to match, but that didn't make much difference when he had the personality of the devil himself.

Now she was feeling sorry for herself. She had to remember that Ian had been a very unpleasant man to deal with as well. She managed to weather that for the three months she was with him. And who could forget how unpleasant Colin could be when reciting all his rules. She managed to turn him around a little, didn't she?

Looking up from her thoughts, she heard the sound of a horse approaching. She watched as small plumes of dust trailed behind the lone rider. He seemed to be riding as if the devil were on his heels.

The rider seemed to change direction when he noticed her standing alone in the field south of the house. He slowed his horse as he approached her. Ginny caught sight of the rider from a few dozen yards away. *Holy shit*, she thought as she saw the perfect jawline, underneath the rim of a low, black hat.

Jumping off his horse before the animal had fully stopped, the man took the reins and came to stand before her. Removing his hat, Ginny was treated to one of the most handsome faces she'd ever seen. Along with his strong jawline, the man had a straight nose, big brown eyes and full lips. His face was covered in day old beard growth and dust. His hair, which at first appeared short, was actually pulled back in a tight, long braid that reached halfway down his back. He was tall, taller than even Colby, and he wore the clothes of a cowboy.

Ginny couldn't speak. He was god-like in his masculine perfection. His skin was deeply tanned, or perhaps it was his natural tone. The man clearly had Native American in his blood. She continued to stare, her mouth dry, at the magnificent creature.

Thankfully, she did not affect him as much. "Good day to you, ma'am. I don't believe we've ever met."

Finally finding her voice, if just to avoid looking like an idiot, she replied, "My name is Ginny. I'm the boy's new teacher." She sounded strong, not as breathless as she felt.

Smiling, he showed off his perfect, white teeth. "Well, that explains it. My name is Antonio Vasquez."

Oh, yeah. "Your Nizhoni's son. She talks about you a lot." Smiling now, Ginny felt herself loosening up.

"You *speak* to my mother?" He sounded surprised.

"Yes, I speak Spanish. Otherwise, I would be in the same boat as Eloise was. What brings you back to the ranch?"

Cocking his head to the side slightly to regard her, instead of answering, he asked a question of his own. "How long have you been here?"

"Not even a week."

"Oh, that explains it. I live here, most of the time. My father became partners with the Millers, so now I own part of the ranch." He turned and pointed at a small cottage just a hundred yards or so south. "That's my home. Although I've been away for a few months now."

"Well, welcome back Antonio."

"Vas," he replied, as if that were to mean something.

"I beg your pardon?"

"People call me Vas. No one has called me Antonio since my father died."

"Did he only use your name when you were in trouble?" Ginny asked, arching an eyebrow. She'd already heard many stories about Nizhoni's only child.

Smiling, he said, "Depended on the tone. If he was yelling, I needed to be on the lookout for the switch." Deftly changing the subject, he asked, "Would you care to walk with me to the corral? Then I can go see my mother and hear all about you behind your back."

Ginny laughed. Besides the boys and their antics, she'd had little to laugh over in the past week.

"Okay. I'm sure your mother won't have much to tell. I haven't done anything extraordinarily stupid yet."

"I can't see you doing anything too stupid." They laughed together, and Ginny told him to give it time.

Before they could reach the barn, Colby walked up. Vas smiled at his long time friend and held out his free hand. Colby shook it, but still had the same churlish look on his face.

"How are you, amigo? I told you I'd be back before it was time to run the cattle to Denver."

"Yeah, you said you'd be back. I see you met Ginny." Colby tilted his head in Ginny's direction as if he needed to point her out. She was the only other person there.

"Where did you find such a pretty teacher for the boys?" Vas winked in her direction, and Ginny barely suppressed the giggle.

"You mean my wife, don't you?"

Ginny's head whipped around to look at Colby. What kind of game was he trying to play now? After all they'd discussed, after all the bad feelings, now he wanted her to play his wife. Not bloody likely.

Vas turned again to look at Ginny. He had a questioning expression on his face. "Wife? I didn't realize you'd married, my friend. Congratulations." His whole speech was meant for Colby, but directed at Ginny.

Ginny was shocked. Turning back to Colby, she asked, "Where did that come from?"

Colby gave her his full attention. "The boys are getting into mischief. You'd better get inside before they cause trouble. I'll help Vas here with his horse."

Whatever, she thought. "It was nice to meet you Vas. I'm sure we'll see each other again soon." With that, she turned toward the house and left the two men to piss on things and get territorial.

"Lo siento, amigo. She told me she was a teacher." Vas explained when Ginny was out of earshot.

"She is, technically. I bought her from a match maker in Denver. We decided to not let it get personal, but I don't need you causing trouble with her. I need her to stick it out longer than the last one did."

"And I wouldn't marry her?" Vas said, with mock derision.

"No, you wouldn't." With that, Colby turned on his heel and headed back to the house.

Chapter 13

It was Sunday morning and the whole Miller family was heading into town for church. Ginny had to admit that she was so curious about the minister that she was looking forward to going. He was probably the type to throw bible verses in your face to prove his point.

At breakfast, Colby spoke to his siblings. "At church, I want you all to refer to Ginny as my wife."

Four heads looked at Colby at once. Nate and Frank looked happy, Georgia looked confused and Ginny looked resigned. Colby hadn't explained his statement the day before to Vas, and she hadn't asked. Although she was curious, it just wasn't worth the frustration of speaking to Colby.

Frank was the first to speak. "Are you two getting married for real?"

"No. I just don't want anyone to come around here to call on Ginny. She has a job to do, and she doesn't have time to socialize."

"Ain't that lying? You shouldn't lie in church," was Nate's contribution.

"It's not lying. Ginny and I did get married, but we decided to not honor those vows."

"Sounds like lying to me," came from Georgia, who was usually so demure that it was hard to believe she said anything to her older brother at all.

"Call it what you like. It's the way it has to be." Colby was letting his vexation show.

"So Ginny is a prisoner here. She's not allowed to have any life beyond teaching Nate and Frank or being a companion to me?" Georgia asked angrily.

Ginny just kept her mouth shut. Although she'd been there a week, she'd had little opportunity to see the family dynamic. The four of them rarely ate together, even for supper. There was always something that kept Colby away until they were all finished. It was usually only Ginny who sat with him while he ate and listened to all the things she'd done wrong that day.

Colby gave his sister his undivided attention. "What would you have me do, Georgia? The last woman I hired ran off with Tim and left me high and dry. You know all the bachelors around here. If they sense that Ginny's available, they'll swarm in like a hive a bees."

Georgia, all her bravery gone, bowed her head. She glanced over at Ginny, looking forlorn in her defeat. Ginny set out to reassure her.

"It's okay, guys. I have no interest in being courted right now anyway. I've got all the boys I need right now."

Colby, who had been feeling bad about how he spoke to his sister, smiled in Ginny's direction. Not because he got his way, but because she had made Georgia feel better. He was going to have to give her some credit. After only one week, his siblings were more taken with her, than Eloise had achieved in over two months.

After breakfast, they all loaded up in the cart and headed toward Sherman. The church was an obvious, white sided building with a small steeple. There was a cross above the double doors. It was small, but functional with an aisle down the middle and five rows of pews. Colby took his usual seat in the last pew, followed by Ginny, Nate, Frank and finally Georgia. The other members of the small town filed in and took their seats. Many of the folks glanced over at Ginny. It was a small town after all, and everyone could recognize a stranger.

After everyone was seated, the minister made a big show of entering the church with his wife. After helping his wife take her seat, the minister walked up to the pulpit, located at the center front of the church.

Ginny had to admit that the minister was a good looking man. Not gorgeous like Vas and Colby, but very boy next door. He had short, light brown hair and piercing blue eyes. His features were pleasant, completely unlike his manner. Almost from the start, Ginny knew she wasn't going to like him.

"Good morning, good people of Sherman." His voice was a booming, baritone that was soothing in its timbre. Unfortunately, the nice voice betrayed the not-so-nice message.

"Let us begin today with Job 11:15-17: 'For then shalt thou lift up thy face without spot; yea, thou shalt be steadfast, and shalt not fear: Because thou shalt forget thy misery, and remember it as waters that pass away: And thine age shall be clearer than the noonday; thou shalt shine forth, thou shalt be as the morning.'"

The minister took a dramatic pause and stared around his flock.

His gaze fell on Ginny, as if noticing someone new for the first time, then continued through the crowd. Taking a deep breath, he continued. "We should all strive to be without sin. Steadfast, as the Bible states. It is this achievement, that guarantees us a place in heaven."

Ginny scrunched up her face for a moment. She never studied the Bible, nor was she apt to read from it unless a patient requested it, but that wasn't at all what she got from that passage. Looking around the church, Ginny watched as other parishioners stared in rapt attention, hanging on every word the minister spoke. *Scary*, she thought.

It went on, for more than an hour. As the sun rose in the sky, the heat in the church got higher as well. Ginny could feel the sweat forming on her body, around her neck and under her breasts. Besides the heat, she had to endure the mis-interpretations from an obvious racist/sexist. The only good part was the singing. Didn't matter that Ginny couldn't sing. It gave her an excuse to stand up and do something besides listen.

After the service was over, the minister exited first and stood outside the door to greet the parishioners. Ginny wanted to leave right away, but Colby put a hand on her arm to stay her.

"What are we waiting for?" she whispered to Colby as the rest of the church filed out.

"The minister will want to meet you. His wife will most likely invite us to dinner. You're about to run a gamut out there. Everyone in town'll be wanting to meet you."

"I figured. It's a small town, and I'm the new shiny toy. I'm ready." It was Ginny's turn to sound exasperated.

"Remember what I said... about us being married." His eyes looked desperate, so Ginny relented.

"I know. I got it."

After the rest of the town had left, the Miller family made their way outside. As predicted, the minister was at the top of the steps, waiting for their departure.

"Good day to you Colby Miller. Good day to you Miss Georgia, Frank and Nate. And who do we have here?" Ginny noticed that the minister's wife stood a half step behind him, waiting to be introduced. Inwardly groaning, Ginny came forward on her own.

Offering her hand, she said, "My name is Ginny Miller. Colby and

I were recently married."

Ignoring her proffered hand, the minister turned to Colby and asked, "Is this true brother Colby?"

"Yes, Reverend Thomas." Got to love a man of few words.

Turning his attention back to Ginny, he grabbed her hand with both of his and smiled warmly. It was the first nice gesture she'd seen him make. "It is truly a pleasure to meet you, Mrs. Miller. I hope you enjoyed the service. I have to say that I'm a little disappointed that I was not the officiant of your wedding service."

Wanting to score points with Colby, in the hopes it would put him in a better mood, Ginny responded to the minister. "We were married in Denver, where we met. Colby didn't feel it would be appropriate for the two of us to travel together if we hadn't been formally married first."

Turning his attention back to Colby, the Reverend said, "Of course. Very prudent of you Colby. Obviously a women's reputation is all she has going into marriage."

Ginny could feel her smile twitch at his statement. *Nope, no smarts available to any woman, hey Reverend?*

Colby nodded his assent. He knew better than to engage the minister in conversation. It ended up being a long, boring, pointless affair. "We should be on our way, Reverend. I have a lot of work these days with the cattle fattening up."

Colby grabbed Ginny's arm and headed toward the cart. The other Millers followed quickly, jumping into the cart before either Colby or Ginny could. The minister could not take the hint.

"Mrs. Miller, please allow me to introduce you to my wife, Mrs. Thomas."

Ginny turned toward the timid looking woman and smiled. "It's nice to meet you. Please call me Ginny."

Both the reverend and his wife looked aghast. "We don't use familiar names unless they're family."

"You used my husband's first name," Ginny replied. She felt Colby's hand tighten on her arm. *Obviously, you did not question the Reverend.*

"Of course, you can see how that would be different." Ginny didn't see, but decided to keep her mouth shut. She just wanted to get home and away from this freak.

Mrs. Thomas whispered something to her husband, who turned back to Colby. "Brother Colby, my wife has requested that you and your bride join us for dinner this evening. As you know, my wife is a fine cook and is preparing a roast." As if any cut of meat would induce someone to eat with them.

Colby sputtered, but was saved by Ginny, as usual.

"That is so kind of you, Reverend. Unfortunately, Mr. Vasquez has recently returned to the ranch, and we have a big dinner planned for this evening. You and your wife are, of course, welcome to join us. Mr. Vasquez's mother is preparing quite the feast." Ginny's plastic smile was radiant. She knew damn well the Reverend and his wife wouldn't be caught dead at the same table as a Native American, let alone someone half Native American, half Mexican.

"Oh, that is very kind of you, Mrs. Miller. But, Mrs. Thomas has already begun to prepare her dinner for this evening. Perhaps another time, shall we?"

"Of course. I'm sure we'll see each other again real soon."

With that, Colby helped Ginny into the front of the cart and walked around and climbed into the driver's seat. Tipping his hat to the reverend, he said, "Good day, Reverend." Not waiting for a reply, he slapped the horses forward and started towards home.

Georgia, who was sitting right behind Ginny, said, "What were you thinking inviting them to dinner?"

Colby gave his sister an eye and went back to running his horses.

Ginny replied, "Your brothers already told me that the reverend doesn't care for Nizhoni. I knew they wouldn't accept but made myself look charitable anyway. It was a win-win."

Nate piped up. "Win-win?"

"It means that everyone got what they wanted. I got to look good to the minister, and we all got out of having dinner at their house."

At this, everyone in the cart laughed, even Colby. The sound was good to hear. Judging by the looks on the younger Miller's faces, it was a sound they hadn't heard in a long time.

Chapter 14

Over the next few days, Ginny saw little of Colby. He and Tim would leave early in the morning and sometimes spend a few nights away to look after the cattle. Ginny could see why Colby was in such a panic to find someone to look after his siblings. Left to their own devices, the boys would have been a terror.

Georgia would spend her days helping Nizhoni and learning how to cook. She had a real gift for combining ingredients, making new and interesting creations. Men would stop by the ranch at times, in the hopes of speaking to her, but Georgia wasn't interested in any of them.

One morning, when Colby was away and the boys were working with Georgia on some treats in the kitchen, Ginny went out to sit on the rocking chair on the front porch of the house. Staying in the shade, an occasional breeze would pass over her, cooling her down despite all the clothing she had to wear. She felt herself dozing, looking out at the barn and corral. That's when she spotted him.

Vas was in the corral, with a horse tied to a rope. He was working the horse, driving her in circles. The horse, on the other hand, had other ideas and would pull and buck and threaten Vas at every turn. Remaining calm, Vas continued on his course.

His movements were graceful, always staying out of the temperamental horse's reach. He moved and swayed, turned in time to music only he could hear. Vas had removed his shirt, and Ginny noticed the sweat on his back and arms. He had a nice body, muscular and tan. Ginny had to admit that watching him work was one of the best things to happen to her since arriving.

Her thoughts began to wander, watching his beautiful body move rhythmically. A daydream started to form in her mind, as she rocked back and forth in the chair, watching. She pictured his strong hands doing something very different than trying to keep a horse in line.

Ginny saw him turn to her and spot her on the porch. His dazzling smile captured her from the distance between him. He put the rope down and jumped over the fence of the corral. Walking slowly across the distance, Ginny couldn't take her eyes off his. He moved with sinewed grace up the steps before stopping in front of her on the porch.

Without a word, Vas reached down and grabbed Ginny's hand to lift her up out of the chair. Ginny's hands automatically reached to touch his chest, surprisingly hairless, but well toned. She felt as his hand reached over to grab her chin and lift her face to his.

Before she could utter a protest, not that she had planned to give one, his mouth was on hers. He didn't bother to go slow, immediately overtaking her mouth with his tongue. Ginny gave as good as she got, demonstrating that she was no spring virgin. Reaching her hands behind his head, she played with his braid and kissed him back. When she felt his hands on her breasts, she pulled away and wordlessly pleaded with him to find better accommodations.

Turning his head this way and that, he opted for her bedroom. Although small, it would afford them some privacy. Sneaking quietly into the house, Ginny led the two upstairs to her bedroom, closing the door after her and leaning back against it, watching Vas turn to look at her again.

"I've wanted you since the moment I met you."

Ginny thought that was pretty corny, but couldn't deny that she had wondered what it would be like to be with him as well. He was too beautiful, but she wasn't looking for marriage. She already had that and look how that was turning out.

It seemed that their clothes just melted away. Once naked, he picked her up and laid her gently on the small bed. Sleeping would have been difficult, but neither of them had sleeping in mind. His calloused hands began caressing her breasts, soon followed by his mouth. He knelt on the floor beside the bed and treated her body like a smörgåsbord. He tasted and touched every bit of her. He reached between her legs and stroked her until she was breathless. When his finger entered her, she was wet and nearly pained in anticipation.

His finger slowly entered, then retreated. Back and forth until Ginny nearly screamed her orgasm. Vas was smart enough to cover her mouth with his, not wanting them to be discovered.

Writhing back against the coarse blanket, Vas climbed up on the bed and positioned himself between her legs. Ginny caught a glance at his manhood and was well pleased with what she saw. Vas brought his face down to Ginny's, staring deeply into her eyes, grinning as he entered her.

At first, he was so large, it was uncomfortable, but his preparation had paid off. She was slick and he was able to slip in without much trouble. He mimicked what he'd done with his finger, sliding in and out. His rhythm was precise and effective. Ginny felt the budding of another orgasm about to take her.

Quicker, she thought, unable to form words in her mind that had now turned to mush. It felt so good, she didn't want it to end, all the while begging silently for her climax. She knew she should feel guilty, but Ginny had too many other things to think about. Actually, she had only one, but it was all consuming. Her second orgasm burst forth like a gun from the barrel.

As she laid panting, she looked up in his eyes. He was smiling, as men are wont to do after getting a woman to orgasm. His smile turned devilish as he leaned down and whispered, "We're not done yet."

Ginny smiled in return, looking forward to whatever was to come next. She never got the chance. At that moment, Nate ran out the front door and woke her up. Startling awake, Ginny sat straight up and looked at the ten year old.

"Sorry, Ginny. Were you asleep?"

Taking a deep breath, she sighed. "No, just resting my eyes." Looking out toward the corral, Vas had not moved. He was still training his horse, still looking impossibly beautiful in the morning sunshine.

That evening, after supper, the family was gathered in the parlor. Georgia and Nate were reading, Frank was drawing on a piece of paper and Ginny was trying her hand at knitting. Georgia had shown her a few of the steps and Ginny was now practicing those steps without actually making anything. Every once in a while, Georgia would look over and give her a tip or tell her she was doing a great job.

Colby walked in at ten o'clock, looked at his family then left to go back into the bathroom. As he was walking down the short hallway, he called to Ginny to join him.

"Frank, Nate, I think it's time for you two to go to bed."

"Awwww, Ginny, do we have to?" Frank was good at whining. He had it down to a science.

"Yes. It's late guys. And you two can be pretty grumpy without enough sleep."

The two boys scampered off. Georgia gave Ginny a look of concern.

"Don't worry, Georgia. I can handle your brother." The last part was whispered and delivered with a wink. Georgia smiled in return and closed her book to go to bed as well.

When Ginny got to the kitchen, Colby was in the bathroom with the door open. His shirt was off, and he was washing himself from the sink. Ginny saw his strong back muscles flexing as he went about his business.

Turning suddenly, he just stared at her for a moment. Ginny became uncomfortable, so she asked, "Do you want me to get you something to eat?" She sounded scared, which she wasn't. Maybe she was just tired.

Drying off with a clean towel, Colby walked out into the kitchen. He was still shirtless, which made Ginny even more uncomfortable. She refused to look at him, keeping her eyes to the floor. Noticing a small knothole in the wood flooring, she went about examining it.

"How was your day?" Colby asked, wondering why she wouldn't look at him. "Anything happen?"

Popping her head up, she answered, "No. The boys are doing really well with their reading and math. We did some biology today. I might have them dissect a frog if I can find something about it in our books."

"Georgia receive any callers?"

"No. She seems more interested in cooking than in boys." Colby was being nice which made her even more uncomfortable. She couldn't help but wonder where this was leading.

"I'm thinking of taking Frank with me next time we go out. It will do him good to learn more about the herd."

Ginny scrunched her face. The boy was thirteen. He had plenty of time to learn about cattle. Right now, he needed to learn patience and understanding. "I would prefer you wait. We have a lot of interesting lessons planned, and I'm sure he wouldn't want to miss them."

Colby let out an exasperated sigh. "Well, Ginny, this is more important. The boy has to learn how to handle himself. I don't see you teaching him that."

"Really. A good education can teach you how to handle yourself, Colby. I'm not denying that he desperately wants to learn the family business, but he's only thirteen. He has time."

"He's practically a man. He's ready."

"Why do you discuss things with me if you don't want my opinion?" Ginny felt her voice elevating and knew she had to rein it in. It wouldn't do any good to get Colby mad.

His eyes turned dark. Oh well, too late. "You've been here less than a month. What do you know about my brothers?" Colby had been wanting to throw down the gauntlet for a while. Now seemed to be the time. After only a few weeks, his brothers seemed more close to her then they had ever been to him.

Misunderstanding his meaning, figuring he thought she was overstepping her position, she answered, "I've talked to them. We're together all day. I know their maturity level, and I can tell you it's not really high."

"What kind of life did you have before now? A boy becomes a man a lot sooner out here then they do in the drawing rooms of the rich in St. Louis."

"You know damn well that I don't know what kind of life I had before here. Do you relish being able to throw that in my face every day? Or do save it for special occasions?"

Before Colby could say anything else to piss her off, Ginny left. She went right to her room and sat on the edge of her bed fuming. The only light came from the moonlight out her window. She undressed and put on her nightgown. She knew it would be a long time before sleep took her, so she moved toward her window to stare at the moonlight.

She saw a strange glow, next to the barn and corral. She thought it was a cigar, since the glow grew brighter, than softer. She could discern a figure, a man, leaning against the barn. He was in shadow, but it could only be two people: Vas or Colby. All the ranch hands stayed in a bunkhouse far east of the house. Taking a chance, Ginny left her room and made her way outside.

In her bare feet, she made little noise, but as soon as she approached the figure, a voice called out, "Colby, that you?"

Well, that at least answered her question about who it was. Thankfully, it wasn't Colby, so she answered, "No."

Vas turned abruptly to the sound of her voice. He put the cigar out on the bottom of his boot and stumbled a bit walking closer.

"Uh, Ginny, whatcha doing out here?"

"Couldn't sleep. I saw you from my window. I... uh, mean... I saw someone. I didn't know it was you." *Nice*, Ginny thought. *Now he thinks you're an idiot!*

His face was still in shadow, but she could see him smiling. That brought a blush to Ginny's cheeks. Thankfully, he couldn't see that in the dark.

"Care to take a walk?" His voice was low and he smelled good, like cigars and soap.

"I don't have any shoes on. I wouldn't want to step on something."

"Alright. How about we sit here for a spell?" Vas directed her to a couple of bales of hay. Ginny sat down, smoothing out the cotton nightgown. She didn't think he could see through it, but she wasn't taking any chances. He probably already thought she was loose to be sitting out here alone with him.

It was at that moment that Ginny remembered her daydream. This added to her discomfort, being so near him.

"Fine night," he said, looking toward the sky.

"So, the boys tell me that you're a bit of a wanderer." Might as well get this conversation going, otherwise they could be exchanging pleasantries all night.

Laughing at her forwardness, he replied, "I thought I might see a bit of the world before I settle down. The boys tell me that you don't know where you come from."

Nothing like a little prid pro quo. "That's right. I remember being on a train, going to Denver to meet myself a husband." Ginny added a little twang to her voice.

"Sounds like a much scarier adventure than anything I ever did," he chuckled.

I've been through worse, she thought to herself. Their conversation continued, Vas telling her all about the places he'd been, the people he met and the bigotry he'd experienced.

"I'm always good enough to work the menial stuff. Damn, I did love it when some man would be shocked because I could put two sentences together, in English. Little did they know that every one of their wives never had an issue with how I looked."

94

Ginny laughed. "I'm sure you showed them," she said jokingly, but was surprised when he got quiet.

In a whisper, he said, "You bet I did."

In those four words, Ginny heard a lot of pain. Little did Vas know that some things never change. They might improve, but not change.

"Not fair being judged like that, huh?"

"Nope. But you get used to it, I suppose."

"You should remember that next time you meet a woman. I find that men often judge us simply because we have breasts and ovaries." Right after the words left her mouth, Ginny knew she'd screwed up.

Vas turned and looked at her. The moonlight lit up half his face, so his expression was clear. Shocked, to say the least. But maybe he was a little more respectful of her too. Ginny certainly hoped so.

"I guess maybe you might know a little about what I'm talking about."

Laughing, she replied, "Yeah, maybe a little."

Vas leaned back against the barn once again and both were silent for a few minutes. The night had cooled off, making it very comfortable to sit about. Ginny felt all the anger she had for Colby melting away. Perhaps she should say the hell with this story and choose Vas. That would show the fates who was in charge.

"So, you and Colby aren't really married, huh?" What a way to break the silence, just as she was contemplating a re-creation of her daydream.

"No. I mean, we were married. Although I doubt the legality of it. We decided to keep things professional, so that we could go our separate ways eventually."

"I heard in town that he's calling you his wife. How's that going play out if you leave?"

"I don't care. He can tell them I died, or ran away."

"What if you wanted to stay? Be with someone else?"

Well, that wasn't subtle. Or had Ginny just started believing she was all that. "I don't know. I haven't given it that much thought."

He turned and stared into her eyes. Before she could ponder anything, Vas leaned down and placed his mouth on hers. His thumb gently rubbed her cheek. He was being gentle and Ginny didn't want gentle. She reached up, grabbed the back of his head and deepened the kiss. Before she knew it, he had reached around her and brought her up on his lap.

The kiss continued until they both heard the sound of gravel on the other side of the barn. Before Ginny could react, Vas had her seated next to him again, his hat in his lap, staring at the stars. Ginny followed suit, turning her head toward the noise, just in time to see Colby round the corner.

Ginny remained silent. Not that she felt guilty, but because she was still mad at him. Vas, however, turned his head to regard his old friend.

"Evening, Colby. Can't sleep either?" Ginny's heart was only just calming down, yet Vas sounded as cool as a cucumber.

"No, couldn't sleep. Thought a walk around would help." Turning his attention to Ginny, he said, "Maybe you should be getting to bed, Ginny. You've got a lot to do tomorrow."

"Since you're taking one of my students, I won't have nearly as much to do. Will I?" Her challenge was apparent, even to Vas who hadn't heard the earlier conversation.

"You shouldn't be out here alone with Vas in your nightgown. Someone might talk."

Ginny made a point of turning her head back and forth. "Yeah, I heard the horses gossiping just the other night. Catty bitches, every last one of them."

At this, Vas laughed, but Colby remained silent. Instead of pursuing the conversation further, Ginny turned and looked at Vas. "Good night, Vas. Pleasant dreams." The last part was said quietly, seductively.

"You too, Ginny. See you tomorrow."

Ginny stood up and walked back to the house. She hoped that it didn't escape Colby's notice that she did not bother to offer him the same.

Chapter 15

The next morning, Ginny had to deal with Nate, who was depressed over, once again, being left behind.

"It ain't fair, Ginny. I can do anything Frank can do."

"It isn't fair," she said, once again correcting him. "I know it isn't, Nate. It's just the way things are. You'll catch up, you'll see."

Nate kicked the dirt with his feet. Ginny had decided at breakfast that Nate could have a day off as well. They were outside trying to decide what to do with their day.

The sun had already climbed up the sky and the day was turning hot. Ginny could already feel herself sweating through her layers. She only had two dresses, plus two more that Georgia had given her. If it got any hotter this summer, she would be doing laundry every other day.

"I know. We can go to the swimmin' hole. It ain't far. We can ride there in no time. Please, Ginny, can we? Can we?"

Ginny was starting to love his expressions. It occurred to her that she might not fall in love with Colby, but she certainly did love Nate. He was everything she'd always wanted in a child of her own.

"Do you think that Georgia will join us?"

"Yeah. You go ask her, and I'll go ask Vas. He'll come too, I bet." Not a second later, Nate was off running toward Vas, who was with another horse in the corral.

Ginny went off in search of Georgia. She had to ask her what they should wear to go swimming. Did they even have swimsuits in this time period? Ginny had no clue. One thing was for sure, she didn't want to go skinny dipping.

It took over an hour to get ready. Everyone had a job to do: Georgia and Ginny collected towels, a blanket and a picnic basket full of food. Nate and Vas got the horses saddled and loaded the goods. Turns out that Georgia had some bathing gowns for the two girls to wear. Over that, Georgia gave Ginny a pair of pants and old shirt to wear while riding. At this thought, Ginny started to panic.

"Listen, guys, I don't remember how to ride a horse."

Vas responded, "Don't worry. I'll stick close by you, and we won't go fast."

"But that's half the fun," Nate whined.

Georgia, seeing the look on Ginny's face, offered, "I'll ride ahead with Nate. You and Vas can take your time." She smiled at them both, although Ginny thought it was meant primarily for Vas.

"Thanks, Georgia. I owe you one."

Nate and Georgia took off in a run. Vas explained that it was better if they went slow since they were carrying the supplies. Ginny thought that Vas could be pretty sweet when he wanted. As they rode on in silence, she thought about their kiss. Truth be told, it was hot. As she had laid in bed that night, she wondered if she wouldn't have taken him up on his offer of sex if one had come.

Vas had other things on his mind. Colby would be pretty mad if he knew about the kiss. Although they both claimed to not be married "officially," Vas felt some jealousy from Colby after Ginny left them the night before. Colby had been his friend for longer than he could remember. He knew Colby didn't want to lose another teacher, but if he made an honest woman of Ginny, she'd stay on with the boys. Vas considered talking to Colby about it last night, but something held him back. He wondered if Colby didn't feel more for Ginny than he let on.

Finally, Vas couldn't take the silence any longer. "About last night..."

When Vas paused, Ginny thought that might have been an '80's movie title. It made her smile. She turned toward Vas and said, "Last night?"

"Don't play coy, Ginny. You know I mean the kiss." His dark eyes shone in the sunlight. Ginny was turned on just watching him.

"The kiss. Yes. I do seem to remember a kiss."

Now it was Vas' turn to smile. "I need to talk to Colby about this."

Ginny felt something inside her tighten. She couldn't explain what it was, only that something inside her was warning her to not let that happen. Shaking her head, she wondered if those powers that be that sent her here in the first place were sending her a message. Grimacing, she thought she didn't care. Although truthfully, she did.

"What do you plan to say?" she asked, her voice betraying her fear.

Vas caught her tone and asked, "You don't think he'd hurt you, do you?"

"What? No. I guess I'm asking if you want to continue our relationship. I didn't mean to make you think that Colby was ever violent. He can be a complete jerk sometimes, but he's never threatened me with violence."

Letting out the breath he'd been holding, Vas felt relief. The last thing he wanted to do was beat up his best friend. But if he ever found out he'd done such a heinous thing, Vas wouldn't think twice about putting things right.

Now it was Vas' turn to feel uncomfortable. Did he want to continue their relationship, as Ginny put it? The kiss had been incredible and he was getting hard all over again just thinking about it. But was he ready to fully commit to a woman? Vas' parents had told him that when he met the right woman, he'd have no problem committing. He'd do anything to spend the rest of his life with that woman.

"I like you. I'd like to get to know you better." That was as far as Vas was willing to go at this point.

Ginny felt him hedging and was actually relieved by it. Maybe he didn't want a relationship with her. Maybe last night they had both gotten caught up in a moment that really meant nothing.

"Well, how about you hold off on that talk just now. How about we be friends first?"

Smiling, Vas said, "Never had a friend who was a woman before."

"Well, you don't know what you've been missing."

The swimmin' hole, as Nate put it, was more like a lake. Not huge, by any means, but large enough to fit a few boats on. It was picturesque, with a waterfall on one side and a shady meadow on another.

"Do you know how to swim?" Nate asked Ginny as they put their stuff down and walked to the water's edge.

Ginny could swim like a fish, but couldn't admit to that since she had no idea who she really was. So, she stuck with her usual answer. "I don't know. I don't feel any fear, so maybe I do."

Smiling, Nate took off his outer clothes. Wearing only his drawers, he jumped into the water and started swimming toward the waterfall.

Ginny couldn't help herself when she called, "Be careful, Nate."

The sentiment made her smile. She could really get used to this mothering thing.

Georgia and Ginny removed their clothes and waded into the water slowly. The bottom was rocky at first, but then they reached the muddy part. Ginny felt the sendiment squishing between her toes and thought that some women in her time pay big money to get this stuff rubbed on their faces.

The water was cold, being fed from snow melt in the mountains. Still, it felt good on the warm day. Holding each other's hands, the women made their way into the water up to their waists. Georgia was giggling and Ginny was smiling. All of a sudden, Vas came running to the edge, throwing himself into the water with a giant splash.

Georgia started to laugh, admiring the view of a half naked Vas, swimming in Nate's direction. Ginny was admiring it as well.

Staring at Colby's sister, Ginny noticed something in her eye that she hadn't noticed before. It hit her like a brick to the head. *Oh my God, Georgia likes Vas.*

Trying to be subtle, and failing miserably, Ginny asked, "You've known Vas a long time now, huh?"

Turning her view back to Ginny, Georgia replies, "Yes. My whole life really."

"He seems like a great guy. I've only spoken to him a few times, but he's very polite. Charming, some would say."

Looking down at the water's surface, Georgia face turned dejected. Lowering her voice, she said, "Yes. There are many women who think so."

"Do you think so?"

Never taking her eyes off the water, Georgia nodded. Then, Ginny saw some tears hit the water.

"Georgia, what's wrong?" Ginny reached over and pulled her face up to meet hers. Georgia immediately turned away and started to make her way back to the shore. Once out of the water, she sat down on a large rock. Following her out, Ginny sat next to her and waited for an explanation.

Taking a deep breath, she explained. "Vas looks at me like I'm his little sister. No matter what I do or say, he just pats my head and walks away."

Trying to be reassuring, Ginny said, "Men are pretty stupid. And they can't take a hint if it hit them on the head. Maybe I could talk to him. Get him to see you for what you are... a beautiful, young woman." Ginny paused as she turned to watch the two boys playing in the water. "Is that what you want? Is Vas who you want?"

Looking Ginny in the eye, desperation marring her pretty face, she replied, "Oh yes, Ginny. He's the only one I've ever wanted. And you know how many men come to call on me. I only compare them to Vas. He's always been the one."

Ginny resisted the urge to roll her eyes. Instead, she decided that she would help. Or interfere, depending on how one looked at it. Ginny had some experience in setting couples up.

"Okay. Then I'll do everything I can to make it happen."

Georgia's face looked confused. "But I thought you and Vas were..."

"Were what?"

"Oh, nothing. I just thought he might be interested in you."

Ginny scrunched her face in confusion. Where would she get that idea? Had either of them done or said anything that would lead the others to assume a relationship? Oh well, it didn't matter.

"I think he likes me as a person. As far as romance, he may have thought of me as his only option, since we haven't gotten him to look at you yet. But don't worry, he will." Ginny smiled and winked.

The two women got back into the water and swam over to the guys. The day turned out to be a lot of fun. Ginny hadn't played in the water for a long time. In her real life, there were so many other things to do. Even on her last beach vacation, she'd spent more time sick, than swimming or boating. Most of all, she liked spending the day with Nate and Georgia, who she was coming to think of as her own family. Even Vas was entertaining, telling stories of his more PG rated adventures.

When it was time to leave, Ginny suggested that Georgia ride with her brother again, then she and Vas would take up the rear. At first, Georgia looked put off, but when Ginny gave her the "remember what we talked about earlier" look, she smiled and thought it was a good idea.

As they rode back to the ranch, Ginny asked Vas, "Georgia certainly has grown up, hasn't she?"

Confused, Vas asked, "You've only known her a couple of weeks.

What makes you say that?"

"Sometimes I can see the little girl she was. But mostly, she's so beautiful, inside and out. Obviously, she's stunning. But she's also so sweet and kind. You know that she's helped me out so much since I came here."

Vas' face remained neutral when he asked, "How so?"

"She's given me extra dresses, because I only had a couple. She's teaching me how to knit and helps me keep an eye on the boys. She helps Nizhoni in the kitchen. Did you know that? Your mother is teaching her how to cook. She's spectacular. She makes the best biscuits."

Shaking his head, he replied, "No, I didn't know that. She's always been a sweet girl." His voice trailed off at the end, as though he was considering something he'd never considered before. Which was, of course, exactly what Ginny wanted.

Smiling, Ginny remained silent the rest of the way home. Once the seed was planted, it takes some time to grow, although Ginny planned to water it a few more times to see if it took hold.

Chapter 16

When they arrived home, Nizhoni informed them that Colby and Frank had come home only long enough to pack up some extra supplies and head east. Some of their stock had wandered off in search of better grazing, so the men needed to round them up and bring them back. They would be gone a few days.

Ginny had to admit that she was pleased by this. For one, she wouldn't have to deal with Colby. But it would also give her time to put her plan into action, getting Vas to see Georgia as something other than a child.

That night at dinner, Ginny made a few more subtle comments, directing Vas to what a good wife Georgia would make. How considerate she was for helping with the boy's schooling and what a wonderful mother she'd be someday. Vas smiled and acknowledged her comments, keeping quiet afterwards, hopefully thinking.

It wasn't until late the next day, after Ginny and Nate had worked through some challenging math equations together, that Ginny bumped into Vas again. He was mucking stalls in the barn, looking hot, sweaty and simply delicious. Ginny had to wonder why she wasn't grabbing him for herself.

"Hi Vas," she said, walking over and sitting on one of the bales of hay.

"Hey Ginny," Vas put the rake down and walked over to where she was sitting. "Where's Nate?"

"He's still working on math. Got to say, not my favorite subject."

Vas smiled and took the seat next to her. Looking at his feet, he asked, "I was thinking about..." When he paused, Ginny turned and looked at him.

Prompting him, she said, "You were thinking about..."

"Aww, Ginny. I don't know how to tell you this."

"May I suggest you just spit it out." He looked at her, and she smiled back.

"I was thinking of courting Georgia."

Ginny's face lit up like the sun. "That's great, Vas. I happen to know that she really cares about you too."

"But... I thought... you and I..." It was almost sexy watching him sputter.

Putting her hand on his arm, he watched her intently. "I'm sorry if I led you on. To be honest, I really like you, but I don't think we were meant to be together. The kiss was... well, it was spectacular. But I obviously have a few things to work out with Colby before I can consider another man. Thanks for making me feel special."

Vas turned his head slightly, then whispered, "You are special, Ginny. And if things don't work out with you and Colby, I know a few guys who would love to show you just how special you are."

Strangely, Ginny felt tears in her eyes. She turned her head, not wanting Vas to see how she felt. She'd had two guys fall in love with her and make her their world. Maybe she was just getting used to the feeling. Colby did not make her feel that way, that was for sure.

Standing up to leave, Ginny said, "Thank you. If I can do anything to help you out, with Georgia I mean, just let me know."

Ginny walked from the barn, feeling both elated and deflated. She was happy that Georgia would get her happy ever after. Still, being stuck in this limbo didn't sit well. She remembered how she sat for a year waiting for Colin to return. She certainly didn't want to go down that avenue again. Maybe it was time she moved things along. But how was she ever going to get Colby to stop being so angry with her and fall in love with her instead?

Chapter 17

Colby, Tim and Frank were gone for four days. A lot had changed in that time. Vas was courting Georgia at a furious pace. Ginny had warned both of them to keep their time together respectable. They had plenty of time to get to know each other biblically after they were married. Ginny caught them kissing a couple of times, always breaking them up and sending Georgia away. Vas would smile at her, but she let him know that she was in charge of keeping Georgia out of trouble, just as much as Nate and Frank.

The trio returned early in the afternoon, with Nate running out to greet them. Georgia and Ginny had taken the cart to town to retrieve a few things from the mercantile. Nizhoni knew that Vas was asking for Georgia's hand, and wanted to make a special dinner to honor it, so she asked the girls to get a few supplies.

It was after three o'clock by the time Georgia and Ginny returned. Georgia stopped the cart in front of the house, so Ginny could deliver the needed supplies to Nizhoni. Jumping down, she rounded the cart to pick up the food when the front screen door slammed against the house. Out came Colby, looking his usual pissed off self.

Walking down the front steps at a face pace, Colby turned to his sister. "Is it true?" was all he asked, but everyone knew what he was referring to.

Georgia's head dropped to the reins in her hands. Barely above a whisper, she responded, "Yes. I love him."

"What?" Colby screamed. Ginny jumped at the sound, watching Colby to make sure he wouldn't do anything violent. Colby gave the impression of bite, but, so far, he'd been all bark. Ginny didn't want to know what would happen if that changed.

Georgia was crying now, sitting in the front of the cart, shaking. Ginny decided it was time for her to interrupt. After all, Colby already hated her, so what difference would it make if he hated her more. She didn't want him ruining the relationship he had with his only sister.

"Georgia, go into the house and bring the supplies to Nizhoni."

Georgia, who had been waiting for help, jumped at the chance to get away from Colby and his anger. Getting down from the cart, she came the long way around the cart, picked up the supplies and ran into the house. Colby was surprisingly quiet while his sister disappeared.

"Come on, Ginny. Let's return the cart and horses." His calm voice did nothing to quell Ginny's fear. He was saving something up for her, she could tell. It was going to be a very unpleasant afternoon. So, swallowing the saliva in her mouth, Ginny climbed back into the cart next to the waiting Colby.

He stopped the cart in front of the barn and proceeded to remove the horses. Once both horses were stabled, with new feed and water, Colby turned to look at her. Ginny stood up straight, trying to give the impression of no fear. She wasn't afraid of him hurting her, just of her losing her temper and making things worse.

"I got to talking to Frank."

Okay, she thought. *Maybe this isn't about Georgia after all. Maybe he just wanted to talk to me about something Frank needs to work on.* Ginny's disposition brightened a bit. Still, something told her to remain silent.

"He's developed quite a vocabulary since you came."

Scrunching her face, Ginny looked confused. Wasn't a better vocabulary a good thing?

"When I asked him where he learned all these new words, he tells me from you."

Well, I am his teacher.

"Did you tell him that you would teach him new swear words in exchange for his good behavior?" Colby's voice was still calm, but the look on his face was decidedly troublesome.

Taking a deep breath, she answered, "Yes. He tried to shock me with his use of swear words when I met him. I saw it as a way for us to connect. I told him that his... vocabulary was limited. That I could teach him how to swear properly. It has been an effective way to ensure Frank's compliance." Thank God for Dilbert cartoons or Ginny would never be able to talk like that.

"Your job wasn't to teach him how to curse. It was to teach him how to read and write." With every word Colby spoke, his voice got higher and higher. His face was turning red and his posture was alarmingly hostile.

Trying to diffuse him somewhat, Ginny said, "I understand that you're a little mad about Vas and Georgia. But you'll see what a great couple they make. He's so sweet to her, and she just adores him."

When Ginny decided on a course of action, she usually expected it to work well. In this case, she couldn't have chosen a worse topic to bring up to try to calm Colby down.

"Dammit, Ginny. Vas told me that you got them together. Do you have any idea how many women Vas has had? It won't be you picking up the pieces of my sister's broken heart when he takes off."

"What makes you think he'll leave..."

"Because it's what he always does. When his father died, he took off, not caring what happened to his share of the ranch or his mother. He'd come back when the money was gone, work a few months, but then he'd always take off again. I knew my sister was sweet on him, but I never encouraged it because Vas is completely unreliable."

"Didn't you take off too?" Ginny had a wonderful way of making things worse.

"That was not the same thing, dammit. I wanted a different life. I was willing to put off marriage. I just wanted to take care of myself."

"I don't know Vas all that well, but maybe he's seen the other side and wants to come back to this life. Maybe he's grown up and is ready to settle down. Just because it's not the life you would have chosen doesn't mean that he might not like it."

"You have no idea what you're talking about. You haven't been here. You barely know any of us, but you seem too ready to make decisions for all of us."

"Bullshit. Sometimes it takes an outsider to see things clearly. Your sister was miserable, because she knew that the only man she ever wanted couldn't look at her as anything other than a child. Frank wants so badly to be a man, that his teenage mind told him that cursing would somehow achieve that for him quicker. And Nate... he's just so desperate for your approval, and you put him aside like he's not worth your time. It's not that I haven't been here long enough, Colby. It's that you're too close and too fucking angry to see what is so damn obvious."

Walking forward, Colby grabbed Ginny's arms and pulled her up to his face. He was so mad that he was seething, eyes blazed. "You will pack your bags tonight. First thing tomorrow morning, I'm going to drive you back to Cheyenne. What you do there, I don't care. All I care about is getting you away from my family."

He shook her twice, then let her fall to the ground. He turned on his heel and walked out of the barn, never looking back to make sure she was alright.

Ginny sat on the ground for a few minutes, rubbing her arms to take the sting out of where Colby had grabbed her. She tried to slow her breathing down and keep the tears at bay. How had she messed up that badly? She didn't think there was anything she could do to make him fall in love with her now. She doubted he even cared about the money he'd spent on her. One of these days, Ginny was going to learn her lesson. Stop interfering and start going with the flow. She would learn if it damn well killed her.

Chapter 18

Needless to say, dinner was ruined. Vas and Georgia were there, along with Frank and Ginny. Colby was off doing God knew what, and Nate disappeared after Colby got home. When Ginny asked where he was, Frank assured her that sometimes he just liked to be alone and would be back before bedtime.

Everyone ate in silence, Georgia giving worried looks to everyone around the table. Ginny hadn't told anyone yet that she was leaving. Her mind wandered to what she would do in Cheyenne. Although she was smart and filled with future knowledge, she didn't know if that would translate to anything useful. She supposed she could find a doctor or hospital and see about a position as a nurse. If nothing else, she wouldn't swoon at the sight of blood.

Frank kept his head down until he finally decided that he needed to get something off his chest. "Ginny. I'm real sorry about telling Colby about the swearing. He sure was mad." The boy looked close to tears. It was breaking Ginny's heart.

Putting her hand on his arm, Ginny tried to reassure him. "Frank, it's okay. I know you weren't trying to get me in trouble. We didn't do anything wrong. And if you want, I'll teach you another one right now, just because your brother's not here."

Smiling, Frank nodded his approval.

"Let's see. Have I told you peckerhead yet?"

Laughing, Frank shook his head. "What's a peckerhead?"

"Well, pecker is another word for a penis. I guess it's just a not so nice way of telling someone that they are being stupid."

"Like Colby?" Frank asked, his good mood dissipating.

"Listen Frank. I know we don't agree with Colby, but you still need to respect him. He's your big brother, and although he seems to be in a very bad mood all the time, he does a lot to keep this family together. It's okay to disagree, but don't be disrespectful. Okay?"

Looking down, Ginny thought she saw a ghost of a smile on his face. "Okay, Ginny. I'll try."

Smiling back, she replied, "That's all I could hope for."

Georgia spoke up for the first time that evening. "Ginny, I was wondering something. I thought that maybe you'd be my bridesmaid at the wedding. Vas and I decided that we wanted to get married right away, like maybe next week sometime. Would you stand up with me?"

Her heart breaking, realizing how much she was going to miss this family, Ginny said, "Of course. I would be honored. We'll talk about it later, though, okay?"

Hearing her voice, Georgia thought that maybe Ginny was embarrassed because she didn't have anything to wear. "I plan on making my wedding dress. I bet if we work together, we can make you something to wear as well."

Ginny smiled, but it was tired looking. "That would be great." *I'm such a coward*, she thought, not being able to bring herself to tell them. Obviously, they were going to find out tomorrow. She hoped that the news didn't rip the family apart. It was amazing how close they'd gotten in such a short amount of time. Ginny had been the youngest sibling in her family, by several years. She was the "oops" baby, the one that neither of her parents ever dreamed would happen. Now, being the older sister in a lot of ways was fun for Ginny. Finally, she could be the superior one.

Just as they were finishing up their dinner, Colby walked into the kitchen. The silence was deafening. No one spoke, and it seemed like no one took a breath.

"Where's Nate?" Colby asked, standing in the doorway.

Frank spoke up first. "He's off sulking somewhere about something. He's not in our room and wasn't in his usual hiding place in the barn."

"Well, I guess I'll talk to him later." Colby came forward, clearing his throat. "Ginny's leaving tomorrow."

Everyone's head whipped around to look at her, while Ginny stared daggers at Colby. He was purposely being insensitive, but what did she expect? He was a grown man who behaved more like a petulant child. Before Ginny could explain, Vas spoke up.

"Where are you going?" He sounded hurt, like Ginny was abandoning him.

"I'm driving her back to Cheyenne. From there, she can arrange transport back to St. Louis."

Georgia looked at her brother. "How? She hasn't got any money."

"Ginny's resourceful. I'm sure she can figure something out."

Georgia and Frank looked incredulous. Frank was sputtering something, but nothing coherent came out. Georgia stared at Vas, as if to try to get him to do something. For the woman he loved, he would do anything.

"That won't be necessary, Colby. Ginny can come and stay with me."

Ginny smiled at Vas and Georgia. It was a nice thing to do. The best part was the look on Colby's face after he said it.

Colby began to breath harder, as if he was doing his best to contain his anger. Now, with the tables turned, it was Colby's turn to look incredulous. Taking a last ditch effort to rid his family of Ginny, he said, "Why would you want to do that? You are marrying my sister. Does Georgia know about you two out together the other night? Ginny only in her nightgown?"

Georgia gasped, but her fury was not for Vas or Ginny. Her anger was set squarely on her brother. "How dare you? How dare you say such a thing about your best friend and my best friend? Vas has never betrayed me, and I know Ginny wouldn't. And to think that Ginny was just telling Frank to respect you despite you being angry all the time. You don't deserve our respect." Georgia jumped up from the table and left through the back door. Vas was hot on her heels, all that could be heard was the sound of him trying to soothe his fiancée.

Frank got up from the table and looked at his brother. "I don't think I want to go out with you anymore. Especially if you're going to act like such a peckerhead!" Frank pushed his way past Colby and went up the steps to his room.

Colby was furious. This could not be happening to his family. Why didn't he go with his instinct and leave Ginny behind? He could have gone into Denver, checked to see if there was any eligible, desperate women there willing to come and live in the frontier. But, no, he felt sorry for her. He felt sorry for himself.

"This is all your fault," was the best he could do, in his state of near apoplexy.

Ginny turned her gaze to his eyes. She could go one of two ways with this. She could get angry again, be childish and lash out at him, or she could try to reason with him. She decided on the latter, but knew that it would probably degrade into the former eventually.

"I don't know where it went wrong, Colby, but I did not turn your family against you. I've tried to be patient. I think I was doing a damn good job with your brothers. Your sister has become a good friend. Tell me what you want me to do, and I'll do it. Just please, don't make me go. I really like it here." Ginny's voice dripped with sincerity, but unfortunately, it was lost on her "husband."

"The only thing I want you to do is leave. You can't fix this, Ginny. It's too late."

"You're finally right about one thing, Colby. I can't fix this. But you can. And you should before you lose them forever." Ginny's eyes were brimming with tears as she got up from the table and left to go to her room. She knew her message was lost. She hoped she'd have one more chance before he made her leave. All she could do was try.

Georgia and Vas went for a walk in the moonlight. They were holding hands, Vas' thumb occasionally stroking the top of her hand. He couldn't begin to imagine how to make this right. Vas knew Colby would be mad about the engagement. He didn't think he would stoop so low to try to get Georgia to believe he'd been unfaithful to her. Not knowing what she was thinking, he felt it best to come clean.

"Colby didn't lie, Georgia. Ginny and I were out together one night, and she was wearing only her nightgown."

"So?" was all Georgia said. She wasn't a fool. She noticed how they looked at each other when Vas first got home. She'd even assumed that Vas was interested. But all that was in the past. Georgia knew how Vas felt about her, and she was secure about it.

"I kissed her. Just the once, though. And never since I started courting you." His voice was pained, like he thought this was going to ruin their budding relationship.

To set him mind at ease, Georgia turned toward her fiancé. "Do you love me, Vas?"

"Yes. Oh God, yes."

"Then I have nothing to worry about. I know it was Ginny who made you see me as a woman. Why would she do that if she wanted you for herself?"

Vas stopped short and pulled Georgia back into his arms. Wrapping his arms around her shoulders, he buried his nose into her hair and inhaled the sweet smell of her soap. How had he not seen her

112

himself? Why did it take Ginny to make him realize that the perfect woman was right in front of him?

"You don't want her to go, do you?" Vas whispered into her hair.

"If I didn't already know I loved you, I would have been certain when you offered her your home. It was so chivalrous. I don't deserve you." Georgia felt the tears in her eyes. She was so proud of Vas for standing up to Colby. She was also proud of herself. She rarely spoke up, but for a friend like Ginny, she felt it was her only option.

"I don't deserve you, my love. Maybe we should go into town tomorrow and speak to Reverend Thomas. We'll take Ginny with us... for moral support." Vas pulled away and looked into his love's eyes. Then he bent down and kissed her soundly, letting all his love for her flow through his kiss. Georgia responded in kind, hoping that all would work out in the end.

Chapter 19

The next morning, Ginny was up at dawn. She had packed her bag the night before, but she had no intention of leaving the ranch. She would live at Vas' cabin until she could figure out what else to do. She didn't want to find out what would happen to her if she couldn't make it work with Colby.

She walked down the steps and placed her bag at the front door. Walking to the kitchen, she wanted to be quiet to see who was there before entering. If it was Colby, she would just turn around and sit in the parlor until Vas came to collect her.

Only Frank and Nizhoni were in the kitchen. Frank had a plate of food in front of him, but he hadn't touched it. Nizhoni, who had missed the blow up the night before, was busy banging pots and pans around, in her frustration and anger.

"Good morning," Ginny said as she entered the kitchen and sat down with a *whump.*

"Buenos dias." Nizhoni must be angry, if she wouldn't comment on what had happened. The woman was a consummate gossip, and it worried Ginny that she wasn't talking to her.

Frank looked worried, but he wouldn't look at her, only his uneaten plate of eggs.

"What's wrong, Frank? I'm just going to be living over with Vas for a while. It will be alright, you'll see." Ginny tried to smile, but she just wasn't feeling it herself.

Frank looked up and whispered, "Nate didn't come home last night."

Standing up from the chair so quickly that she knocked her chair over, she screamed, "What!?"

Nizhoni turned from her stove and stared at the two of them. "¿Qué?"

Speaking in Spanish, Ginny explained that Nate hadn't come home. Nizhoni turned to Frank and spoke in Navajo, a language all the Millers had mastered over the years. Frank replied in kind, then turned to Ginny.

"I don't know where he is. When he wasn't in his bed this

morning, I checked all his favorite hiding places to make sure that he hadn't fallen asleep. But I couldn't find him anywhere."

"Does Colby know?" Ginny asked, her heart racing at the thought that Nate might be hurt somewhere and they didn't know where.

"No. I didn't want to talk to him." Frank looked on the verge of tears, not wanting to admit just how mad he was at his older brother.

Ginny turned on her heel and left the kitchen. Figuring that Colby was already awake, she went outside, toward the barn, calling his name. She saw two figures walk out of the barn and look at her. One was Colby, the other Tim.

"Nate didn't come home last night." Ginny was breathing heavy, most likely from the solid weight that was sitting on her heart.

"He's just hiding, Ginny. He'll come home when he's hungry." Colby sounded annoyed, as usual, but Tim looked a little worried.

Ginny was desperate to get through to him. "Frank has already been out looking for him this morning and hasn't found him in any of his usual hiding places. He didn't come to dinner last night and wasn't at breakfast this morning."

Colby scrunched up his face and went back toward the house, Ginny hot on his heels. Walking up to his brother's room, he first looked under the bed. Whatever he was looking for, he didn't find because he looked more confused. Then, Colby spotted something under Nate's pillow. Grabbing it, Ginny realized it was a piece of paper. After unfolding the single sheet, Colby read what it had to say. Ginny saw his skin turn white, right before he pushed past her and ran back down the stairs.

Running outside, Ginny heard him call for Tim. "Nate's taken off. We'll need some of the ranch hands to help in the search. Round them up and get them on horses. Have everyone meet here as soon as possible."

The weight was heavier, and Ginny thought she just might throw up. Nate ran away? How could that be? Frank ran outside of the house to join them. Colby sent him to Vas' house to bring him over to help with the search.

After Frank ran off toward Vas' cabin, Ginny asked, "What does the note say?"

Instead of answering her, Colby stuffed the note in his pants pocket and walked toward the barn. He began to saddle a horse, ignoring her as she stood waiting, waiting for anything he would give her.

"Go back to the house, Ginny. I'll have Nate home by this afternoon."

"Where did he go? Why did he go? Please Colby, I have to know." Desperate, heartsick, Ginny grabbed his arm, pleading with her eyes for any information.

Pulling abruptly away, he turned to her. His eyes, for once, weren't angry, but hurt. He shook slightly, as if he was holding back something he wanted to say. Instead, he took out the note and handed it to Ginny.

Ginny opened the note and began to read:

> Colby,
>
> *I won't stay here if Ginny ain't here. I'm going to Cheyenne*
> *to meet her. I will live with her from now on. Goodbye.*
>
> Nate

Ginny gasped. He left because he was mad that Colby was getting rid of her. She thought he must have overheard them in the barn, since it was after that when he disappeared.

Feeling somewhat more empowered, Ginny said, "I want to go with you."

Colby was leading his horse out into the corral. He went back in the barn to saddle another horse. As he did his work, he replied, "Impossible."

"What do you mean? I want to help." *I need to help*, she left unspoken.

After saddling the second horse, he asked, "And what can you do? Can you ride? Can you track? You'll just end up getting lost yourself, and then I'll have to go out looking for you too."

"Somehow I doubt that you would bother to look for me if I didn't come back," Ginny said caustically, not caring about his feelings at the moment.

"Damn right," he said, under his breath, but still a stage whisper loud enough to be heard.

"Please Colby, let me help." When he turned his back to her again, she got rash. "If you let me go and help, I promise to leave as soon as Nate is home. I won't even make you drive me. I'll walk away. I just need to know that he's okay. If you leave me here, I swear I'll go crazy."

Ginny had never felt this way before. She remembered when her nephew had been hit in the head with a baseball during a game. It was touch and go for a while, with all of the family huddled in the hospital, waiting for news from his mother whether he'd pull through. But this, this was like Ginny was the mother. She'd never felt anything this close to being maternal before. Was it the environment that made it happen so fast or was Nate just that kind of special kid?

Colby was moved by the sound of her voice. In the past few weeks, his brother and Ginny had formed a bond that Colby didn't have with him after ten years. She sounded as if her heart was breaking. He thought back to her begging to let her stay. She'd said she would do anything he wanted, as long as she could stay because she "liked it here." Closing his eyes, trying to put himself in her shoes, he said, "Alright. You can come with me." Ginny gasped and he added, "But if you slow me down, I'll leave you behind. He's my brother, after all."

Putting up her hands in supplication, Ginny said, "Of course, of course. I won't slow you down, I swear. Just tell me what you want me to do. Should I get some supplies from Nizhoni?"

In the hopes of getting her away from him, he nodded. Ginny flew away, towards the house. The last thing he heard was Ginny calling to Vas that he was in the barn. A moment later, Vas came in for his instructions.

They had three teams of two. With the two ranch hands, everyone had a partner to watch their back. Colby was going to stick Ginny with Vas or Tim, but decided he needed his two best trackers not to be distracted by her. So, in the end, he took her himself.

Ginny had arranged supplies for everyone in saddle bags. With Nizhoni's help, each bag contained food, ammo and some basic medical supplies. By the time everyone had gathered, Ginny had changed into the pants and shirt that Georgia had given her the day they'd gone to the swimming hole. She had also found a hat and long coat, to keep her warm at night.

The six set off east, figuring that Nate wouldn't take the mountain pass to the north or use the road into Cheyenne. He wouldn't want to be discovered that easily. Vas and Tim would probably be able to pick up a trail, but they would still have to split up in case Nate got lost and ended up somewhere unexpected.

As they approached the wooded area east of the ranch, Tim looked up at the sky. "Could be a bad one."

"Bad what?" Ginny asked, having so far held her own on the horse. She thought that whoever she was may have been a rider, since she found herself doing things automatically, without thinking about it first.

Vas pointed toward the horizon. "Storm, Ginny. Looks like a real soaker too."

Ginny's face began to crack slightly. She was determined not to be a burden, but the thought of Nate alone, cold and wet and possibly lost was eating at her soul. He was a smart kid, she told herself. He would be alright.

After entering the woods, Colby directed each team where to go. "Ginny and I will head south, toward the river. He might try to follow it out of the woods. Tim, Vas, both of you head northeast and see if you can pick up his trail. Douglas, you and Ben head north and see if there is any sign. If anyone finds him, one man take him home while the other lets the rest of us know. Got it?"

Everyone agreed and set off. Thankfully for Ginny, the forest was dense enough to keep Colby from racing off on the horse. Unfortunately, it was too dense to get through in a hurry and find Nate quicker.

They'd been riding for over an hour when the wind picked up. Ginny couldn't feel it in the forest, but she could hear the tops of the trees swaying. She was cold, but not from exposure. She feared they wouldn't find him in time. *Don't borrow trouble, Ginny. It does you no good,* her mother used to say when she worried needlessly. Ginny wondered what her mother would say about this.

Without any preamble, the rain started to come down. They had just reached the river. Not yet swollen from the rain, they were able to cross easily. After they reached the other side, Colby came along side her.

He nearly had to yell, as the they were no longer in the woods and the rain began to pour down in buckets. "This river runs east. It eventually hits a road going north toward Cheyenne. He may be following it."

"Would he know about it? Have you guys been here before?"

His face was exasperated, again. "Of course he does, Ginny. Do you think I would waste our time."

Ginny took a deep breath. With every ounce of patience she had, she said, "Of course not, Colby. Sometimes I don't think before I speak. Lead on."

Colby's eyes held some regret, but then he turned his horse and led her along the path beside the river. Soon, they had to enter the forest again, as the river began to swell in the continued downpour.

Ginny didn't think she'd ever been this wet before, except when swimming in a pool. She felt heavy, from all the clothing that had sucked in every available ounce of water falling from the sky. As miserable as she felt, she could only imagine how Nate was doing. She had no idea what supplies he'd thought to bring or if he had any materials to make a shelter. The one good part of the rain was that Colby couldn't tell that she was crying.

After a couple of hours of following the river, the pair stopped to let the horses rest. Hiding under a thick, evergreen tree, Ginny leaned against the trunk, feeling forlorn. Colby found the horses some grass to nibble on and walked back to stand next to Ginny.

Seeing her face, he set out to reassure her. "He's a smart kid, Ginny. He knows how to take care of himself out here. He'll be alright."

Turning her face to his, Colby saw the tears in her eyes. It struck him how much Ginny had become a mother to his brother. After losing their own mother less than a year ago, Nate had seemed lost. He rarely spoke, and when he did, it was usually only to Frank. In the past few weeks, he'd come out of his self-imposed shell. For the first time in a while, Nate was laughing again, joining in activities, and best of all, acting more like a ten year old boy. Colby wondered if some of the stunts that his brothers had orchestrated hadn't been cries for attention. When Ginny started to shower them with attention, they hadn't needed to cause anymore trouble.

Reaching over, Colby used his gloved hand to wipe away a tear falling down Ginny's cheek. Her reaction startled him. She pulled away and looked shocked.

"What's wrong, Ginny?"

Staring at Colby, she couldn't believe that he didn't know. It was the first time the man had shown any affection toward her since her arrival. Ginny wasn't talking about anything sexual. Colby hadn't so much as high fived her for a job well done.

"I... What are you doing?" she asked, clearly confused by his change of heart. Wasn't it just yesterday that he was screamed at her to get out of his house and go to a strange city, without any resources, just to be away from him?

Colby looked away. For the first time, he saw his behavior from someone else's point of view. What he saw made him cringe. Instead of addressing their issues, he said, "We better get going. I don't want to burn too much daylight just standing around." With that, he walked away to collect the horses.

Ginny watched him leave and wondered if things might be changing between them. That when they found Nate, Colby would be willing to give her another chance and let her stay. God she hoped so, since she knew she had so much more to do with this family.

Chapter 20

They rode on together, without speaking, for another couple of hours. Ginny was amazed to find out they had only gone about twelve or fifteen miles from the ranch. It seemed like they'd been riding for days and should be near Denver by now. Fifteen miles in her time period usually meant less than twenty minutes by car, not four or five hours by horse.

The swaying of the horse was lulling her into a false sense of security. She kept looking around for any sign of Nate, but truthfully, she didn't know what to look for. Short of a large sign saying, "Over here," she was lost.

The only sound besides the rain was some distant thunder. Although they were in the woods, Ginny still worried about lightning. There certainly wasn't any thing she could do if one of them were struck.

As if conjured by her own mind, a flash of lightning struck one of the trees, directly behind Ginny. A large chunk of wood and leaves came crashing down next to her, spooking the horse so bad that he took off like a jackrabbit. The only thing Ginny had time to do was hold on tight. The horse passed Colby, who was able to keep his horse from taking off.

They were racing through the forest, dodging branches. Ginny kept her head down and was screaming, "Whoa," for all the good it did. The horse, clearly unhappy at his task as it was, was even more displeased at the prospect of lightning and falling debris.

A low lying branch slashed across Ginny's face, knocking off her hat and scraping her cheek. Ginny hoped that the forest would open up so she could sit up and pull back the reins. She didn't dare try it now, or she might be taken off the horse by all the branches.

Suddenly, Ginny saw Nate. He was crouched by the river, trying to fill his canteen. Before Ginny could scream, the horse stopped up short, bucking on his hind legs and sending Ginny to the ground. With the wind knocked out of her, she barely registered the fact that her escapade had caught Nate unaware, making him fall into the river.

With what strength she had left, Ginny ran down to the river, ripping off her coat as she went. She spotted Nate heading toward her on the fast moving water. Without any time to think, Ginny jumped into the water, grabbed Nate and reached out to grab hold of a tree that had long ago fallen into the river. She and Nate were pressed against the side of the tree, with the water pushing them against it, keeping them from moving. The pressure was tremendous. They had to get out of the river.

Ginny moved so one arm was draped around the tree, then she could use her other hand to help Nate climb on top of the log. The current kept trying to pull him under, making her job all that much harder. The river was cold, slowly sapping what little strength either of them had.

With a mighty heave, Ginny pulled Nate up by his belt. She was screaming at him to climb up, but the rushing water drowned out most of the sound. Nate turned his head, and she saw raw fear in his eyes. After all, wasn't this how his parents had died?

Putting on a confident face, she said as loud as she could, "Nate, you have got to climb up. Use all your strength."

"But what about you?" he asked, tears forming in his eyes.

"As soon as you're out, I can get out. I can't move with you here." It was a lie. Ginny didn't think she'd be able to climb out regardless, but she needed him to get out. Without a thought of herself, she would do anything to save the boy.

Nate nodded his understanding and started to climb. Ginny pulled as hard as she could, not feeling as though she was getting very far. Just as she thought they were making headway, something cracked and Ginny got sucked under the log.

Miraculously, she was able to grab a branch on the other side, barely pulling herself back to the log. The current was a little softer, with the log taking the brunt of the force, but she didn't think she'd be able to hold on for long. Nate had both arms over the log, with his chest plastered against it. He was crying, not able to move.

"Nate, please try again. Try to pull yourself up."

His eyes flew open, and Ginny realized that he thought she was gone. After seeing her there, still clinging to the dead tree, he found a small reserve of strength and started again to pull himself up. Meanwhile, Ginny held onto the branch, praying she could hold on just long enough for Nate to pull himself out.

No matter what Nate did, he couldn't get his legs up. The current under the tree was too strong. Ginny tried to pull herself closer, but was pulled away by the same assault. Just when she thought they would have to let go and try again down river, Colby appeared by the river's edge. Reaching down, with one hand he pulled Nate to the shore. From the cold and terror, Nate could only flop down on the ground.

Colby leaned out on the tree and reached out his hand. Ginny was afraid to let go, knowing she had only one chance to grab his hand or be swept down river. Looking up at his face, she saw something she hadn't seen on him before: fear. Before she could say anything, it was gone, replaced by determination.

"Ginny, grab my hand. I swear I won't let you go." He must have been shouting, but over the sound of the river, Ginny could barely hear him.

Knowing that this could only end one of two ways, and generally speaking, heroines didn't drown, Ginny reached out and grabbed his hand. Colby pulled her up, onto the log, then helped her onto the river bank. She flopped next to Nate, who had his eyes closed and was breathing steadily.

She touched his cheek, and he turned and looked at her. Smiling, he started to cry and shake. He grabbed her and wrapped his arms around her.

"It's okay, Nate. We're all okay." Ginny held the boy until he calmed down. By then, she felt like she could stand. The three moved further up the bank, away from the river.

Chapter 21

Colby knew he had hurt his family by ordering Ginny to leave. Seeing her under the tree, crying with worry over his little brother, he realized that she could no more leave than he could. His family needed her, and it appeared that she needed them as well. Not remembering who she was must be frightening, and Colby hadn't made it any easier on her.

As they rode together through the forest, he kept stealing clandestine looks. She paid him no notice, her worry etched in her face. They would find his little brother, but then what? Could he make it up to his family, to Ginny?

He hadn't been fair, and he was even less mature. After all, he'd brought her here to be a mother to his brothers and when she was, he got jealous of her. Colby wasn't the warm and fuzzy type. And since being forced to return, he hadn't even been the nice type. He wasn't willing to sit with his brothers as they fell asleep, and he wasn't going to listen to his sister ramble on about suitors.

But Ginny was willing, able, and more than capable. So why had he wanted her gone so badly? The answer hit him and made him catch his breath. He was falling in love with her. She was strong and independent. She was smart, funny and beautiful. Ginny had everything he was looking for. But, she was unavailable. She had suggested the original idea of keeping things professional. She wasn't interested in a relationship with him.

The more he thought about it, the more he realized why she'd made the suggestion. Hadn't he been standoffish? Hadn't he made it clear that he wanted nothing to do with her because he thought she was only there to take advantage? Faced with that, Ginny had made the proposal in order to save herself. It was either him or the whorehouse, and what woman would choose a brothel over being a governess?

Then she came, and she never once complained. She did the job he'd assigned her. Maybe her methods were strange, but one thing was certain, she had gotten through to his siblings. They trusted her, liked her and maybe even loved her. Nate definitely did, or he wouldn't be out traipsing the countryside to live with her instead of him.

Ginny even earned Nizhoni's friendship and trust. An accomplishment that Eloise had never been able to do. Everyone seemed to take to her as soon as they met her. Vas liked her immediately, although Colby knew that Vas liked most women immediately. Seeing them together that night in the dark with Ginny in only her nightgown, had nearly sent him over the edge. He hated to admit that he was somewhat relieved when Vas chose Georgia instead of Ginny.

Having finally come to terms with his feelings, Colby wondered how he would make it right with his family. Obviously he wouldn't send Ginny away. But could he make her love him as much as he was starting to love her? Or had that ship sailed away on his bitterness and anger? He couldn't imagine her ever wanting him now, but he was determined to show her the other side of Colby Miller. The one that could be nice, sweet and generous. He would even marry her again before Reverend Thomas, to make it official.

As Colby was setting plans in his head, he heard a loud crack, followed by an even louder crash. Without thinking, he set to calm his spooked horse down. As he tried to keep his horse from throwing him, he saw Ginny fly past him on her own horse. It was obvious that she had no control over the animal.

It took a moment to get his own horse calm enough to go after her. By that time, she was gone, hidden from view by the trees. He couldn't even hear her with the sound of the rain. He went as fast as he could, through the trees, worried that he would be pulled off if he went any faster. That was his biggest fear for Ginny.

It seemed like a long time before he spotted her horse, eating some grass he'd found in a small clearing. But where was Ginny? He hadn't passed her, he was sure of it. Looking around frantically, he saw her coat, lying on the ground. He ran over to it, and then saw a sight that froze his heart. Both Ginny and Nate were in the river, holding onto an old tree.

As he ran towards them, Ginny went under. Colby felt his heart stop until he saw her come up on the other side of the tree, still clinging to it. Colby didn't think he'd ever be as scared as he was at that moment. Two of the most important people in his life were in mortal danger. If either let go, they would be swept away and would surely drown. He didn't want to imagine his life if that happened.

Reaching the river's edge, Colby grabbed his brother and pulled him on shore. The current had been sucking him under. It took a lot of force to get him out, like sucking a watermelon through a straw. Then he turned and saw Ginny. She looked relieved. It finally hit Colby that Ginny had become a true mother to Nate, willing to surrender her own life in exchange for his. In that moment, Colby knew that he couldn't lose her, not to the river and not to his own bitterness.

Reaching down, he held out his hand. "Ginny, grab my hand. I swear I won't let you go." He had never meant anything more in his life. It occurred to him as he pulled her out of the water, that he would gladly exchange his life for hers.

Chapter 22

Walking back to Colby's horse, Ginny held Nate in her arms directing him where to step so he wouldn't fall. They were both bone cold, exhausted and soaking wet. As Colby went to pick up their possessions, Ginny examined Nate for any injuries. He wasn't talking, just staring into space.

When Colby returned with Ginny's coat and Nate's backpack, Ginny gave him a worried look. "I think Nate is going into shock. We need to get him warm and dry as soon as possible."

Colby stood up and looked around. "I remember an outcropping not too far from here. It'll be dry, and I'll be able to build a fire to keep him warm."

Colby put Ginny and Nate on his horse and walked them to Ginny's horse. Climbing up on the other animal, he set off in the direction of the shelter. It took less than a half hour to reach it, but by the time they arrived, Nate was shaking.

Ginny dropped from the horse after handing Nate to Colby. She surveyed the outcropping. It was just what she expected, a thick, flat piece of rock jutting out to provide a small shelter underneath. The space went back underneath, surrounded by rock walls, making a small cave. Fortunately, it was both dry and unoccupied.

The ground had some rocks lying around, so Ginny moved those out of the way. Using her long coat, she laid it down on the ground. Then she found her saddlebag that contained a clean shirt. She removed Nate's clothing and put him in the clean shirt. Colby handed her the blanket from his horse. Although the edges were wet, most of it that was under the saddle was still dry. Ginny took it and covered the boy.

Colby set out to find some firewood. Ginny laid down next to Nate and wrapped herself around him. She had removed her outer shirt and pants, hanging them from a rock to dry out. She had only a pair of long underwear that Georgia had given her to keep her warm. They were soaked as well, but Ginny wasn't about to go naked.

Colby returned and started a fire. The small shelter soon filled with its warmth and Nate stopped shaking. As Colby built the fire, he could hear Ginny talking to Nate, telling him how everything would be alright, that he was alright. Colby took a deep breath and told his brother the one thing that he thought would calm him more than anything.

"Nate, Ginny's not leaving. I was wrong to try to make her go. If she wants, she can stay as long as she wants."

Nate's eyes cleared for a moment as he looked at his brother. "Really?" he asked, voice earnest.

Smiling a sad smile, knowing that he had caused the boy so much pain, he answered, "Really."

Turning to look up at Ginny, Nate asked, "Are you gonna stay, Ginny? Please say you'll stay."

With a sincere smile, she answered, "Of course. I can't think of anywhere else I'd rather be."

With a sigh of relief, Nate cuddled under the blanket and fell asleep, as if the news was all he needed to hear to be comfortable again. When his breathing evened out, Ginny moved to sit with her back against the wall of the small cave. She was a little chilled, but the heat from the fire helped keep her from shivering.

Colby, who had retrieved his saddlebag, was busy making a spot for her to get comfortable. He pulled out his only clean shirt and handed it to her. Ginny was grateful for the extra clothing. He motioned for Ginny to join him. They sat side by side, backs against the cave wall, Nate only a few feet away, fast asleep.

Ginny figured this would be when they had it out. That all the nice things Colby had said were only to placate his brother. She would be able to stay, but he would still be the same stubborn, prickly individual he was before.

Handing her a flask, Colby said, "I don't think I've ever been as scared as when I saw you two in the river."

Ginny gladly took a long draw of the whiskey and replied, "It wasn't too great being in the river either."

Colby chuckled. Ginny was surprised that he actually took something she said correctly, not jumping down her throat for being a smart ass. "No, I can't imagine it was."

The two fell silent for a moment, when Colby finally resolved to have his say. Turning toward her, looking into her eyes, he said what needed to be said. "You are the most incredible woman I've ever met. I can't believe that you would risk your life for my brother when you've only known him a few weeks. I doubt I could ever repay you for that."

Her smile was weak and cautious. "You don't have to repay me, Colby. I did it because he means so much to me. Your whole family means that much to me."

Looking down, scratching his forehead, he whispered, "Everyone but me, right?"

Ginny, who hadn't taken her eyes off him, replied, "You haven't exactly ever made me feel welcome, you know."

Still avoiding eye contact, he said, "I know. I feel pretty awful about that."

Ginny turned to watch the rain drops fall from the leaves of the nearby trees. The sounds were soothing, like listening to one of those CD's of nature sounds, with waves crashing, crickets chirping and rain falling. All they ever did for her was make her have to pee. But now, it was nice.

Not sure how to broach the subject, but knowing this was to be where they would forge new ground, find their way, she asked, "Why didn't you... what could I... what happened?" She stammered, not knowing what to ask or how to ask it. Mostly, she was afraid of saying the wrong thing and setting him off again.

"Three years ago, I finally got to leave the ranch. I wanted to be a lawyer. My parents always said I could argue anything to death. So, when the ranch was doing well, and my parents had enough help, I went to Denver and started apprenticing with a local lawyer.

"His name was Barney Strohman, and he taught me a lot. But in the end, I decided to enroll in a law school back East. Part of me wanted to learn as much as I could, but there was also part of me that wanted to be away from here. I wanted to live an exciting life in a big city. So, I saved every penny I could, and with a recommendation from Barney, I got accepted to Columbia."

"Wow, Columbia. That's a good school, huh?" Ginny knew that it was a good school in her time but not so much about it in this time period. Still, he obviously wanted to get very far away, and New York City was really far.

"Yeah, I guess. There's not too many law schools to chose from. Anyway, I was set to leave when my parents died. I received a telegram two weeks before I was supposed to leave. Needless to say, I rushed back to the ranch. It wasn't long before I realized that I wouldn't be able to leave again."

"Why never again?" Ginny asked, trying to keep him talking.

He finally turned and looked at her again. "How can I leave? My brothers can't handle the ranch, and it wouldn't be right leaving it to strangers." His voice held that same old exasperation, but Ginny bit her tongue. Some habits die hard.

"What I mean is... your brothers will eventually grow up and will be able to take care of themselves. If none of you want the ranch, you could sell it and move on. It's just a setback, Colby. It doesn't have to be forever."

Shaking his head, he said, "My parents worked so hard. All they wanted was to leave us something when they were gone. Wouldn't be right to sell the ranch."

Staring out at the trees once again, Ginny thought about what he said. "Your parents did give you something, Colby. If they were like any decent parents, they just wanted you to be happy. Besides, I don't think Frank will ever leave this valley. You can see it in his eyes. He couldn't picture himself anywhere else in the world." A smile came across Ginny's face.

Seeing that smile, Colby said, "How did you do it? How did you get so close to them so quickly?"

"I don't know. Frank tried so hard to shock me with the cursing. It only made me laugh. When he saw that I could give him what he wanted, I guess he decided I wasn't so bad. And Nate... well, he's just such a special kid." Ginny turned and looked him in the eye. "He needed someone so bad, and so did I. He just managed to crawl into my heart, I guess."

"Nate has a way of doing that, even when he was younger. I remember the day he was born. He had these big, blue eyes. He grabbed my finger and held on so tight."

Ginny's breath caught in her throat. He sounded like a father, and she couldn't help but love the sound of it. She knew he loved his family, but this was the first time that she'd heard it in his voice. Before, she had only seen the side of him that looked upon his brothers and sister as a burden.

Not being able to help herself, Ginny asked, "Do you ever want your own children someday?"

Colby stared out at the dripping trees and smiled. He would remember that question as the first thing Ginny had ever said that could mean that she would be willing to have him. "Yes. I would like to be married to someone special and have kids of my own."

He turned his gaze to his feet and muttered, "Don't know how good a father I would be, though."

Seeing how forlorn he looked, Ginny replied, "I think you'd make a great father. You're obviously a good provider and an excellent protector. You're willing to sacrifice yourself for your family. Sounds like some great qualifications to me."

Turning his gaze to hers once again, Colby felt like he was home. Just staring in her eyes, he felt complete. He would have to do anything and everything in his power to make sure that this woman was his forever.

"Thanks," was all he could say. Not taking his eyes off hers, he reached over and brushed her cheek with his thumb. Ginny's tender look turned to shock.

In for a penny, in for a pound, he thought as he broached the topic of her staying as more than a nanny.

"I was wondering if you might like to... alter our original arrangement."

Squinting her eyes in suspicion, she asked, "Our original arrangement?"

"Yeah. You know the one about our marriage being in name only. You earning back what I paid for you, then leaving." Colby's eyes were intense, knowing that her rejection would devastate him.

Ginny turned to look over at Nate. He was still sound asleep, breathing steadily. She realized what this was. This was her ticket to sex and moving on. Judging by the look in his eyes, he was already in love. Just as the romance novels dictated.

Taking a deep breath, she looked back at him and asked, "What did you have in mind?"

Colby let out a breath he hadn't realized he was holding. She hadn't rejected him outright, so he still had a chance. "I was thinking that we consider our marriage valid. Or..." he stumbled a bit when her expression looked doubtful, "I could court you proper. Then we could say our vows again, before Reverend Thomas."

Ginny turned to stare out at the trees again. She thought about what he said. If he were to court her proper, as he put it, it could take weeks or months before she had her best sex ever. On the other hand, if they were in love, would she leave again quickly? Turning once again to gaze at Nate, she didn't want to leave this family. Her heart broke a little knowing that she would eventually have to do just that.

Steeling herself against the inevitable, she made her decision. "Not that I'm opposed to you having to be nice to me to convince me to remarry you, but I don't think I want to wait." Ginny knew she would have to leave eventually, but she didn't want to drag this storyline out and make it even more difficult on herself.

Now it was Colby's turn to look shocked. "What do you mean, exactly?" he sputtered, not believing what he may have just heard.

"Can't you take me home as your wife? As if you really did just marry me?"

Colby was breathless. If he wasn't completely fantasizing this entire episode, he had just heard her ask him to take her to his bed. A prospect that made him hard.

Testing the water to make sure he wasn't going crazy and hearing things, Colby bent his head down towards Ginny. When she didn't pull away, he brushed his lips against hers. Still, she didn't pull away. Taking his hand, he caressed her cheek, and used his thumb to pull her lips apart. He needed no further invitation to taste her mouth with his tongue. She tasted of whiskey and a sweetness that could only be his Ginny.

When he pulled away from her, Ginny had a glazed look in her eyes. He smiled smugly. Colby realized that for the first time in his life, he was at peace right where he was. He didn't feel the need to move on or away. He felt like he was right where he was supposed to be.

Seeing the smug look on his face, Ginny said, "You can knock that grin right off your face, Colby Miller. You're not that good a kisser."

His smile only grew more radiant. "How would you know? How many men do you remember kissing?"

Truth was she could remember every man she'd ever kissed, from her real life through all her romance lives. Not that she could explain that to Colby. Regardless, she had kissed one other man, that she could remember as Colby put it, while living in this body. And she was not about to tell Colby about it.

Allowing him this one victory, she conceded, "Fine. It was a nice kiss. But without anything to compare it to, how do I know there isn't something better?" Ginny raised her eyebrow in challenge.

Growling, Colby muttered, "You'd better not go around finding out, Mrs. Miller." When the words left his mouth, Colby got a flash of their future. It was a name he would pass down to his children. Again, he felt only peace.

Pulling his wife toward him, resting her head on his shoulder, he said, "Get some rest, Ginny. We'll set out tomorrow back to the ranch. It will be a long day trying to find a suitable spot to cross that swollen river."

With Colby's warmth against her, Ginny finally succumbed to the exhaustion she had been feeling. Between the riding, the falling and the river, her body had had enough. It was time to let go. So she did.

Chapter 23

Ginny woke up at dawn, surprised that she had slept through part of the day and all of the night. She was stretched out next to Nate, who was still breathing softly. Disoriented at first, Ginny soon remembered what had happened and how she had agreed to be married to Colby for real.

In the first light of day, Ginny began to wonder if that was such a good idea. After all, Colby had treated her so badly, for the past few weeks, she didn't know if she could summon up any warm and fuzzy feelings toward him. She found him attractive, that was never an issue. But his personality, up until yesterday, wasn't anything but annoying.

Could she put that aside and have sex with him? With Ian, in Scotland, he had an annoying personality at times, but she was still able to appreciate his finer qualities. Don't even get her started on Colin, her Regency English Earl, who abandoned her for a whole year. Still, she was able to forgive him and move on. And now, she had Colby.

It seemed to her that unless she could find something in him that could churn her butter, she was better off not sleeping with him yet. Ginny could be shallow when discussing a fine piece of beefcake, but she would never act on those feelings. Despite her situation, as a romance novel heroine, she had to have some feelings for a man before she up and slept with him.

Rather than fret over the possibility, she would just go about getting Nate home. Colby had said it would be a long day, so maybe something would happen that would light a fire inside her. Or, if it didn't, she would just have to make him court her after all. After their talk yesterday, she knew there was something about this man she could care about, and not just his siblings.

Ginny propped herself on her elbow and looked for the man in question. Still asleep, Colby was propped against the same rock they'd shared the night before. His eyes were closed, his arms crossed across his body, his chin touching his chest. Just seeing him at peace made Ginny smile. She'd meant what she'd said about him being a good father. Perhaps that would be the grease to get the wheels of their relationship going.

As if sensing her attention, Colby lifted his head and stared back at Ginny. His blue eyes sparkled in the early morning sunlight. His expression said he was eager to get their journey going, so he could have his wedding night. The look made Ginny's stomach drop. If she thought he had any doubts, she certainly couldn't think that now. It was clear that Colby had no doubts about where he wanted this relationship to go.

Ginny smiled and rose from behind Nate. Careful not to hit her head, she left the enclosure and found some privacy behind a group of trees. After relieving herself, she found a clear puddle to wash her hands and face with. Refreshed, she returned to their makeshift campsite and found Colby stoking the fire and Nate sitting up against the rocks.

Seeing her again, he looked relieved, like he thought she'd left for good. Smiling at her young charge, she said, "Good morning, Nate. Colby."

Smiling back, he replied, "Good morning, Ginny. Colby's gonna make us some breakfast, then we have to get back to the ranch." His voice grew morose as he spoke the last part.

Colby, who knew why, said, "Nate, you know you have to be punished. You should have come and talked to me. You shouldn't have worried Ginny so by running off. What if we didn't find you?"

Staring down at the ground, playing with a dried leaf, he responded, "I know, Colby." His voice sounded so much like the little boy he was, but his response was very much the man he would become.

Trying to back Colby up, she asked, "What will his punishment be? Because I was pretty worried." Ginny figured he would be grounded or denied something. Never did she consider what Colby had in mind.

"He'll choose his switch and he'll get ten licks."

By sheer willpower, Ginny didn't gasp. She should have known, but it just never occurred to her. This was a different time, and she knew she should say something to deter him, but Ginny also knew it wasn't her place. She would speak to him privately, though, the first chance she got.

The chance came a few minutes later, when Nate went off to get some privacy. Whispering, Ginny asked, "Ten licks?"

135

Colby knew the moment he'd said the punishment that Ginny would object. She had become like a mother to Nate with an inherent need to protect him. Rather than be annoyed, he asked, "What do you think would be fair?"

"I'd rather not hit him, but I know that's probably not a possibility."

"Ginny, he took off alone. He could've been killed yesterday and taken you with him. I've got to teach him a lesson." Although his voice was calm, he still sounded annoyed.

"I know. He does need to learn a lesson, but do you think hitting him will help? Nate wants more than anything to be old enough to help out like Frank does. Maybe if you tell him that this stunt has proven that he's not ready to join you on rides, it will have more of a lasting effect. And that if he wants to join you, he will have to prove how mature he is. Together we could probably come up with some very unpleasant tasks for him to accomplish to prove himself."

Colby was stunned. This woman never ceased to amaze him with her ideas. The more he thought about it, the more he liked the idea. After all, the whipping would be forgotten with the pain, but her idea would last for a long time, and maybe have him really consider his actions first. Hadn't Colby taken a switch to both his brothers after their previous stunts, and yet they continued to pull their antics.

Before Ginny could object, Colby had her in his arms and was kissing her, hard. He would get them home as quickly and safely as possible, but then he would have her. He would give her exactly five minutes to wash up before he carried her to his bedroom and made their marriage official.

When Colby grabbed her, Ginny had only a second to think he might hit her. When he kissed her, she felt bad that she thought he was capable of such a thing. Whatever she said, he seemed really pleased with. Not only had she stated her case without him getting mad at her, she had won. So, Ginny kissed him back.

They only pulled apart when Nate returned. "Ewww. Can't you two do that somewhere else? Gross!"

Pulling his mouth from hers, looking Ginny in the eyes, Colby said, "Someday you might not think it's so gross, kid. You'll be willing to drive all the way to Denver to find a girl for yourself."

Nate, not catching the nuance of his statement, replied, "Just kill me if that ever happens. Let's eat breakfast and get home. Please."

After breakfast, they packed up their supplies and made sure their fire was out. Colby took Nate with him on his horse, and Ginny took her own once again. After yesterday, Ginny wasn't thrilled about getting back on the beast. But, with sunny skies and no lightning to be seen anywhere, she hoped it would be safe.

Chapter 24

The day was a long one indeed. They had to ride a number of miles out of their way to find a safe place to cross the still swollen river. Once across, they found Vas, who was looking for them. When he couldn't find any trace of Nate, he decided to join forces with Colby and search the river.

With Colby in the lead, Vas held back to talk to Ginny.

"What happened?" Vas' voice sounded worried that Colby hadn't been on his best behavior with either of them.

"Nate fell into the river, and I had to go in to get him."

"Dear God. It's a wonder you two are still here."

Glancing at his face, Ginny saw wonder and respect. "In all fairness, he fell into the river because I scared him. My horse..." Ginny stated while pointing at the offending animal, "decided to take off on me. When he finally decided to dump my ass, it was right by Nate, who then fell into the river."

Vas felt bad about laughing, although it didn't stop him. "Damn, Ginny."

"We were clinging to a log when Colby arrived to fish us out."

Turning his head to stare at his friend, Vas asked, "What's gonna happen to Nate?"

"We decided that rather than spank him, we would have him prove to us that he can be mature."

"How're you gonna do that?"

Shrugging her shoulders, she replied, "I dunno know. We'll figure something out. I do know that he won't get a chance to ride with Colby anytime soon."

"Well, that'll hurt him. There's nothing he'd love more than that."

"That's the idea."

Vas left them to search out Tim and the others to bring them home. It was late afternoon when they arrived back at the ranch, to a much relieved Frank, Georgia and Nizhoni. He was sent right to the bathroom to wash up, then Nizhoni gave him something to eat and he was sent right to bed.

"We'll talk in the morning, Nate. First thing, you meet me by the barn. Understood?" Colby said, keeping his voice menacing.

"Yes, sir." Nate turned with shoulders slumped and headed to his bedroom. Frank was hot on his heels hoping to hear any tales Nate had.

Ginny and Colby decided not to tell Nate that his fate had changed. Better to have him worry over his beating all night. Hopefully, the impression would last longer.

"You must be exhausted, Ginny. Would you like me to draw you a bath?" Georgia asked. She had sensed that something had changed between her brother and Ginny but wasn't about to question it. Whatever it was, it was better.

Ginny turned to Georgia and said, "That sounds wonderful. Thank you, Georgia."

Colby, who had been stealing glances at Ginny throughout the meal, said, "Don't stay in too long. Some of us might like some hot water as well."

The room fell silent as everyone tried to interpret Colby's tone. Georgia, innocent as a babe, looked curiously at her brother. Nizhoni, who had lived a long life, smiled in appreciation. Nothing got past her. Ginny glanced at the carnal look Colby was giving her and felt her stomach flutter. Was there enough attraction for her consent? Would she consider sharing his bed, even after weeks of torture? Hell yes, she decided. She'd seen the real Colby, the one not marred by bitterness. The one who wanted to be happy and make a life with the woman he loved. She might not love him, but she couldn't deny the attraction.

With a flick of her head, she told him to meet her in the other room. Georgia went about preparing the bath, and Nizhoni cleaned up the kitchen. Ginny got up and left the kitchen, Colby hot on her heels.

Ginny went to enter the parlor, but Colby escorted her outside instead. Heading for the barn, he pulled into an empty stall. When Ginny tried to talk to him, he ignored her attempt and began to nibble on her neck instead. Feeling herself being distracted, Ginny playfully tried to push Colby away. He could not be deterred.

"Colby, can we talk for a minute?" she asked, voice innocent, but tinged with the passion he was igniting in her.

"Hmmmm?" was his only reply. His mouth was better used for other things.

"About our marriage?" Ginny was soon forgetting her arguments, as she got caught up in the moment.

Pulling away, he asked, "What about it? Do you want to be married proper before we..." Colby's cheeks turned pink, as he suddenly realized that his bride was a virgin. Even is she wasn't, she obviously didn't remember one way or the other.

Putting a hand on his chest to reassure him, she said, "I don't know if I've ever... you know..."

Placing his own hand over hers, Colby said, "It's alright. We can wait, Ginny, until it's right. We can go see Reverend Thomas tomorrow and talk about a real wedding ceremony. I want you to be a true mother to my brothers. And a true wife to me."

Part of Ginny thought it was corny and stupid. She was, after all, a 21st century woman, not a 19th century prude. The thought of having this man all over her made her heartbeat quicken. But there was another part of her that thought that wasn't right. She could sleep with him and maybe move on, but it just didn't seem like the way it should be. Ginny thought she should smack herself in the head. Obviously, she was getting too caught up in these romance novels.

As she stared at Colby, she tried to decide. Yes or No? Sex or Wait? Possibly move on or continue to live this life? In a flash, she knew what she was going to do.

"Colby. I can't deny that I really want you. I want more than anything to come to your bed tonight. But, I also think that we should be officially married first. I doubt John, by the back of his wagon, constitutes an official marriage. I'm sorry." Ginny thought he would get mad, but he surprised her instead.

"I think that's a good idea. We can go into town tomorrow and speak to the minister. He'll be pleased as punch to be able to marry us."

Not hearing any sarcasm or annoyance, Ginny asked, "Really?"

Colby smiled at her. "Honest and truly."

Ginny smiled back. After one more brief kiss, Colby escorted her to the bathroom and the hot bath that Georgia had so kindly drawn. Before she could enter the bathroom, he whispered, "Do be quick, Ginny. If you're not out soon, I may have to come in and find out what's taking you so long." With a wink, he disappeared out of the kitchen.

Ginny was left to wonder if she'd made a stupid mistake in turning him down for the night. What could she have possibly been thinking?

After a frustratingly sleepless night, Ginny woke up later than usual. By the time she entered the kitchen, only Frank and Georgia remained. Nizhoni had already left to attend her garden.

Sitting on one of the available chairs, Ginny asked, "Where are your brothers?"

Frank, who was stuffing his face with food, responded, "Colby took Nate to the barn for his punishment."

"Don't speak with your mouth full," Ginny said automatically, having heard it from her mother a thousand times growing up. "How long ago did they leave?"

It was Georgia this time who spoke. "Maybe ten minutes. Colby looked plenty mad, and Nate looked even more worried." Georgia looked worried as well.

"Ginny, is it true? Are you and my brother getting married for real?" Georgia asked before Ginny could go outside and find out what was going on.

"Uh, yes. We're going to talk to the minister today."

"That is excellent news. Vas and I need to speak to him as well. Do you think that maybe we could have a double ceremony? We could be each other's bridesmaids. I could help you make a dress. What do you think?"

Ginny stared at her for a full minute before responding. "I, uh... that would be great." Truth was, Ginny didn't care. One way or the other, she was going to marry Colby. If her soon-to-be sister-in-law wanted to share a wedding, fine with her.

"Are you sure? If you want your own ceremony, I won't be offended." Georgia's expression gave her away. She looked terrified of rejection.

Ginny felt terrible. "Georgia, truly, I would love to have a double wedding. I'm more worried about you. Are you sure you don't want to have your own ceremony?"

"Absolutely not. I already consider you my sister and so wanted you to be my bridesmaid. That you can officially become my sister would be a dream come true, especially as I marry the love of my life."

Ginny didn't know what to say, mostly because she was trying not to gag. Such sentimentality wasn't part of her makeup. But, seeing how much it would please Georgia, she couldn't resist making her happy.

"Then it's settled. We'll marry together."

Bursting with joy, Georgia started going on about all the plans they needed to make. Before she could go on, Ginny stopped her.

"I want to go and help Colby with Nate. Can we chat later?"

"Chat?" Georgia asked, perplexed.

"Talk, discuss, converse..."

"Oh, yes. Of course."

Finally able to disengage herself, Ginny left and went straight to the barn. When she entered, she didn't know what to expect, but certainly not what she saw. There was Colby, standing under a ladder, with Nate halfway up coming down. Nate had tears in his eyes, but wasn't blubbering. When Colby saw her, he motioned for her to remain quiet.

Ginny sat on a nearby bale of hay and watched the two.

"Do you see what I mean, Nate?" Colby sounded calm, reasonable.

Shaking his head up and down, Nate remained silent.

"Please don't ever do anything like that again to me or to Ginny. If I'd lost either one of you, it would have killed me."

Colby's voice was so full of emotion, that it almost made Ginny cry. She could feel his pain, and it was like a stab at her. Why had she said they should wait?

"Ginny, what should Nate do today as far as his lessons are concerned?" Colby had turned toward her, his brother tucked under his arm.

Snapping to attention, Ginny responded, "Read the next three chapters of your reader. Prepare a detailed report of what those chapters contain." Ginny kept her voice solemn, to match the seriousness of their discussion.

"Well, you heard her. Get going." Colby said, smacking his brother on the bottom to get him moving.

Before he could leave, Nate looked at Ginny and said, "I'm real sorry to make you worry, Ginny. I'm real glad that you're gonna stay."

Ginny smiled and said, "Me too, kiddo. Get going now so I can talk to your brother, okay?"

Nate smiled and left. Colby sat next to her on the bale of hay and leaned back against the barn wall. He took a deep breath and released it again. Then he gave her a sideways glance.

"Did you think I was gonna hit him?" he asked, mockery in his voice.

"No, I didn't. I came out to help you drive the point home," Ginny replied, fake derision in her voice.

Laughing, he asked, "Do you want to know what I said to him?"

Ginny turned and looked at him. "Yes, please." She hardly used any sarcasm at all.

Patting her on the leg as he got up, he said, "Too bad. It's between us men." With that, he began to leave the barn.

Ginny jumped up and pulled on his arm. "Come on, Colby. Tell me." She was proud that she barely whined when asking.

"What will you give me if I tell you?" This was a side of Colby that Ginny had never seen. Playful, funny, joyous.

Squirming a bit, she asked, "What do you want?"

Putting his hand on his chin, acting as though in deep thought, he replied, "I don't know." Turning his gaze to meet hers directly, he said, "A kiss, perhaps."

"That's it? Done." With that, she stretched up on her tippy toes and kissed his cheek.

"You'll have to do far better than that, my soon-to-be wife." Colby grabbed Ginny, threw her over his shoulder and entered the same empty stall he had her in the day before.

He closed the door and laid her gently on the hay. Climbing on top of her, he put his face inches from hers. She could stare into his beautiful blue eyes as he bent closer to kiss her.

Before his lips touched hers, he said, "I believe that you are supposed to kiss me. Not the other way around."

Ginny pushed him over and climbed on top of him. She moved her face to inches from his and pulled her long hair over so it fell on only one side of her face. Lowering herself closer, she whispered, "Is this better, Colby?"

His eyes widened and he panted out, "Yes. So far, so good."

With mockery in her eyes, she placed her lips on his. Using her hands, she turned his face and deepened the kiss. When she began to use her tongue, Colby flung her back over onto her back. He was hungry and if he didn't stop this, his good intentions on waiting until they were truly married would mean nothing. But, he decided, one more kiss wouldn't hurt.

It was now his turn to grab her face and shove his tongue in her mouth. Ginny was giving as good as she was getting, so Colby didn't fear taking advantage. When his hands moved on their own and found her breasts, he knew he had to stop. Ginny wasn't making it any easier on him by running her hands up and down his back.

Before all good sense could leave him, he pulled away, laying himself beside her in the clean hay. He adjusted his pants for better comfort, but the only thing that would help would be bedding Ginny. She rolled to look at him, hand under her head, hay in her hair. She was so beautiful, Colby worried that he would grab her again.

"I guess we need to show a little more restraint, huh?" she asked, smiling.

Returning her smile, he replied, "You just plumb make me forget myself, Ginny."

Putting on a more serious face, Ginny asked, "What are we going to tell the minister today? You've already called me your wife. What excuse will we give him for wanting to get married again?"

Colby leaned over and mirrored her position. "I was thinking about that. I thought we could tell him that since you didn't have a proper church wedding the first time, you decided that we should do it one more time. Just in case."

"Just in case, what?" Ginny asked, perplexed by his strange logic.

"Just in case you're carrying my child." The only thing missing was Colby saying, "Duh!"

"Oh. So our fake wedding wouldn't cover babies?"

"Ok, just tell the reverend you liked him so much that you wanted him to perform the ceremony."

"Lying in church. Good idea, Colby. Do you want me to go to hell?" She sounded appalled.

Laughing, he asked, "As opposed to telling him that we were already married?"

Ginny's eyes widened. "That was all you, Colby. I didn't say a word. My only sin was going along with your lying, and I didn't have a choice. You were very convincing in your arguments."

They continued to spar, back and forth for a few more minutes, until Ginny's stomach growled, and Colby's willpower began to fail. Before he could grab her again, he sent her inside to eat breakfast and attend the boys.

As Ginny sat down to her plate of eggs, she realized that her scoundrel of a husband never did tell her what he'd said to Nate. And she had paid his price and everything. She figured she would just get it out of Nate later. Smiling as she ate, Ginny took a deep breath in relief that maybe she was doing everything right. Little did she know, what lay right around the corner.

Chapter 25

The six of them took a cart to town: Colby, Ginny, Vas, Georgia, Nate and Frank. Ginny had wanted to keep the boys at home doing their schoolwork, but Colby pointed out that leaving them alone was a bad idea. Although they had changed and their behavior had improved, there was no reason to tempt fate, especially after Nate's latest escapade.

They went to the reverend's house, knowing he wasn't likely at the church at this time of the week anyway. Mrs. Thomas answered the door, apron on and covered in flour. She seemed truly surprised to see the group massed outside her doorway, but was too polite to say anything. With a cheery smile, she welcomed everyone in and showed them to the parlor. Colby gave the boys a penny each to buy some candy at the Mercantile and told them to stay out of trouble. If they got bored, he'd said, they could go to the feed store and watch Noah do his work.

Once the group was seated, Mrs. Thomas asked if they would like any refreshments. "I have some lovely lemonade, if you'd care for some."

Ginny smiled. The woman was so demure, it almost seemed illogical, like she was more child than adult. "That would be great. Perhaps I could help you..."

"Oh, no. Please stay here. I'll have the reverend come in."

Not more than a minute after she left, Reverend Thomas walked in. He seemed genuinely pleased to see them there, until he spotted Vas. Although he remained civil, it was pretty obvious he was curious why he had joined their party.

Reverend Thomas was brought up in a small town in Texas. His father, a minister as well, had brought him up on stories about the Texas fight for independence. His family had owned land, and his grandparents were slave owners. Thomas remembered his father explaining the order of humanity. The white male population were ordained by God to lead the world with other races existing to serve. It was a heady responsibility, he would think as his father preached.

His mother, a tiny, timid woman, would spend her days in service to the men of his family. It had never bothered him to see his father punish his mother. Most women had to learn their place, which was far below that of their men.

"Good day to you, Brother and Sister Miller. Miss Georgia, I must say that you look lovely this morning. What is it that brings you here today?" It wasn't lost on Ginny that he hadn't even bothered to address Vas. She let it go, for the time being.

Colby, who had been relaxed, had stiffened noticeably as well. "Thank you for seeing us, Reverend. We're here to arrange a wedding ceremony."

Thomas looked surprised. "A wedding? But, dear Brother Colby, you're already married, correct?"

"Legally, yes, Reverend. But, my wife has decided that she has always wanted a church wedding, so we're here to arrange one." Colby kept his voice even. He knew that when he mentioned that Georgia and Vas were to marry as well, it could cause problems. The last thing Colby wanted was more problems.

At this news, the reverend seemed pleased. He assumed that Vas and Georgia were there to be witnesses. "That is splendid news. As you can see, I don't do many weddings, so any day you wish for the ceremony to be, I'm most likely available."

Before they could explain the double wedding, Mrs. Thomas returned with a tray of lemonade. She gave a glass to Colby, Ginny, Georgia and Reverend Thomas. No glass was given to Vas. She left before anything could be said.

No one said a word, so Ginny decided she'd had enough. "Reverend, is your wife returning with another glass?"

The minister stiffened and replied, "Of course not."

"But you have another guest in your parlor, sir." Ginny's voice was growing more cross.

"Ginny, it's not necessary." This came from Vas. His face pleaded with her to drop it before it got out of hand.

Too late for that, Ginny thought.

Placing her glass on the side table, Ginny rose from her seat. Colby placed a hand on her arm and gave her a look of warning. Although she didn't want to cause them any trouble, some things couldn't go unsaid.

Sitting slowly, she turned to the minister and said, "I really love

Jesus, don't you?" Her voice was jovial, almost childlike in it's admiration.

The reverend, who had been stealing himself for a fight, looked perplexed for a moment. Then he replied, "Yes, I do, obviously, as I've made it my life's work to spread his holy gospel."

"Jesus taught us charity and kindness. He taught us the value of humanity above greed and selfishness. He taught us that to include was a virtue. Would you agree, Reverend?" Ginny's eyes were wide with wonderment.

"Of course," he said, still not seeing where Ginny was going with this.

"I read that he used to hang out with society's rejects: The poor, the sick and the women." Ginny's voice was sweet, no sarcasm or contention.

"Did you? And where did you read that?"

Instead of answering, she kept on her train of thought. "He was honest and charitable. He would never deny someone help based on ignorance. He was truly an archetype of decent behavior." Ginny was on a role, almost sounding like a minister on a pulpit. *Can you give me a hallelujah?*

"What's your point, Ginny?" This came from Colby, who had the old exasperation in his voice.

Keeping her eyes squarely on the minister, she said, "What I mean is this. By denying Vas a glass of lemonade, the Reverend is spitting on the lessons that Jesus taught us. If he is truly a minister of God, then Vas could be the devil himself, and he should still be charitable and kind. Turn the other cheek and all that, hey Reverend?" Ginny's voice had turned from sweet and innocent, to sarcastic and pissed.

"He is a half breed. His mother is a heathen and his father was a Mexican," sputtered Thomas, clearly unused to having anyone, never mind a woman, question his faith.

Standing up once again, Ginny looked down at the man. "So what! He is still a man, born the same way you were. He is a good person, who happens to be in love and willing to make a life long commitment to Georgia. How is that any different than what Colby and I want to do? Or what you did with your wife?"

Oops! Ginny thought when she saw his face turn white as he turned to stare at Vas and Georgia. She'd forgotten that they hadn't mentioned yet that there was a part two to their reason for being there.

The Reverend stood up and looked down at Colby. "I suggest you control your wife, Brother Miller. She is out of her place here."

Before Colby could speak, Ginny said, "I don't need Colby to speak for me. I, too, am a person. I can defend myself."

The strike came out of nowhere and sent Ginny to the floor. It wasn't the first time she'd been hit, and it never got any easier. She saw stars. But before Colby could do anything, she got up and cold cocked the reverend in the face. It was a pleasure to see the minister down on his knees.

Colby came up behind her and grabbed her. As the reverend stared up at her, clearly confused, she spat, "Don't you ever touch me again. Unlike your timid wife, I fight back." With that, she pulled away from Colby and left the house. Damned if she was ever going to set foot in that church again.

Georgia and Vas, who finally came to their senses after the shock of seeing Ginny hit the minister in the face, quietly took their leave as well. Only Colby remained behind.

Reaching down, he gave the Reverend his hand to help him up. As the man stood, Colby said, quietly, but menacingly, "If you ever lay a hand on my wife again, I will kill you. No real man lays a hand on a woman. It ain't right. Good day, Reverend." Then he turned and walked out of the room. As he left the house, he saw Mrs. Thomas hiding behind the stairs. The smile on her face was telling enough.

As they collected up the boys, nobody said a word. When Frank and Nate saw Ginny's budding shiner, they wouldn't stop asking questions about it. They were almost halfway home when Ginny finally spoke up. "I'm sorry. But he wouldn't have married you two anyway."

It was Colby who responded. "He may have, Ginny, if Vas pretended to convert."

Ginny was incredulous. "So, he would have to lie? What the hell's the point? And if you think for one second that his dislike of Vas has to do with religion, think again."

Vas answered this time. "Well, it could have saved us a trip into Laramie or Cheyenne to get hitched."

Everyone was surprised when Georgia spoke up. "No, Ginny's right. I want our ceremony to be about love. Short of my already being pregnant, he wouldn't have married us."

Colby turned toward Vas. "She ain't pregnant, is she?"

Ginny placed her hand on Colby's arm. "You don't think much of chaperoning skills, do you?"

He softened at this and kept quiet. They all remained quiet for a few more minutes as they contemplated their new dilemma. Colby and Ginny were fine, although their wedding was questionably legal. But Colby wouldn't allow Vas to take Georgia until they'd done it right. After all, she was his only sister.

"Is there a Justice of the Peace or judge that could perform the ceremony?" Ginny wondered if that was even an option in this time period.

"No. If someone needs to go to trial, the sheriff transports them to Cheyenne."

"Are there any other ministers?" Ginny was grasping at straws, but what else could she do. She felt responsible for Vas and Georgia putting off their wedding, all because she couldn't play nice with the bigot.

"We'll just have to make a trip into Cheyenne. We'll only be gone a couple of days. Tim can handle the ranch until we get back." Colby was being suspiciously reasonable. Ginny wondered if he was as desperate to have her, as she was him.

"We can spend the wedding night in a nice hotel," Vas said, staring at his bride. Georgia blushed a nice crimson color and turned her head to giggle.

"What about the boys?" Ginny asked. She thought she could threaten them to make sure they were good, but with those two, who knew.

"They'll be fine for a couple of days, Ginny." Colby took her hand and looked at her. "We won't be getting much alone time from now on. Let's enjoy it." His smile melted Ginny's heart.

Despite his previous cantankerous attitude, Ginny now saw something very sweet about Colby. He was a gentleman, but he was also a playful boy. She could see how he wanted to please her, but also take care of her. Ginny turned away suddenly and looked at the landscape.

No, no, no, no, no, she kept repeating in her head. *I can't fall in love with him. It will hurt that much more when I'm gone.* Her palms grew sweaty and her heart beat too quickly. This was going to be bad.

Using his free hand, Colby turned Ginny's face toward him. When he saw the tears, he grew worried. He kept it to himself until they reached the ranch. Asking Vas to take care of the cart, Colby took Ginny out into the field, southeast of the house. As they were walking, he felt himself feeling real fear. What if she didn't want him anymore? What if she'd changed her mind? What if she'd gotten her memory back and was in love with someone else? As much as Colby didn't want to know, he wouldn't put it off.

They found an old boulder sticking up through the ground and took a seat. Then Colby took Ginny's hands and asked what was wrong.

Ginny wasn't about to be honest with him. He would have her locked up in an insane asylum if he knew the truth about her. So, she told him the first thing that came to mind. With her ability to lie compromised, her words were very close to the truth.

"I might be falling in love with you, Colby."

Colby let out the breath he'd been holding. Smiling like a cat who'd caught a big, fat mouse, he said, "And that's something to cry about?"

"No." Ginny hedged while she thought of something to say. Anything, really. Stupid or otherwise. It finally hit her. "What if I get my memory back and it's bad? What if I'm not a good person?"

Colby laughed, but quickly coughed to cover it up. He didn't want to hurt her feelings, but to hear her say she might love him, that was about the best thing he'd ever heard in his life. It was better than when he found out he'd been accepted to Columbia.

Taking her face in his hands, Colby leaned down and kissed Ginny gently on the lips. "We'll get through anything together. We're a team, right? You, me, my family. If you love me, there ain't nothing we can't get through."

Ginny recognized the corniness of the words, but couldn't help but be touched. He was so perfect. But, in the beginning of any relationship, don't people feel like everything is perfect? Keeping that in mind, Ginny smiled and said three little words that shocked her husband. "Let's not wait."

His eyes grew big as the meaning of her statement finally

registered. Sputtering, he asked, "Are you... Are you sure?"

Taking her hand and rubbing his stubbled cheek, she replied, "Of course I'm sure." She let a big sigh and revealed, "You have no idea how much I want you right now, Colby Miller."

Colby felt his heart pound in his chest and his breathing become labored. "Oh, I have some idea, Ginny Miller. Can't be any worse than what I've been feeling since shortly after meeting you."

Ginny turned her head and looked befuddled. "But, you hated me."

Laughing, he said, "Naw. I was just pretending. Sometimes men like to behave like asses to impress their women."

Smiling and shaking her head, Ginny reached out and hugged him. She seemed to fit so perfectly in his arms. Resting her head on his shoulder, she inhaled his scent. Then she felt something else. Colby's hands were trying to unbutton her shirt. Pulling back she looked at him.

"Now?" was all she asked.

Colby looked around to see if they were alone. That was when he spotted his two brothers, out the barn window, with their spyglass. He quickly covered Ginny up and said, "Maybe not now... later... tonight. Come to my room. Please."

His politeness was her undoing. "Tonight. I promise."

Chapter 26

Dinner took forever. The boys wouldn't stop their questions about what happened with Reverend Thomas. Colby merely stated that they wouldn't be attending church any more. That made things worse.

"Did the Reverend hit you, Ginny. Cause if he did, I'll have to put him straight," Frank said, with all due seriousness.

"Me too," shouted Nate. "Papa always said it ain't right to hit a girl."

"Isn't right, Nate," Ginny said as she took another bite of her food. She and Colby had hoped to keep what happened from the boys, but maybe that wasn't such a good idea.

Colby gave Ginny a look from across the table. Ginny read his question and shrugged. They couldn't keep the truth from the boys. Either they would find out from them or from some twisted gossip in town.

Ginny took the first stab. "Yes boys, Reverend Thomas is the one who hit me. He thought I was being insolent and needed to learn my place."

Nate looked confused. "What's your place, Ginny?"

"Well Nate, the Reverend thinks my place is to be silent, never speak up for myself or anyone else. I think the exact opposite."

Frank scrunched up his face. "What, 'cause you're a girl?"

It was Colby who answered. "Yes, that's how the Reverend feels. I happen to think Ginny's pretty smart, don't you?"

Both boys readily agreed and also supported Ginny in her ability to speak up. Ginny knew there were a few other things that needed to be said.

"Just so you know, the Reverend was not willing to marry Georgia and Vas. That's what caused the argument in the first place."

Nate gasped as he stared at Georgia and Vas. "Nu-uh," Nate declared.

Georgia turned her gaze to her plate and Vas took her hand. "That's right, Nate. Too many people in this world frown on people like me marrying someone as pretty as your sister."

"I also want you two to know that I only hit the Reverend after he hit me. I don't condone violence, but that man had it coming."

Two sets of eyes stared widely at Ginny. "You hit the Reverend?" Frank asked.

Colby answered, "Better watch out you two. Ginny's got a mean right hook."

Chastising him, Ginny said, "Colby, please. I really shouldn't have done it, but something tells me that no one's ever let him know that his actions have consequences. I only wish his wife would stand up for herself too."

"Regardless, we now have to travel to Cheyenne to get married." Colby looked directly at the boys. "You two will need to stay here and help Tim while we're gone. We'll be gone no more than three days. I don't want to come home and find out you've gotten into mischief. Understood?" Colby held Nate's gaze a moment longer than Frank's. The message was obvious. That morning in the barn, after he ran away, they had made some sort of deal. Ginny still didn't know what it was, but it was having the right effect on Nate at that moment.

"Yes sir," they both responded.

"Good, that's settled. Frank and Nate, help Nizhoni with the dishes."

"Awwww," they both whined, but got up and brought the dishes to the sink.

Georgia was right behind them, "I'll help too. That way we can finish up and have time to play outside a little before bed."

Vas and Colby started to discuss their upcoming trip, while Ginny helped clear the table. In no time, everything was cleaned up and decided. They would leave in two days, provided the weather was good. Colby and Ginny went to sit on the front porch and watch the boys play with a hard ball Georgia had made for them. Vas and Georgia took a turn around the yard.

Ten minutes later, Tim and Eloise arrived with stupefied looks on their faces. Eloise came up on the porch with her hands on her hips and looked directly at Ginny.

"Did you hit Reverend Thomas today?" she asked, gasping every word as if it couldn't be possible.

Ginny, who had been rocking slowly, turned her gaze toward their guests and said, "Yup."

Tim snickered, but one look from his wife, and he stopped

immediately. "How could you do that? He's a man of God."

With a fake whine, Ginny responded, "Well, he hit me first."

"He told me what you said to him. You had it coming."

"Now Eloise, that ain't fair..." Tim started to say, but Ginny finished for him.

"Really, Eloise. Would you allow Tim to hit you for speaking your mind?" Ginny knew she should get control of herself. Although she could admit that a good face slapping was exactly what Eloise needed.

She gasped again. Ginny thought if she kept it up, she would probably pass out. "You have to admit that the Reverend had a point."

Shaking her head slowly, Ginny asked, "Meaning?"

Eloise drew herself back and whispered, "Meaning that you don't welcome murderers and thieves into your home."

Completely missing her meaning, Ginny asked, "You think I'm a murderer and a thief?"

Using Colby's favorite exasperation looks, Eloise said, "No, not you. The Indian over there." Eloise casually shrugged her shoulder in the direction of Vas and Georgia, who were now playing ball with the boys.

Ginny turned to look at Colby, who just shrugged. "Do you know something that we don't, Eloise?" Ginny asked, trying to take the high road, knowing it wasn't going to be easy.

Whispering again, she stated, "All Indians are. And don't get me started on the Mexicans. Vas had no chance with parentage like that."

Before Colby could stand, Ginny put a hand on his arm. But it was Tim, who came up behind his wife and spoke in a low, but menacing tone. "Now, Eloise. Don't be saying anything stupid. I've known Vas and Nizhoni a long time, and they're both fine people. I've worked with plenty of ranch hands from all over, and the one thing I've noticed is that you can't judge a book by its cover."

Turning toward her husband, seeing that she would get no support, Eloise turned on her heel and walked back in the direction of their home. Tim looked down and said, "I'm real sorry about that, Colby, Ginny. I'll go talk to her. She's just been so worried about the baby and all." Then Tim took off walking fast to catch up with his wife.

"Well, that was awkward," Ginny said, watching the pair leave. Tim tried to take his wife's arm, but she brushed him off and kept going. "Wouldn't want to be in that bed tonight."

"Oh, Mrs. Miller, you won't be. Seeing's how you and I have a date in another bed."

Ginny felt herself blush from Colby's words. He reached over and grabbed her hand. Picking it up, he placed a gentle kiss on the back and winked at her. Ginny smiled and went back to watching her new family.

In the silence, Ginny began to think about her lives. Ian had been great in the sack, though, overall, they had little compatibility. He wanted to own her and control her, and she wanted none of that. He was gorgeous, strong and brutish, able to protect her and able to command an army. There were definitely aspects to him that appealed to her, but the whole package wasn't there.

With Colin, he had the perfect personality to fit hers. He took her seriously, and listened to her opinions. He had an acerbic wit and could be just as sarcastic as Ginny. He too, was a handsome specimen, but it only added to his appeal, but didn't define it. And still, she didn't feel like she'd fallen in love with him. Maybe it was because he'd abandoned her, and that would have taken some time to get over.

Even when she considered Miles, who had the looks and, most likely, the talent in bed, she never felt anything more than friendship. Miles was like that extraneous character in a book, where you never find out what happens to him, but are always left to wonder.

So what was it about Colby that was different. God knew he treated her like dirt for the first few weeks she was here. Knowing now why he was so bitter, she didn't hold it against him, but why did she feel something extra? Maybe because he was an American, like herself? No, Ginny thought, she'd never been that shallow. Was it the easy drawl he used when he spoke? Ginny couldn't put her finger on it. Maybe she was just so vulnerable, having lived two lives already not her own. Maybe her lack of experience in the love department was finally catching up to her. Feeling her head starting to ache, she gave up. If she was in love, she was. If she just thought she was, oh well, too. What was to be done?

There was only one thing to be done. Come to Colby's bed that night. If she couldn't be sure about love, she wanted to be sure that he was every bit as satisfying in bed.

Chapter 27

After the boys and Georgia had gone to bed, Ginny went to the bathroom and washed up. She filled up the tub halfway, not wanting to wait for a full tub and began to wash herself all over. When she felt clean, she got out, dried off and brushed her hair. As she was leaving the bathroom, Colby entered the kitchen and stopped to whistle at her.

"Mrs. Miller, you look mighty fine this evening. Any plans?" he asked, with a twinkle in his eyes.

Ginny, being herself, took the low road. "I have a date with a handsome man. I might even put out tonight."

A look of confusion came over Colby's face. "Put out?" he asked.

Ginny walked up next to her husband and whispered, "You know. Take off all my clothes and ravish him to near death. That's the plan anyway."

Colby turned his head to look in her eyes. "Lucky man."

"Indeed. See you around, Colby." Ginny turned and went up to her room. She would give him ten minutes, figuring after her word play it would only take him five. Then she would go to his room. Ginny was feeling pretty good about how the evening was shaping up.

Ten minutes later, Ginny knocked lightly on Colby's bedroom door. The door opened immediately, with Colby grabbing her arm and pulling her inside. He closed and locked the door behind her. Ginny got her first glimpse of his bedroom.

It was obvious that the room used to belong to his parents. There were many womanly touches, from the colorful quilt and matching pillows, to the flower prints on the wall. There was even a vase with fresh flowers next to the bed. The room smelled clean and fresh, with the window open to allow a small breeze. The rug on the floor was soft and clean. Ginny remembered Nizhoni beating it just the other day.

Colby came around to stand in front of her. "Are you nervous?" he asked, concern in his eyes.

"No. I know you'll take good care of me." Ginny meant the words, as Colby was the protector of his family.

He reached his hand up to cup her cheek. "I'll always take care of you, Ginny. After tonight, you'll be mine forever. No more business arrangement. We'll be married for real. You alright with that?"

Ginny took in his vulnerability for a moment. He wanted this so badly, and she had to admit that at the moment, she wanted it too. But then, nobody gets married thinking that someday they'll grow apart and leave each other. In the beginning, it's all wine and roses and lovemaking. It takes something more to make it last.

Ginny couldn't be concerned with the far future right now. She knew this fantasy wouldn't last. She could only live in the moment, and right now, the moment told her to agree and make love to this man.

"I'm alright with that, Mr. Miller. I'm definitely alright with that."

Smiling, Colby lowered his mouth to hers and began to kiss his wife tenderly, but passionately. He entered her mouth, tasting her and letting her have her fill of him as well. Without a thought, Colby picked up his wife and placed her lightly on the bed. And that was when it happened.

Squeak.

Ginny stopped kissing Colby, but he simply moved to her neck. As he climbed into the bed next to her, she heard it again.

Squeak.

Ginny stiffened and Colby stopped and looked at her with confusion.

"What's the matter, Ginny?"

Instead of answering, Ginny bounced a little on the bed.

Squeaky, squeaky, squeak.

Her eyes widened, but no words would come to her. After a moment, Colby understood her dismay. Colby went about testing the bed as well.

Squeaky, squeaky, squeak.

He bowed his head, realizing that the bed would make too much noise. And, as if to cement that into their heads, they heard Nate call out, "You alright, Colby?"

His voice gruff, Colby responded, "Yeah, Nate. I'm fine. Go back to sleep."

Colby stood up and helped Ginny from the bed. His face said it all.

Ginny felt a case of giggles overcoming her and she pressed her hands against her mouth to keep them from escaping. When Colby looked at her, it was too much. As quietly as possible, she started to giggle, her whole body joining in.

Colby watched her for a moment before he couldn't help but join in. After a minute, he grabbed Ginny and kissed her again. When she finally stopped shaking and started to respond, he pulled away and whispered, "What should we do now?" He lifted his eyebrow to punctuate his question.

Taking a deep breath, she asked, "How didn't you know about this?" She pointed to the bed.

"I usually just get in and go to sleep, Ginny. I guess I don't move much to make it squeak more."

Still whispering, trying to hold the laughter at bay, Ginny asked, "How did your parents do it?"

Colby opened his mouth to say he had no idea, when a memory came back to him. He wasn't more than twelve at the time. He remembered waking up and hearing the squeaky cadence coming from his parent's room. He figured they were joking around and went back to sleep. It occurred to him that Frank came along not too long after that.

Groaning, he put his head in his hands. Ginny put her arm around him and asked, "Don't think about it. Let's just figure out what we're gonna do now."

"If it weren't your first time, I would take you against the door." His voice, gravelly with passion, made her toes curl in anticipation. If she was sure it wasn't her first time, she would take him up on his offer. But that was the problem with possessing a body with amnesia. She wasn't sure of anything.

"I could grab my blanket and we could head out to the barn."

Ginny thought about hay poking into her. If they kept to the blanket, it would be alright, but then she would have to smell the horses. The whole thought just didn't do it for her.

"I don't know. Isn't there anywhere else?"

Colby thought for a moment and suggested, "We could go out into the field. No one would be able to see us in the tall grass. We could make our own little nest out there."

"That sounds good. Just let me grab my shoes and I'll meet you by the front door." Ginny unlocked the door and went a few doors down to her room. She put on her shoes and was just about to leave when she bumped into Georgia.

Confused, since Georgia had gone to bed before she had, Ginny asked, "What's the matter, Georgia? You okay?"

"I need to talk to you, Ginny. I don't want to do it when the boys could overhear us."

"Uh, well... how about you and I take a walk tomorrow. Just the two of us. That way, none of the boys will be able to overhear us."

"Frank and Nate have a way of sneaking up. I really don't want them to hear us. Do you think we could go for a walk over to the barn right now?"

Crap, crap, crap, Ginny thought. But what could she do. It was clear that Georgia was upset about something and she was terrified that one of the guys would overhear their conversation.

"Alright. Go down to the kitchen and wait for me there. I'll just make sure Colby is sleeping so we can be alone." Ginny smiled reassuringly, as Georgia disappeared down the steps.

She needed the patience of a saint at this point. She'd been waiting for the unbelievable sex for nearly a month. She'd put up with bad attitudes, mischievous children, racist ministers and nearly being drowned to get here. Was it too much to ask that one thing go right?

Ginny found Colby standing in his room, with the blanket in his hands and a confused look on his face. "What was Georgia doing up?" he asked.

Putting a hand on his chest, Ginny took a deep breath and let it out. In a calm whisper, she replied, "Georgia wants to talk to me about something. She doesn't want any of you to overhear, so she's asked me to take a walk to the barn for a chat. Can you give me a few minutes alone with your sister to find out what's bothering her." Ginny produced a set of sad, begging eyes for her husband. He turned his head and sighed.

"Fine, but only a few minutes. I'm about to explode, Ginny."

Smiling at her husband, she said, "I know. Me too. But she's your sister, and she has no other women to talk to. I'll be back before you know it." With that, she placed a kiss on his cheek and went downstairs after Georgia.

❖❖❖

The two women walked the short distance to the barn. Outside, they found a couple of hay bales to sit on. They had a view of Vas' house in the distance. Ginny leaned back against the barn and waited for Georgia to get to what she wanted to ask. As she waited, she thought about how this was the spot where Vas had kissed her. She quickly squashed that thought. After all, she was sitting next to his fiancée. It took a few minutes for Georgia to finally speak up.

"I don't have many people to talk to," was all she said.

"I know. It's been pretty hard on you since your mother died, huh?"

Feeling her tense up, Ginny placed a hand on her shoulder. "I know I'm probably not much older than you, but I will always be honest with what I know. So, is there something you wanted to ask me?"

Georgia took a deep breath and let the words tumble from her lips. "Have you and my brother had... well, you know... have you been with him yet because I know that it's part of marriage and Vas has hinted at it a few times... well, more than a few times... but the truth is I'm terrified and don't know if I can do it."

Ginny stared at Georgia for a full minute before answering. Licking her lips, considering her answer, she decided she would have to fib a little. Georgia needed reassurance, and someone telling her that they hadn't had sex yet either would not be reassuring.

"Georgia, it can be very frightening the first time. But, let me ask you this: Do you love Vas? Do you trust him?"

"Of course I do. I wouldn't marry him if I didn't."

"If you trust him, then you must know that he wouldn't do anything to hurt you, right?"

"But my mother told me that the first time often hurts." Georgia's eyes pleaded with her to tell her that it wasn't true.

Looking down, steeling herself, she met Georgia's gaze once more. "Yes, it can sometimes be painful the first time. But, if you have a sweet, caring man who..." How was she going to put this? "Who, prepares you for the moment, it's not nearly as bad as it could be."

Georgia scrunched up her eyes and turned her head quizzically. "Prepares?"

"You've kissed Vas, right?" Ginny would have to take this slowly.

Unfortunately, she had a husband, who at that moment, was waiting not so patiently for her to return.

Turning her gaze to her lap, she answered, "Yes, of course. You've caught us a few times."

"Did those kisses make you feel different? Like your skin was heating up and you insides were all... fluttery?"

"Yes, they did. Especially in my... well, you know where."

"Yes, I know where. That's all part of the preparation." Ginny launched into a short version of the medical reasons why a woman's body produced a lubricant for sex. She explained exactly what would happen, why it led to pregnancy and how Georgia's own menstrual cycle played a part. When she was done, Georgia looked relieved.

"I see. I wish my mother had explained that to me earlier."

"I have no doubt that she would have. She just didn't get the chance."

Looking sad, Georgia said, "I wish they were here. They always liked Vas, and I know they would be happy for us."

"I know they would be happy, because you're so happy."

Standing up, smoothing out the front of her nightgown, Georgia announced, "Well, I should be off to bed. I suppose Colby is waiting for you, huh?"

Standing beside her sister-in-law, she said, "Yes, but he can wait. This was more important."

Startling Ginny, Georgia gave her a quick hug. "Thank you, Ginny. I couldn't ask for a better sister."

The two women walked back to the house. Ginny made sure that Georgia had closed her door before creeping back into Colby's room. She closed the door over and turned to tell Colby she was sorry when she saw him, sound asleep, taking up most of the bed and snoring softly. Ginny watched him for a moment and wondered if she should wake him up. Part of her screamed, "Hell yes, wake his ass up." But, there was another part who thought she should let him sleep. After all, they would be going to Cheyenne in a couple of days and would have plenty of opportunity then.

Creeping from the room, Ginny returned to her own. Crawling between the covers, she wondered if they would ever have sex. Laughing softly to herself, she considered how crazy a romance novel would be without sex. *Never in a million years*, she thought.

Chapter 28

Early the next morning, as the sun was just creeping into the valley, Ginny was woken up by a presence in her room. When she opened her eyes, she startled at first, seeing Colby so close to her face.

He chuckled softly and asked, "Why didn't you wake me up, Mrs. Miller?"

Recovering quickly, she reached up and felt the stubble on his cheek. "You were out, Mr. Miller. I wanted you wide awake, not stumbling around in the dark."

Colby kissed her, and Ginny knew she was in trouble. Before she could stop herself, she reached up and grabbed his shirt and pulled him fully on top of her. They fumbled with the covers for a moment, before he settled himself between her legs, kissing her neck and playing with her breasts.

"This is a great way to wake up. Thank you," Ginny said absently, as he continued his sensual assault.

Colby reached down and lifted up her nightgown. His hand started to feel its way up her leg. Ginny wanted her clothing gone, along with his, and was about to say so when the boys started yelling at each other from the other side of her door.

"Give me that. I told you to stop taking my stuff, Nate. Ain't yours to take!"

"It is mine. You stole it from me first."

Then came Georgia's voice. "Boys, you're gonna wake up the house if you don't keep your voices down. Get downstairs to breakfast." That was followed by the trampling of feet down the steps. Colby let out a heavy sigh and shook his head.

Picking her up out of bed, he ordered her to get dressed. "I'll be downstairs waiting with some breakfast. We're going on a picnic. To be alone. Without anyone disturbing us. Agreed?"

By the look on Colby's face, Ginny would have to be stupid not to agree, even if she didn't want to. Which of course, she did. Very much so. She shook her head with an affirmative, then went about getting dressed as quickly as possible.

She was downstairs in a couple of minutes, entering the kitchen in enough time to hear Colby explain that he and Ginny would be gone for part of the morning. He told Nate and Frank what he wanted done by the time he got home and asked Georgia to supervise.

"Any questions," he asked, knowing that in his current mood, there had better not be any.

All three shook their heads. When Ginny entered, all three heads looked at her for help. "Well, if that's settled, Colby and I will just be going. Mind your sister, boys. If we get back and there's been trouble, you won't be liking life too much. Georgia, don't take any excuses. Okay, bye."

With that, Colby and Ginny left out the front door and headed to the barn. Colby quickly saddled his horse, climbed up and pulled Ginny to sit on his lap. They were off to find some peace and quiet and hopefully, sex.

They stopped by the same swimming hole that Ginny had visited earlier with Nate. She couldn't think of a better spot, since they could have privacy, then enjoy a nice swim afterwards. The air was filled with the sweet smell of flowers that were growing near the water's edge.

Ginny watched as Colby laid a blanket down on the soft grass. He retrieved the basket with the food and set it aside. As Ginny was reaching down to feel the water, she turned to see Colby had already taken off his boots and socks. In the next few moments, he had his shirt and pants off as well, keeping his long drawers on. It wasn't like Ginny couldn't see his excitement level. Colby hadn't taken his eyes off her the whole time he'd been undressing.

Standing there in his near nakedness, Colby held out his hand. Without a word, Ginny approached him, while removing her shirt. She had opted for her blouse and pants, rather than the cumbersome skirt and seven layers of underwear. She did have on a tight fitting, corset top with chemise. Riding a horse without any support would have been murder.

She opened her pants and let them drop to the ground. She kicked off her shoes, slipped off the pants with the socks. Now she stood before him in the short chemise. She reached in front and loosened her stays. Colby's eyes widened as Ginny's plump breasts popped out of the tight fitting top. She could hear his breathing get ragged as he reached for her.

Colby kissed her immediately, running his fingers in her hair and caressing her face. Before she could think, he had her lying on the ground next to him, pulling apart her top and fondling her. As his mouth kissed other parts of her face and neck, he whispered sweet endearments. Ginny got lost in the moment, enjoying his attention.

The only sounds were the birds chirping in the trees and their desperate breathing. When his hand reached up her leg, Ginny opened up for him, allowing him to explore her further. His fingers found her sensitive nub and began a rhythmic motion. Without thinking, Ginny reached down and grabbed him through his drawers, soliciting a hiss from Colby.

She looked at him and demanded, "Take those off."

Smiling his compliance, he stood and pulled down his drawers to reveal himself to her for the first time. Seeing him naked, Ginny had that stab of love once again. She was too old to mistake lust and love, but at that point, it didn't matter. She knew what she wanted and dammit if she wouldn't get it.

Lowering himself slowly to the ground, he settled once again between her legs. He pulled down her chemise to fully expose her. He examined each breast in turn and decided on one. Taking the nipple into his mouth, he sucked gently as his fingers once again found her nub. He used one finger to enter her, finding her impossibly wet. Colby felt his control slipping.

He looked at her as he slipped his finger into her, watching her face as she shivered from his invasion. "I have never wanted a woman like I want you right now, Mrs. Miller."

Ginny picked up her head and raised herself on her elbows. She sat up and grabbed his face in her hands and kissed him. "Then take me. Now."

"My pleasure," was his response. He lowered her to the ground, kissing her as they went. Ginny reached down and grabbed hold of him. He was so hard, but after waiting so long, it wasn't a shock. The situation had become dire, with need and want.

He moved her legs to open her up more. Then he whispered his warning. "This may hurt a little, my love. I promise to go slow. If you tell me to stop, I will."

Ginny, laid back against the blanket, her hair all spread out around her head, said, "I'll be fine. Please don't wait any longer."

Lowering himself on top of her, he reached down to direct himself inside of her. Just as the head had pushed through the entrance, they heard hoofbeats. Colby stopped to listen, to make sure whoever it was wasn't coming near them. As it became obvious that the direction of the rider was searching them out, Colby cursed.

"Goddammit, somebody better be dead."

Colby only had a moment to retrieve his drawers and pull them on before the rider broke through the trees. Using his body to shield Ginny, giving her a little time to straighten herself, Colby saw Vas get off his horse. Vas respectfully turned and looked away as Ginny and Colby dressed.

When they were decent, Colby turned back to his friend and asked, "What could be so important, Vas?" His voice was low, nearly growling.

Vas turned around and walked over. "I'm really sorry, Colby. You know I wouldn't have come out here unless it was important." Vas looked over at Ginny, he looked almost angry at her.

He continued, not taking his eyes off Ginny. "Some people showed up shortly after you left. They were claiming to be Ginny's kin."

"What?" This was from Ginny. Her family was here? Her real family? Ginny forgot all about her unspent passion and looked back at Vas. "Who were they? Did they say what happened to me?"

Vas turned toward Colby. "They said she ran away to avoid a marriage."

Colby turned toward his wife. He didn't appear angry, just sad. "Well, I guess we'd better go and see what this is all about."

After packing up their picnic, the three rode back to the ranch. As they approached, Ginny saw a carriage sitting in front of the house. Both boys were climbing on top and looking inside. The coachman was showing them around it.

Vas took both horses as Ginny and Colby walked toward the house. Ginny started to feel a strange intimidation. She still couldn't remember anything, but for some reason, she knew this was going to be bad. Pushing past the feeling, she recognized it for what it was. "The big problem." It was the "thing" that would conspire to keep the two lovers apart. As predictable as it was, when forced to live it, it made Ginny very uneasy.

The boys spotted them and came running over. Their voices were full of excitement.

"Ain't it grand, Ginny. John was showing us the coach. You should see the inside," Nate was so excited he probably didn't even realize he had spoken so much in front of Colby.

Frank chimed in next. "There are two men. One says he's your pa. I don't know who the other is, cause he wouldn't talk. Looks kinda angry. You want us to protect you, Ginny?"

Forcing a smile to her lips, Ginny said, "Thank you, Frank, but that won't be necessary." Lowering herself to Frank's level, she whispered, "If I need protecting, I'm sure your brother can handle it." She winked at him and followed Colby into the house. The boys went back to examining the coach.

They entered the parlor, side by side, and faced the two gentlemen sitting in opposing chairs. An older man, with short, salt and pepper hair, stood up first and faced Ginny. There was no tenderness in his eyes. He looked every bit a harsh taskmaster.

"You've put us through a great deal of trouble, Cassandra. We've had to travel halfway across this country to find you."

At the sound of his voice, Ginny was slammed with her memories. In an instant, she knew who she was and what had happened to her. She'd been waiting for those memories for weeks, but wasn't so happy to have them. All she knew was she was in big trouble. Swaying under her father's gaze, Ginny turned to Colby and promptly passed out cold.

Chapter 29

Ginny woke up in her own room, with a wet compress on her forehead. As she reached up to remove it, Georgia appeared and moved her hand away.

"Don't fret, Ginny. Just let me take care of you." Georgia sounded worried, which was a sharp contrast to her usual, upbeat self.

"Where are they?" Ginny asked, knowing she would not have to explain who "they" were.

"Downstairs, talking to Colby and Vas. Your father told quite a story. He paints you in a very bad light. Do you remember anything yet?" Her voice was filled with worry.

"What did he say?"

"He said that you are engaged to Mr. Fitzhume. He said that to avoid the marriage that you deemed 'beneath' you, you ran away with another man. I believe his name was Robert. They tracked down Robert, who told them that you had run away from him, and he hadn't any idea where you'd gone. He indicated that they had to hurt Robert to get the information from him. Somehow they tracked you to the matchmaker and then to here."

Ginny closed her eyes for a moment. As far as stories went, it wasn't far off. She had run away from the marriage with Reginald Fitzhume. Not only had the man raped her, he had beat her in a way that left no visible marks. She hadn't been able to walk for days and stayed hidden in her room until she was able to face her father.

She told her father that she had no wish to marry Reginald, but he would have none of it. Her father had gambled away most of the family's money, and this was the only way to replenish the coffers. Reginald was very rich and very willing to take care of Cassandra's family in exchange for the marriage.

When Cassandra had told her father of her fiancé's cruelty, he told her to get used to it. If she had been born a man, she could have worked to pay off their debt. But since she was merely a girl, and his only child, her only use to him was by marrying well.

"I do remember now. And I did run away from my fiancé. But not because I was some spoiled brat." As the words left her mouth, she realized that Cassandra was just that. She'd had people waiting on her her whole life. She'd never done anything productive. She used her beauty to get anything she wanted. She'd had dozens of suitors, but she had chosen Reginald because he was the richest and the most influential. What she hadn't known at the time was that he was also a sadistic bastard, who liked his women screaming in pain.

"How'd you lose your memory?" Georgia asked.

"Robert was a gardener at my father's home in St. Louis. He helped me escape. Once I was away, he said he would help me hide, but I didn't want him to get into trouble, so I left him one night while he was sleeping. I was wandering the streets, when a group of boys tried to rob me. One of them hit me with something. The next thing I remember was the matchmaker finding me."

"Let me go get Colby. He'll know what to do." Georgia got up and left.

Ginny sat up in bed and thought about what Cassandra had done. She had to be truthful with Colby. She owed him that much. To say she was a different person now was an understatement. Lamentably, Ginny would have to pay for the sins of Cassandra.

A few minutes later, Colby entered the room. His face looked much like it did in the early part of their relationship. Disappointment and exasperation mixed with anger. Apparently, he had bought into most of her father's stories.

He closed the door and leaned his back to it, folding his arms across his chest. He didn't say a word, just stood there and stared at her as if he was seeing her for the first time. Ginny guessed that he probably was.

"Don't listen to all my father's assertions." Ginny refused to take so many steps back. They'd come so far together.

"I suppose I should hear your side of the story." Would he listen? He didn't sound too reasonable, but Ginny had no choice but to carry on.

Ginny decided to start at the beginning. "I was a spoiled, rich girl. Exactly what the men outside Denver accused me of being. I wouldn't lift a finger to help with anything. I had maids do my bidding. My mother died when I was very small, so my father always coddled me. I was his only child. Although he remarried, they never had any more children."

Colby stared into the corner, not looking at his wife. He'd spent the last half hour listening to her father and fiancé, as they went on and on about her. How she was spoiled, but also how she had shown signs of her mother's mental illness. He listened attentively, but didn't believe much of their tale. There was a certain ring of desperation to it.

"When I turned eighteen, I started looking for a husband. I attended all the society balls and soirées in St. Louis. I was the belle of the ball, so to speak. I had my pick of just about anyone. But I chose Reginald Fitzhume." Her voice shook when she said his name, but she continued on with her story.

"I chose him for incredibly selfish reasons. He wasn't terribly attractive, but he was unbelievably rich. When my father had told me of our money issues, I realized that I didn't want to live without that kind of security. I figured I could manipulate Reginald easily. After all, he would be the luckiest man in the world to get to marry me." Her disgust in her own behavior was evident, but Colby remained silent.

"Reginald wanted me so badly, he went to my father and offered to buy me. Since I had no dowry, Reginald would settle a large sum on me, payable to my father, in the event I married him. My father agreed and told me that we would be wed. The next day, my father dropped me off at Fitzhume's house. He said that Reginald wanted to ask me properly. My father left and told me he would pick me up later.

"I was surprised when Reginald answered the door himself. He said that his staff had the day off and showed me to his parlor." Ginny's voice grew distant and she felt herself grow cold. Although the attack hadn't happened to Ginny, she carried the vivid memories of it as if it had.

"He locked the door and told me to take my clothes off. I laughed at him and he punched me in the side of my head. I fell down and he raped me. When he was done dispensing of my virginity, he went about torturing me for an hour or so. He..." Tears sprung up in Ginny's eyes. She felt herself sway again, but this time, Colby was there to steady her.

"I'll kill him," was all he said, but those three little words told Ginny that he believed her.

Taking her hand and placing it against his cheek, she said, "You can't. You would do no good getting yourself hanged. But thank you for believing me."

"Anyone can see that he ain't right, Ginny. I mean... Cassandra."

"Please keep calling me Ginny. I'm not that girl anymore. I won't ever be that girl again."

Colby bent down and kissed her gently. Pulling away, he said, "I told you we could work out anything. Whether they like it or not, you're still my wife. I'll protect you."

Not caring how corny it was, Ginny kissed him back. It might be trite and predictable, but she felt like a million dollars at that moment. Did she love him? She thought maybe she did. He was willing to fight to protect her. What could be more romantic?

"Stay here. I'll go and take care of our guests." Colby got up and went to the door. "I love you, Ginny Miller." With that, he left, closing the door behind him.

Ginny wanted to hear what he said, so she waited a few moments and left her room to sit at the top of the steps. There, she could hear every word.

Colby entered the parlor, where Ginny's father and ex-fiancé were seated. Georgia had served their guests some tea and promptly left. Vas sat across the room, not moving even when Colby reappeared.

"Mr. Thompson, as I stated earlier, your daughter is married to me. She entered that union without duress. We have been living as husband and wife for a month now. I'm sorry to you, Mr. Fitzhume, but the reasons are immaterial. Our union was sanctioned by a minister. It cannot be undone."

Cassandra's father stood up and paced the room. Finally, turning back to Colby, he asked, "You would want her, even though she is unstable?"

"I don't know what you experienced with her in your home, sir, but here, she has been a wonderful mother to my siblings and an excellent wife to me. Perhaps her 'issues' only manifest in your home."

The insult was clear and Thompson was enraged. "How dare you? I have called men out for far less than that. I will not be leaving here without my daughter. She had no right to marry you. She has an obligation to her family."

Colby relaxed against the wall. "Mr. Thompson, I've had extensive training in the law. I assure you that I know what is legal and what is not. Despite your assertions, your daughter was never obligated to marry Mr. Fitzhume." Colby could barely keep the disgust from his voice as he glanced toward the other man.

Colby could see why Ginny had thought she could manipulate him. He seemed meek. He was not much taller than Ginny, skinny as a rail and his face was covered in scars from a bad case of spots. His beady eyes were almost black. His hair was short, but looked unwashed. All in all, the man was creepy.

"This is an outrage. You can't keep my daughter here against her will." Thompson looked around the small parlor, taking in its simple furnishings. "I will never believe that she would stay here without any force from you."

Colby kept his eyes on his guests when he called out, "Ginny, come on down here."

"Why do you keep calling her that? Her name is Cassandra."

A moment later, Ginny appeared at the doorway. When she saw the look on Fitzhume's face, she became incensed. She walked over and stood in front of him. "How dare you show up here!" Then she drew back and punched him in the mouth, much like she'd done to Reverend Thomas. Colby had her before she could throw herself on the prone man.

Pulling his wife back, he looked over at her father. "I guess that answers your question, then. I'm thinking that your daughter does not want to go with you. Get out of my house and be on your way."

Vas, who had stood up at the violence, crossed his arms against his massive chest. "Gentlemen, allow me to escort you to your vehicle."

Thompson, whose mouth was still gaping open, walked in a daze to the door. Fitzhume, finally recovering himself, stood up and brushed off his coat. Taking a small handkerchief from his pocket, he dabbed the corner of his mouth. He followed Cassandra's father out the door and into the carriage.

Vas went and removed Nate and Frank from the carriage. Without another word, the two were off, heading back toward Sherman. The boys ran into the house to find out what was going on. They found Colby and Ginny sitting at the kitchen table. Colby looked concerned and Ginny looked as stunned.

Nate looked at his big brother, worriedly. He'd never seen Ginny like this. Colby rubbed her back in small circles and soon she began to relax.

"They're gone, Ginny."

"No, they're not."

Vas spoke up. "I saw their carriage leave, Ginny. I believe they got the message."

Ginny looked up at Vas. They had no idea. This was, after all, a romance novel. That meant that her father and ex-fiancé would not give up so easily. They would be back and something unpleasant would ensue. In the end, they would live happily ever after, and then she would be gone.

"They won't give up so easily."

Colby said, "We'll be on our way to Cheyenne tomorrow, Ginny. Even if they go back there, it's a big enough city that we're not likely to run into each other."

Ginny thought about what he said. What if her father kidnapped Nate or Frank, to ransom for Ginny's return? What if they ambushed them on the road to Cheyenne? What if they went to the sheriff claiming she was being held against her will? Ginny's head hurt with all the possibilities. If there was one thing she knew, it was that she was unlikely to just go with it. Ginny wanted to head off disaster, sparing her new family any pain. She still felt strange getting so caught up in the fantasy.

There was one thing that she knew needed taking care of before they had to confront whatever her father had planned.

"Vas, can I speak to you privately for a moment?"

Everyone in the room fell silent. Colby looked hurt, but covered it up quickly enough. The boys went out the back door, to get into some sort of mischief. Colby and Georgia went back through the front of the house. Vas took a seat next to her and waited.

"I was wondering if I could borrow your cabin today?"

"Borrow it?" Vas, looking very tasty as usual, lifted an eyebrow in question.

"Before we leave tomorrow, I want some alone time with Colby. As you saw this morning, we've been trying, but something keeps getting in the way. You can stay here tonight, which I'd ask you to do anyway to help keep Georgia and the boys safe."

"I would give you two anything, Ginny. Of course you can use my cabin tonight." Vas' smile was weak, but only because he knew she was hurting.

"Thank you. I'll let Colby know. I can trust that you won't try anything with Georgia tonight, right?"

Vas produced a devilish smile. "I plan to wait until we're legally wed, Ginny. Now, we might enjoy each other's company, but I swear that I will not steal her virtue."

"That's a good boy. Thank you." Ginny stood up and went in search of Colby to give him the good news.

Chapter 30

Ginny found Colby in the barn with his brothers, talking about what needed to be done while they were gone.

"Frank, you and Nate will need to clean out the stalls and fill them with fresh bedding. There are two fences that need repairing not too far from here. I think you two can handle it. I'll be asking Tim to stay at the house until we return. I expect you to be respectful of Eloise, since she'll likely come as well."

"Yes, sir," the boys said in unison.

"Now, about your schoolwork..." Colby turned and noticed Ginny standing in the doorway of the barn. When Colby stopped talking, the boys turned to see what he was looking at. Both gave each other a knowing smile.

"Frank, Nate. Would you mind if I spoke to your brother for a minute?"

"Sure, Ginny. We'll go take a look at that broken fence. Right, Nate?"

"Yeah, sure." Both boys scampered off and out of the barn.

Ginny didn't hesitate when they'd left. She ran over to Colby and threw her arms around him. Colby pulled her close and wrapped his arms around her, partly for love and mostly to make her feel protected. They stood there for a few minutes, Ginny enjoying the feeling of him wrapped around her.

When she did finally pull away, it was to kiss him. They both got caught up in the feeling, Colby holding on to his control and not dragging her into the nearest stall. It wasn't lost on him that they still hadn't had sex yet, and he wasn't sure his body could take much more.

Colby pulled away first and brushed some stray strands of hair from Ginny's face.

"Are you alright?" He wanted to ask what she needed to talk to Vas about, but didn't want to invade her privacy. She had revealed a lot of pain to him today, so he couldn't blame her if she wanted to solicit Vas' help with something.

"I'm okay. I asked a favor of Vas. I asked if we could use his cabin tonight. He promised to stay at the house and not ravish your sister, in

175

exchange. I think it's really important for us to be alone."

Colby was shocked. He figured it would be months before she would have sex with him, especially after remembering what that monster Fitzhume had done to her. He must have been making strange sputtering sounds because Ginny placed her hand on his cheek.

"I know. But I want you to wash away the stain. Okay?" Her voice cracked. In her real life, Ginny had never experienced the level of violence that Cassandra did that past afternoon. Nor was she willing to experience it again.

"I will make you forget it, Ginny. I will show you what it is supposed to be like."

His speech made her smile. This one was a keeper, she could tell. Her heart broke a little, knowing that the conclusion was near and she would be on her way. She refused to think about it at the moment. There were far more pressing things to think about, like her best sex ever.

After dinner, everyone sat out on the porch and watched the sunset. It had been a long day, filled with a lot of pain, but Ginny felt good. This family did that for her. They were close knit and happy. That was exactly what she needed and wanted.

After the sun set and darkness came over the valley, Ginny told the boys to get ready for bed. "Colby and I are staying at Vas' cottage tonight. If you need anything, ask Georgia. Okay?"

Frank, the more world weary brother, just smiled. Nate, asked, "Why would you stay there when you've got rooms here?"

It was Colby who answered. "Ginny and I haven't been alone since we were married. We just want tonight to be alone before we leave."

"But why?" Nate whined.

Georgia said, "You'll understand when you're older." This answer seemed to dissatisfy Nate even more. But, before he could respond with more whining, Georgia took a hold of his hand and directed him into the house.

Colby turned to Vas and asked, "Where will you sleep? I'd prefer you in the parlor." Colby's voice was stern, leaving no mistaking his reasons.

"I was going to sleep in your bed, Colby. I've waited this long for your sister, I'm not about to take her before our wedding." There was a hard glint to Vas' eyes. He would not allow his honor to be besmirched.

"Very well. And thank you for loaning us your house. I really appreciate it, old friend."

The two men smiled and Vas punched Colby in the arm. "You two better get going. The night ain't getting any younger."

Colby offered Ginny his arm and they started walking across the field toward Vas' house. Neither spoke, they were just enjoying the stars in the clear sky. Neither seemed in too much of a hurry to get to their destination, rather, they were content to just be close.

Colby was aware of the sway of Ginny's hips as they made their way in the short grass. Occasionally, he would feel her breast brush against his arm. The feel of her body was nothing compared to her scent. After her father and ex-fiancé left, Georgia had taken her and given her a bath, with some sweet smelling soap. He could now smell the lavender, along with the mild smell of sweat on her skin. With the faint aroma of pine in the background, it felt like home. And to Colby, the ranch hadn't felt that way since his folks had died.

Ginny's thoughts ran toward the past. She remembered how frustrated she'd been not being able to remember anything about this body she possessed. Now, she would give anything to live in that blissful ignorance again. Images, of not only her assault, but her spoiled and snobby behavior, filled her head. How she would mistreat people she felt were beneath her. She was exactly the person she railed against in Regency England. Although she couldn't change this past, she would definitely be a better person while the fantasy lasted.

Coming up to the house, Colby held the door open for her. The house was much bigger than it appeared. The first floor held a large living area, a dining area and a kitchen. It was open concept, a term that people living in her century enjoyed. There was a single loft over the living space. Although Ginny couldn't see up the steps, she assumed that was where Vas kept his bed. She wondered briefly if his sheets were clean.

Colby walked her to the couch and went into the kitchen area. She heard him banging around, but didn't bother to watch him. Her thoughts had turned to the limited future. She knew that her father would not give up, but wondered when his treachery would happen.

She figured it would happen on their journey to Cheyenne. Not knowing exactly what was coming, she would pull Tim aside and make sure he stayed with the boys and was armed.

Colby returned with a plate of bread and cheese. "You didn't eat much at dinner. You need to keep up your strength."

"I wasn't thinking about food, Colby." Her voice carried a touch of Colby's famous exasperation.

His grin spoke of pleasure unspoken. "Don't you worry about that, Mrs. Miller. All in due time."

So the two ate a few bites and washed it down with water. Vas often ate at the ranch house, so he kept few supplies at home. Nizhoni often said that if her son had to prepare a meal for himself, he would end up dead of malnutrition.

"Would you like to take a walk around and look at the stars?" Colby asked, not really wanting to put off the seduction of his wife, but giving her an out is she wanted one.

Ginny turned and looked at him incredulously. "Geez, Colby. How long have we been waiting for this?" She turned thoughtful, then gave him a set of her saddest eyes. "Unless, you don't want me." Her voice, unlike her expression, was playful.

"I won't be having you misunderstand me like that, Mrs. Miller. I just want to be sure you're ready."

"What happened, happened, Colby. I can't change it. All I can do is look forward to you not having to take my virginity, thus making the experience more pleasurable."

Colby looked down to his lap at that reminder. Ginny hurried to make it right. "It's not that I don't wish you were the only one. As far as I'm concerned, you will be my first." Although clichéd, Ginny meant it.

Colby stood up and held out a hand for his wife. Placing her hand in his, he helped her stand and walked her to the steps.

"Why don't you go on up and get ready. I'll be up after I clean up a bit."

Ginny walked up the steps and found a large bed, with a wooden frame. *Thank God*, she thought as she sat down and there were no squeaks. She promptly removed every stitch of clothing and got under the sheets. Ginny positioned herself in the most provocative way she could, leaning back against the pillows and headboard, with the sheet just barely covering her chest.

Colby made his way up the steps and stopped short when he spotted Ginny. He figured she'd have her shoes and stockings off. His mouth must have been wide open, because his wife started laughing.

"You've never seen a naked woman before?" she asked, humor and desire evident in her voice.

"Never one this beautiful." Ginny thought she might just orgasm right there. There was just something so artless about this man. He said what he meant and meant what he said. He didn't play games, anymore than Ginny did.

Ginny watched intently as he removed his clothing. She'd had her preview that morning, but still felt her mouth become dry at the thought of him naked once again. *This is finally gonna happen,* she thought as each piece of clothing fell to the floor. First the shirt, then the shoes and socks, and finally the pants were left in a less than neat pile on the floor. Ginny cared little about his housekeeping skills at that moment.

He was not only naked, but extremely happy to see her. He sauntered over to the bed and lifted the covers. Sliding in next to her, Ginny felt the bed sink with his weight. Before she could move, Colby took her in his arms, pulling the sheet out of his way. He cradled her gently as he reached down and began kissing her. Gently at first, but that changed as soon as Ginny demanded, wordlessly, that she wanted more.

Colby leaned his wife slowly to the bed, stretching himself out next to her. He used his hands on her breasts, teasing her nipples with his fingers, as he continued to kiss her soundly. Ginny, who had never backed down from him before, demonstrated how aggressive she could be, dueling her tongue with his. His hands moved over her body, enjoying the softness of her skin.

Colby moved down to kiss her neck, while his fingers moved down to explore her depths. As he probed the tender folds of her femininity, he heard her breathing change, increasing, yet shallowing. As his finger entered her, Ginny's head threw back and closed her eyes tight.

Ginny thought it was so silly that something so simple could cause so much sensation. Yet, it did. She felt his finger withdraw, then enter her again. Colby used his thumb against her clit and the dueling sensations shattered her reserve.

When Colby heard Ginny moan, felt her wet for him, he almost jumped on top of her. Sweat beaded his forehead as he tried not to rush the moment. His mouth moved slowly down to her breast, taking the nipple into his mouth and suckling it tenderly.

Ginny couldn't figure out what he was waiting for. She was obviously ready, driven crazy by his attention. All she could think about was having him inside her, to help drive away all the bad memories. Yet, he continued to take his time, move from one body part to another, driving her more crazy by the second.

When he finally started to climb between her legs, Ginny had a flash of the rape. Panic started to rise inside her, like she was trapped and couldn't move. Her eyes widened in terror and she began to involuntarily push against Colby.

"Wait, wait... Please." Her pleas made Colby move aside quickly, moving off the bed completely. He stood beside the bed, staring, afraid to touch his wife.

Ginny's heart calmed immediately and she realized the problem. With Colby on top, she would feel confined. Maybe for this first time, she should be on top. If she felt that control given back to her, she knew she'd be alright.

Turning to look at her husband, Ginny said, "I'm sorry."

Colby sat next to her, still not touching her and replied, "You have nothing to be sorry about. I went too quickly. I'm the one who's sorry."

At his tender explanation, Ginny almost laughed. *Too fast*, she thought. *Not bloody likely.*

"Actually..." she said, trying not to sound amused, "I was thinking that maybe it would be better this first time if I could be on top." When she saw the look on his face, she hastened her explanation. "I mean, when you were over me, I felt trapped, powerless. I thought if I could be on top then I'll be able to handle it better. Don't you think?" Her face was pained and Colby put his arm around her.

"I want you to be comfortable. And as for you on top, I was just wondering how you knew about that."

How did she know about that? Other than the rape, she had no other knowledge of sex. "It stands to reason. I mean... well... it does stick up."

Grinning like a boy given a special treat, he said, "I never thought of it like that." Then Colby turned his attention to his now flaccid penis. "I'm afraid I'm no longer ready."

"I can take care of that." Ginny reached down and began to rub her husband provocatively. He soon got back into the spirit of the moment. Ginny continued her exploration of her husband, running her fingers up and down his shaft, cradling his balls in her hands.

"Ginny, if you keep that up, this will end real quick."

Ginny pushed her husband down against the sheets and straddled him. Leaning down, she grabbed his hands and brought them up to her breasts. Colby needed no further encouragement, and rubbed and teased each breast. Ginny pushed her hair over to one side and kissed her husband with every emotion she had: passion, lust, security and love.

Ginny lowered herself down slowly onto the head of his erection, using her hand to guide him in. As she took him in, slowly, she watched the play of emotions across Colby's face. Primarily, she saw relief. Whether that was because of how long they'd waited or because he never thought this moment would come, she didn't know. His stare became intense, watching her to make sure she was alright.

Ginny was more than alright. She moved smoothly, up and down, creating the friction that would lead to their mutual orgasm. She had to concentrate to keep her movements even. It had been so long coming, that Ginny was too afraid of it being over too quickly.

Colby's hands moved to her hips, helping keep the rhythm. When he felt himself about to let go, he increased her tempo, moving her hips quicker, watching to make sure she was almost ready.

Ginny's orgasm was glorious. She had felt it building but had no idea that it would spring forth so explosively. Her muscles clenched, with a heat that spread throughout her body, starting in her middle and spreading to each limb. Her fingernails raked his chest, then, without ceremony, she fell forward, her face inches from his. Colby's eyes were still closed, his face scrunched from spilling his seed deep inside her.

When his eyes opened, his hands grabbed her face, and he kissed her tenderly. He wanted to say so much to her, tell her how it had been better than he could have imagined. Colby wanted to say that he had never felt such completion, such fulfillment. That he finally understood all the love poetry. How she completed him.

Instead, he moved her next to him and pulled her up against him.

Kissing her forehead, the only words to escape his mouth were, "I love you."

Ginny closed her eyes, and replied, "I love you, too." And she thought, for the first time in her life, she just might mean it. They moved under the covers, Colby lay behind her, cradling her body with his own. She felt his love, his protection and with it, came peaceful sleep.

Chapter 31

It was completely black when Ginny was startled awake. She laid still for a moment, trying to figure out what it was that woke her. Still disoriented from sleep, she struggled to remember where she was. Slowly, it came to her: Vas' house, Colby and her finally had sex.

Then she heard the sound that woke her. A scream, from outside, coming toward the house. The disembodied voice was calling for Colby. It sounded like Nate.

Turning toward her bed partner, Ginny shook Colby awake. He woke in an instant, sitting straight up and looking at her.

"What... What is it?"

"I hear Nate screaming for you," Ginny said as she climbed out of bed and promptly fell over in the dark.

Colby lit the kerosene lamp next to the bed. "Get dressed. I'll go outside to see what's going on."

Colby grabbed his pants from the pile he'd left on the floor and went down the stairs. Ginny grabbed her clothes, pulling on each piece as quickly as possible. When done, she ran down the steps and left through the open front door.

She saw two figures in the dark and cursed herself for not thinking to grab the lantern. Deciding not to run, figuring she would break an ankle on something, Ginny walked toward the two as fast as she dared. She knew this was it. The "it." Whatever her father had decided to do, it was happening as she walked toward her husband and his brother.

When Ginny finally reached the two, she saw that Nate's arms were wrapped around Colby. With the limited moonlight, Ginny saw streams of tears running down Nate's cheeks. Colby was trying to soothe him, but was clearly getting aggravated. Ginny got down on her knees and looked up into the boy's eyes.

Taking him from Colby, Nate started to hug Ginny hard. She could hear him babbling something, but couldn't tell what it was.

"Nate, look at me," Ginny said as she pulled him away and grabbed his face with her hands. "You have to tell me what's going on, or I can't help you."

Nate took a shuddering breath and spoke in a whisper. "They took her."

Colby practically yelled, "Took who!?"

This sent Nate back to shivering and sniveling. Ginny shot Colby a look to shut up, but doubted he could even see it in the dark. Settling her tone down, she lifted Nate's face again and asked, "What are you talking about, Nate?"

"I was asleep, but I heard a crash downstairs. When I walked out of my room, two men were taking Georgia. She was screaming. I started to scream for Vas, but one of the guys hit me and sent me flying back into the room."

Colby took off in a run toward the ranch house, with Ginny towing Nate behind her. By the time Ginny had caught up, Colby was in the parlor, with Vas sitting on the couch holding his head. Georgia and Frank were nowhere to be seen.

Every available light was on and the parlor was as bright as day. Ginny ran to the back of the house, in search of Nizhoni. Vas' mother was fast asleep outside, in a small tent she kept for herself. Ginny asked for some supplies and went back to Vas in the parlor.

Vas was speaking when she came in to check to see if he was hurt. "I tried, Colby. There were two of them, and they caught me by surprise. I don't know what they hit me with, but... They took Georgia. Why would they do that?"

It was Ginny who answered. "Because my father never does anything on his own. He probably hired the men to kidnap me. The men were looking for a girl, not knowing it wasn't me." It wasn't hard to figure the plot out. It may give them the advantage when going after Georgia.

Colby stood up. "I'll go and saddle my horse. There is only one way they could have gone safely in the dark. I'll try to head them off at the pass." Ginny would have giggled at the line if the situation weren't so serious.

"You are not going anywhere without me, Colby. She's going to be my wife."

Ginny knelt in front of Vas and started to look at his head. Probing the large welt on his right temple, Ginny asked, "Where's Frank?"

Colby started to look around him fruitlessly, when Vas spoke up. "He was downstairs with me. He'd had a nightmare or something and asked if he could sit with me awhile. When I heard the noise outside, I told him to stay put. He might be hiding somewhere."

Nizhoni entered the parlor and started talking in rapid Navajo. Ginny had no idea what she was saying until Vas told her that his mother had a remedy for him. Ginny spoke back to her in rapid fire Spanish to make it quick.

Meanwhile, Colby and Nate went looking for Frank. When they couldn't find him, they came back into the parlor. Looking at Ginny, Colby asked the question he'd been dreading. "Do you think Frank went after them on his own?"

Ginny wasn't about to sugarcoat her answer. "Yes. But I don't think he'll try to get her away from them. I think he'll just keep an eye on them unless they try to do something to Georgia."

Nate had a sudden idea and went to the kitchen to see if he was right. Upon his return, he said, "Frank's rifle is gone."

"Dammit. He isn't this stupid." Colby looked itchy from standing there. "I'll go saddle the horses."

Before he could leave, Ginny said, "Make it three, Colby." Then she turned back to Vas, checking to see if he had any other wounds.

Colby turned to her and said, "I haven't got time for this, Ginny. You'll just slow us down. You don't know the trail like we do." His voice was a mixture of anger and desperation.

Ginny stood up and stared at her husband. "Like I slowed you down searching for Nate? Georgia was taken because of me. If worse comes to worse, I'll use myself to get her away from them. I won't have your sister in the hands of Fitzhume. We already know how that will turn out."

Colby's eyes widened. Ginny didn't know if it was the thought of his sister with that monster or the fact that Ginny would sacrifice herself to save Georgia. Either way, he didn't look thrilled at the notion of her joining the search party.

"No. You're not coming. Say what you want, but you will stay here if I have to lock you in my bedroom." He turned and left without another word.

It was Vas who filled the sudden silence. "Ginny, you got to stay here and take care of Nate. Colby and I know what we're doing. We will get her back." The last words came out with a strength that reassured Ginny. But, in the end, Ginny knew that she would have to be there to resolve this. That was what happened in romance novels. She needed to put herself in danger, so her hero could save her. Then again, when did she ever do things the way they were supposed to be done?

She nodded her head and went back to caring for his wound. "Any dizziness or nausea, you need to let me know." Her words were half-hearted at best. Nizhoni appeared with a poultice to put on the bump. Ginny figured it was some sort of analgesic or anti-inflammatory, but didn't ask and for that matter, didn't care. Her mind was working on other things, like what to do to help her husband and soon-to-be brother-in-law.

Colby screamed from outside for Vas to join him, although the words were far less polite. Ginny, Nate and Nizhoni all went to the porch to watch them go. As they rode off, it occurred to Ginny that she may not know the the trails, but she had two people with her that did. And then the plan started to work itself out in her head. She had little doubt that Georgia would be returned to them by morning. Hopefully in the same condition she was in when she left.

When the three entered the house, it was Nizhoni who spoke up first. "¿Usted no se va quedar a solo aqui?"

Just sit here? she thought. *Not bloody likely.* So, in the next ten minutes, Ginny explained her plan to both Nate and Nizhoni. They argued over a few points, then came to a consensus. Nizhoni left to get the necessary supplies, Nate went to saddle the horses, and Ginny went to change into something she could ride in. They all met again outside the barn.

Ginny asked Nizhoni if she was sure about the trail she was going to take them on. The old woman just tsked her disapproval at being questioned. As they climbed up on their horses, the old woman went on about how she had been in this valley for most of her life and she knew it better than even her son or Colby. After fifteen minutes of riding, she finally quieted down, much to Ginny's relief.

It was dark when they set off, and Ginny realized that she had no idea what time it was. None of them seemed tired, with all the excitement acting like ten cups of coffee, flooding their systems. The going was slow, especially as they began their climb up the mountain. This narrow pass was far east of the one Ginny took when she first came to the ranch. She probably wouldn't have even called it a pass, but Nizhoni navigated it as if she could see in the dark.

Through the narrow passages, Nizhoni led, Nate stayed in the middle and Ginny took up the rear. Nate was good on a horse, but he was only ten. Her plan did not involve putting Nate in any danger. As a matter of fact, after Nizhoni got them to the road leading to Cheyenne, she would take Nate home and leave Ginny to find the others. That had been one of the sticking points. Nate wanted to stay with Ginny, but neither Nizhoni or Ginny would allow that. The only reason he came with them now was because neither women would leave him at home alone.

Minutes turned to hours, as they continued their climb. They stopped only once to allow the horses a break. Ginny knew they had climbed in altitude, as it became harder to breath. If she had been hiking, she probably would have given up by then. Thankfully, the horses were doing all the hard work. Just when Ginny felt they would never stop climbing, they reached a plateau and were able to ride along side each other for a few minutes.

"¿Cuanto mas?" Ginny asked Nizhoni how much further they needed to travel. Instead of answering, they cleared some trees, and Nizhoni pointed to the road. The sun was just breaking over the horizon.

Ginny came up beside Nizhoni, and they tried to calculate where everyone would be. If, that is, the bad guys were bringing Georgia to Cheyenne. Based on the timing, Nizhoni speculated that the bad guys were probably already past them on the road to Cheyenne, but that Colby and Vas were at least thirty minutes behind.

Not bothering with Spanish, since Ginny knew Nizhoni could understand English, she said, "Okay. Take Nate home and I'll see if I can catch up to the bad guys." They had taken to calling them that since they had nothing else to call them. Ginny had a few names she could have used, and that Frank would have loved to learn, but it was just easiest to call them bad guys.

Ginny set off down the road and Nizhoni turned her horse to return home, when Nate spoke to her.

"We should wait for Colby and Vas, to let them know Ginny's on her way."

Nizhoni, who was wise after so many years on earth, considered what he'd said. In Navajo, she asked him if he was worried about his new teacher.

"Of course. She's really special, ain't she?" Nate felt the tears forming in his eyes. Nizhoni had been wonderful by keeping them fed and making sure their clothes were clean, but she wasn't the loving type. She didn't offer hugs and kisses, she wouldn't read them books or talk to them. Ginny had offered him everything he'd lost when his mother died. She had become the missing piece in his life that he'd longed for. Having all his physical needs met was one thing, but having his emotional needs met was just as important, especially to a ten year old.

They allowed the horses to graze, while waiting for Colby and Vas. Nizhoni had been wrong about the timing, as it was only fifteen minutes later that the two came over a small hill. When they recognized who was stopped at the side of the road, Colby's face turned murderous. Nate was suddenly afraid of his older brother, as he'd never been before.

Getting off his horse, Colby barked, "Where is she?"

Nate looked at his shoes, and Nizhoni simply raised her eyebrows, as if to ask, "Where is who?" Colby wasn't having any of it.

"Nizhoni, you know damn well who I mean. Where is Ginny and why aren't you three at home where we left you?"

Vas, who despite the fear he held for Georgia, had to ask, "And how did you get here before us?"

Nizhoni went off in Navajo to her son and his friend. Colby turned toward Vas during the speech, eyes rolling. Finally, Colby put his hands across his eyes and called a halt to her complaining. He decided a more civil approach was warranted.

"Please Nizhoni, where is Ginny? Did you see Georgia? Please tell me."

Nizhoni explained that Ginny was only twenty minutes ahead of them and if they hurried along, they would catch her. Turning toward her son, she told him that she took a little used passage, that she would have been happy to explain where it was if anyone had bothered to ask her.

Grumbling, both men took off on their horses at a gallop, hoping to catch up with Ginny before she encountered the kidnappers. Colby knew that his wife was not the most confident rider, so he was surprised when most of the work was done by the time they'd caught up.

Chapter 32

Ginny hated horses. They were big, smelly and had brains of their own. The horse she'd used to find Nate had taken off on her and thrown her. There was no love lost between her and the animal between her legs. However, Ginny had to admit that she was not only getting used to riding, but maybe enjoying it just a little.

Now that she had the memories back from Cassandra, she did indeed know how to ride. Her father loved horses and collected many different breeds. Cassandra had learned to ride at a young age and made it a practice to ride almost every day. With this new found knowledge, and along with it, confidence, Ginny was galloping down the road to save Georgia.

She crested a small hill and stopped short. Ahead of her, maybe a mile or more, she saw a lone rider coming down a path, back to the main road. Off in the distance, north of the road, she saw a couple of buildings, a homestead. Even from the distance she was at, she could tell that the buildings had seen better days. The rider, apparently not noticing her, turned his horse toward Cheyenne and continued on his way.

Ginny was no detective, but she knew a plot line when she saw one. Take one abandoned barn, add a few kidnappers, see one leaving toward a major city and what do you have? Ginny would bet dollars to donuts that Georgia was in that barn, with at least one of the bad guys holding her hostage until her father could come to claim her.

Ginny made her way at an angle toward the buildings. There was some scrub brush and tall grass, but nothing that could hide her completely. Deciding on stealth over speed, Ginny dismounted her horse and walked him parallel to the abandoned buildings, using a small grove of trees as cover. As she entered the tree line, which was maybe only a few hundred feet from an abandoned cabin, Ginny tied her horse and made her way through the tall grass.

The closer she got, the lower to the ground she put herself. The element of surprise was all she had going for her, since she hadn't thought to bring a gun. As if that would have made a difference, she thought realistically. Ginny had only shot one gun in her life, and it had been a paintball gun. She was pretty certain she wouldn't be able to pull a trigger, unless in the grimmest of circumstances. Working in a downtown ER made a person never want to inflict that kind of damage on another human being.

As she came up alongside the cabin, she poked her head around to see something that made her heart stop short. There, on the backside of the barn, peering through the slats, was Frank. Rifle in hand, he had his attention on something inside the old barn. If Ginny needed anymore confirmation of her theory, this was it.

Ginny didn't want to startle Frank and risk him shooting her or alerting whoever was inside to their presence. She searched the ground around her feet and found a small rock. Thinking about her complete inability to throw, she hurled the rock as close as possible to Frank's position. When she saw him turn his head in her direction, she waved her arms briefly and indicated for him to return to the cabin.

Frank saw her and shook his head, pointing frantically toward the barn. Ginny knew he wouldn't be reasonable. After all, it was his sister in the barn with some men not opposed to felonious behavior.

Looking out to make sure no one was outside to spot her, Ginny made her way over to Frank's spot. Without saying a word, he indicated for her to look inside a crack in the wood siding of the barn.

Ginny peered inside and saw Georgia, sitting on an old chair, her hands and ankles bound. The place had obviously been cleaned out when the last tenants had moved on. On the far side of Georgia, were the stalls, five of them total. The doors to the stalls had been removed, so the stalls were open to the barn. There was nothing much left inside except some tall bales of hay on the side closest to where Ginny was peering in.

The kidnappers had their horses tied to the open stalls and were standing by them. They had their heads bent over, speaking in hushed tones. Every few seconds, one or both of them would sneak a look at Georgia, who was staring off into space. Ginny saw the men snicker, then one of the men, a tall, dirty looking scumbag, with stringy brown hair, called out to their hostage.

"Yer a pretty one. Bet you ain't no virgin anymore. Bet if we were to have a little fun, no one'd be the wiser." At this, his friend, a good half foot shorter than his partner, with bright red hair and a pale complexion, snickered. His mouth showed an unfortunate lack of teeth.

Ginny felt her insides tighten. The visions of her afternoon alone with Fitzhume were flooding back, narrowing her vision and causing her to step back abruptly. Frank, who hadn't heard the men, motioned to ask her what was wrong. Ginny shook her head and dragged Frank a few feet away so they could talk.

Whispering, Ginny said, "You need to go to the road and wait for Colby and Vas. You need to tell them where to go. Where's your horse?"

Frank, who had been shaking his head at her words, startled at the strange question. "I tied him up by those woods over there." Frank pointed further down the road toward Cheyenne.

Ginny took his face in her hands. "You need to go and get my horse and get Colby here now. Those men are going to hurt your sister."

As soon as the words had left her mouth, she recognized her mistake. Frank turned toward the barn and was raising his rifle. Ginny grabbed him back and shook her head. She took the rifle forcibly and pointed to where her horse was tied.

Sounding as angry and mean as she could, while still whispering, she said, "You listen to me, Frank. This is not a debate. You will go and get my horse and get your brother. I will help your sister."

Ginny could see just how young Frank looked at that moment. He'd carried the weight of helping his sister on his own for the past few hours. He would be a good man someday, just not that day. He nodded and headed toward the small grove where Ginny's horse was tied. When she was certain he was gone, Ginny turned back to the barn and looked in the crack. Now the two men were taunting Georgia, touching her face with their dirty fingers. More than once, Georgia tried to bite them.

"Yeah, she's pretty feisty," the red head growled, as he almost lost a finger.

"She'd be the prettiest thing you'd ever have, Duncan." Tall and ugly made a snorting laugh at his joke. The red head, Duncan, pushed him hard to show his displeasure.

Without seeing how Duncan would handle the insult, Ginny searched for a way into the barn. As if put there by God himself, Ginny found a hole big enough for her to crawl through. The best part was that it was directly behind the tall stack of hay bales, still allowing Ginny the element of surprise. Thankful that she was wearing pants, Ginny crawled through the hole and entered the barn. Once through, she reached through the opening and grabbed Frank's rifle. She was being quiet, but it didn't matter much. Both men were now screaming horrible things at Georgia, trying to get her to react.

If there was one thing Ginny hated, it was a bully. The strong should protect the weak, not exploit them. Her very blood began to boil, to the point where she thought she just might be able to shoot the two men, except she hadn't asked Frank how to fire the rifle. It had a trigger, but Ginny couldn't even tell if it was loaded. Holding the weapon in her hands, she knew what she had to do.

Glancing carefully around the hay, Ginny saw that both men were too preoccupied with taunting Georgia to notice her presence. Coming around the side of the bales, Ginny moved as closely as possible to the red head. Without any warning, she raised the gun with both hands, and like a baseball bat, she brought it down on the man's head. There was a sickening thud as the man sank, first to his knees, then falling over on his side.

The taller man was too shocked to react at first. Ginny quickly closed the distance between them, turning the rifle around as she went. With the butt, she slammed it into the man's testicles. Ginny almost laughed at the sound, like all the air had been sucked out of the room. After the man fell to his knees, clutching himself as if he could hold himself together, Ginny brought the gun down on his head. A moment later, he was out.

Looking from one man to the other, to make sure they were truly knocked unconscious, Ginny felt herself begin to shake. Before it could get out of hand, she took a deep breath and looked to see that Georgia was okay. She found the girl staring at her incredulously. Georgia's eyes were wide and she seemed to be hyperventilating. With a solid course of action, Ginny turned toward the girl and began to untie her.

Once her hands and feet were released, Ginny grabbed Georgia and pulled her to her body. The two women held each other, keeping the fear and shaking at bay. Ginny could feel Georgia crying, and knew that she was crying as well. For make believe, it just couldn't get more real, Ginny mused to herself.

❖❖❖

Frank reached the horse in no time and untied the mare from the tree that Ginny had tied it to. Without any thought but what he needed to do to save his sister, Frank mounted the horse and rode off down the road toward the ranch. He wasn't entirely sure if Colby and Vas had passed by yet, but since he didn't see any sign that horses had passed, he took the chance.

Frank had the horse riding at a full gallop. Although on a normal day he would have slowed down as he reached the top of hill, not knowing if anything was coming the other way, Frank wasn't thinking about anything but finding Vas and Colby. And find them, he did. Frank and Vas nearly collided, but Vas was able to steer his horse over at the last moment. Frank's mare spooked and reared back, throwing his fore legs into the air, and Frank onto the ground. Without any warning, Frank hit the ground hard, slamming the back of his head onto the hard packed dirt. The wind was knocked out of him, and he was knocked unconscious.

Vas and Colby turned their horses and came back. Dismounting quickly, they reached Frank's side at the same time. Colby grabbed his little brother and was checking to see if he was alright. When he didn't respond, Colby felt himself begin to fracture. Not even a year after his parents had died, he was now losing two other members of his family. As he held the boy tightly in his arms, something happened to Colby. The anger, the pain and the futility did not explode out as he may have thought. But, instead, they came crashing in to a hard ball of fury sitting inside his gut. Colby knew that he would kill Ginny's father, no matter what happened. No one messed with his family.

Suddenly coming back to himself, Colby realized that Vas was speaking to him. Turning to look at his long time friend, he struggled to recognize the words coming out of his mouth.

"Do you think Frank knows where they are?" Colby was seeing things clearer. He now saw the deep fear in his friend's eyes. Vas was terrified and barely holding it together.

"I figure he probably does. Ginny may have sent him off to get us."

Vas began to chant, low and to himself. Colby recognized the chant as one used for healing. As they waited to see if Frank would awaken, Colby began to pray. He wasn't much into prayer, but after everything his family had endured, he figured God owed him one. He would take anything. He repeated his plea, inside his head for what seemed like hours, but was only a few minutes.

As they waited for Frank to come around, Colby checked to make sure nothing was broken. He seemed to be in one piece, with a large knot growing on the back of his head. During his examination, he kept his prayer going, over and over again. *Please God, let him wake up. Please God, let him wake up.*

Just as Colby felt the anger begin to ignite, Frank's eyes fluttered open, then closed again. Colby leaned over his brother and brushed his knuckles against his temple. Frank's eyes opened once again, but he didn't seem to be focusing.

"Frank, it's Colby. Where's Ginny and Georgia?" His voice was soft but firm, hoping to illicit a response.

"Huh?" Frank tried to sit up, but Colby and Vas kept him lying down.

"Frank, where's Ginny?" Colby didn't care for the touch of desperation in his voice, but truthfully, he was desperate. If he didn't get to them in time, he would never forgive himself.

Frank looked in Colby's direction and turned his head, as if the motion would clear it. He reached his hand up and pointed down the road. "Old homestead, not far from here. Hurry." With that, he eyes rolled back, and he was out cold once again.

Colby jumped to his feet and looked down at Vas. "I need you to take care of my brother."

Vas, who looked as if he would argue, nodded instead. "I need you to take care of my future wife." Vas knew there wasn't anything that would keep Colby from doing just that, but if he was going to miss out on dispensing some revenge, he needed Colby to do twice the damage.

"Count on it." Colby grabbed his horse and took off down the road, looking for the old homestead where his wife and sister were being held.

Chapter 33

Ginny placed Georgia gingerly back on the chair, letting her get used to the idea that she had been rescued. Taking the binding that the men had used on her, Ginny tied up the two men. As she went about her work, Georgia spoke for the first time.

"They thought I was you." Her voice was steady, but whisper soft.

"I figured. Why didn't you tell them they had the wrong girl?"

"I did, at first. They didn't believe me. Then I thought that if I convinced them, they might just kill me, so I kept my mouth shut." Her voice shook when she spoke again. "I thought I was going to die. I figured that when your father arrived, he would obviously know that I wasn't the right girl, and he would kill me. All I could think about was Vas. How we would never have a life together."

Ginny completed her task and came to stand by Georgia. She pulled her to her feet and hugged her again. The next words to leave her mouth, as sentimental as it sounded, Ginny was beginning to truly believe. "I only believe in happy endings, Georgia. Not just for me, but for everyone I care about." Georgia's body began to shake as she sobbed. All the pain and fear had to be released. After a couple of minutes, Georgia relaxed and sagged against her new sister.

Ginny heard a group of horses coming toward the barn. Relief washed over her. Frank had found Colby and Vas and brought them back. Ginny grabbed Georgia's face with her hands and looked her in the eye. "How would you like to see Vas right now?"

Georgia, whose face was red and puffy from crying, smiled. "I would like that very much."

Walking away to open the doorway to the barn wider, Ginny saw that the group coming toward the barn was not Colby and Vas. Rather, it was her father and Fitzhume, along with the other man, she presumed to be the other kidnapper. Rolling her eyes, Ginny chastised herself for not knowing better. *How many damn novels do you have to read, or live through for that matter to not have seen this coming, you dumb ass?*

Before Georgia could walk out and greet the party, Ginny grabbed her and the rifle and dragged them behind the stack of hay. Georgia was shocked and began to fight against her, but the look that Ginny gave her quelled her belligerence. Ginny pulled Georgia close and whispered in her ear.

"That's not Colby and Vas. It's my father. Crawl through this hole and go hide. I'll meet you in a second."

Georgia started to shake her head, but again, Ginny stopped her with a look. Ginny mouthed that she would be alright, not trusting herself to make any sound with the men so close, if they weren't already inside the barn. Georgia got down on her stomach and crawled through the same hole that Ginny had used to save her. It was Ginny's plan to crawl through right after Georgia, but then she heard the men arguing. Obviously, they had found the two unconscious kidnappers and were about to start searching for her. She needed to give Georgia more time to run, so she hid the rifle behind the hay and walked out to meet her father. Knowing the whole time that Colby had to be on his way. At least she hoped he was.

When Ginny came into view, her father turned and looked relieved. Fitzhume, however, looked anxious. Not anxious that he'd done anything wrong, but anxious to get started on whatever he had planned for her. When the third man looked over at her, she saw his shock.

"Well, Mr. Damien, it seems that I won't have to kill you and your associates after all." Her father sounded so calculated, that for a moment, Ginny felt chills go down her body. Her memories were very clear when it came to her father. He never lifted a finger to do anything for himself. His only aspiration in life was to be waited on by someone else and to treat those people with as little respect as possible.

But now, hearing his voice, she realized that he was very desperate. Without the money that Fitzhume would give him upon their marriage, Cassandra's father would be penniless. What he owed far outweighed what he had left to sell. If left to that, Ginny had no doubt that her father would kill himself rather than work for a living.

The kidnapper realized that if he spoke up and revealed that this was not the woman he'd taken, he would be in serious trouble. So, he kept his mouth shut and wisely asked for his money. Fitzhume, who hadn't taken his eyes off Ginny, reached into his suit coat pocket and withdrew a wad of bills. Leaving his compatriots behind, the kidnapper walked back out the barn and was heard galloping away.

"I'm glad to see you came to your senses, Cassandra. I was hoping that I would not have to use any force to get you to do your duty."

"I would hardly call having me kidnapped 'coming to my senses,' father."

It was Fitzhume who responded. "You won't be showing me any disrespect when we're married, Cassandra."

"I can hardly marry you, when I'm already married." It was a matter of biding her time, Ginny knew. The longer she could keep them talking, the longer her husband had to ride in and save the day.

Reginald Fitzhume was not worried about his reluctant bride's attitude. He'd dealt with reluctant women before. All his life, Reginald was overlooked. He could admit that he wasn't a classically handsome man, but his money seemed to open doors that would have once been thought not only closed, but barred shut. He was confident that Cassandra's father would make her see reason. Fitzhume was well aware of his financial woes, some of which he helped to cause, all in the name of winning the fair Cassandra. He would not only have her, he would own her, possess her. She would be kept away, only for his own enjoyment. The thought made him harden in anticipation.

Rather than responding to her irrelevant remark, he smiled. His excitement grew seeing how the blood drained from her face at his smile. This was power, he knew. Handsome men come and go, but those with deep pockets were always the ones who enjoyed the power.

"I seriously doubt your marriage was legal, Cassandra. Besides, no one in St. Louis will ever know." Her father seemed almost bored by her protest. "We really must be going. We need to reach Cheyenne by nightfall, then take the first coach in the morning to Denver." Taking one, long disdainful look around the abandoned barn, he said, "I really have no desire to stay outside civilization any longer."

Watching her father take out a handkerchief and rub off his fingers, Ginny wondered about her father's sexual orientation. He was more fastidious than most women she knew. Watching his mannerisms, he appeared more feminine than her. She pictured him spending the week at the ranch and thought it might just kill him.

"I assure you both that my marriage is completely legal. And I'm prepared to tell any minister you put us in front of just that." Ginny used her memories to form a perfect pout of her mouth. She seemed to remember that Cassandra used to practice such a look in the mirror for when she would ask for something from her father. Up until a few months ago, it would have worked. And maybe that was why they were in such financial straits.

Fitzhume walked casually in front of Ginny. She waited to hear his acerbic response when he backhanded her. Ginny hit the ground hard, landing on her hands and knees. When the shock wore off she thought, *twice in one book. Seriously?*

Something primal was released in Ginny. She'd felt it before, playing her other roles. She'd felt it a little when the minster had whalloped her. But now, she was fighting for her dignity and her life, because she was certain that this man would take one, and then the other.

Holding her injured cheek, Ginny stood up slowly and looked Fitzhume in the eye. At first, his expression was smug, but slowly it began to change to reticence. Maybe he was worried that she would lash out, based on the look of pure hatred on her face. He would soon find out.

Ginny raised her hand, as if to hit him back. As she swung her arm around, Fitzhume easily caught it in his hand. He held out her arm, slightly lifting her off the ground. Pulling her closer, he looked down into her beautiful face and sneered, "You will obey me, woman, or you will pay the consequences."

Ginny's murderous gaze was unchanged. She responded, "Fuck you." With that, Ginny brought up her right knee and smoothly connected it to his balls. She would have sworn that his eyes crossed before he let her go and dropped to the ground. As he lay on the ground, clutching himself tightly, Ginny walked around him and kicked him square in the ass. She didn't think it would necessarily hurt him, but she had already caused him incalculable pain. Now she was going for humiliation.

Cassandra's father came to her side and grabbed her arm. He looked almost rabid when he screamed, "What have you done!" His entire life hung in the balance and Ginny saw that he blamed her for his downfall. Grabbing both her arms, he fairly shook her, yelling one epithet after another. His voice roared so loud that neither Ginny nor her father heard Colby ride up.

"Take your hands off my wife." Not screamed, but still very effective in getting her father to finally release her. Ginny fell down next to Fitzhume, who was still too occupied with his own pain to touch her.

Her father charged her husband and knocked them both over. They were wrestling on the ground, each taking and delivering punches. As they rolled back and forth, they became covered in the dust and hay. Ginny scrambled around the hay bales to retrieve the rifle. She could use it to bash her father's head in if necessary.

Finally Colby, who was much younger and stronger, was able to gain the upper hand and straddled the older man holding him down. Cassandra's father looked at Colby with such hate, spitting his anger as he tried to free himself.

Ginny found the hidden rifle and came around the stack in time to see that Fitzhume had recovered enough to protect himself and her father. In his hands was a revolver and it was pointing right at her husband. Colby and her father were oblivious to the danger, only focused on one another. Ginny watched as the Fitzhume cocked the gun and leveled it at Colby. Without time to think or reach him, Ginny raised the rifle, pointed it at Fitzhume and pulled the trigger.

The rifle bucked in her hands so hard that she went flying backwards. Assuming that she probably missed by a mile, but giving Colby time to react, she looked up from the floor to see Colby and her father switching their gazes from her, and the now prone Fitzhume on the ground. The man wasn't moving, but Ginny wondered if he were faking it to draw them closer.

Ginny stood up slowly and walked over to kick the gun further from the still man. As she reached his side, she realized that it wouldn't be necessary. A man can survive a gunshot wound, even in this time period, but he couldn't survive missing part of his head.

Ginny took in the whole picture. Fitzhume lying on the ground in a pool of blood. Brain matter and skull detritus plastered on the wall of the nearest stall. The looks on the her father's face and also on Colby's. What had she done? Had she really just killed another human being. She started to shake as she grabbed her head and shouted the thought: *This is make believe. This is make believe. This is make believe.*

Colby stood up and grabbed the dead man's gun so his father-in-law couldn't retrieve it first. Walking to his wife, he gingerly touched her shoulder, not wanting to startle her. When she looked up at him, eyes wide and brimming with tears, he grabbed her and held her tight. She had saved his life and no one had ever done something like that for him before. And, for the second time that day, Colby prayed. He prayed that his wife could survive what she had done, because it was obvious to Colby that this was hitting her very hard.

Chapter 34

Pulling herself together by burying her feelings deep down, Ginny pulled away from Colby. Without giving him any eye contact, she said, "I've got to go find Georgia. I sent her out of the barn to look for a hiding place."

Cassandra's father still lay on the ground, not moving or speaking. As if his world were imploding, he seemed disinclined to exert any energy whatsoever. He lay on his back, staring at the ceiling, eyes glazed over. A part of Ginny wanted to rail against him, blame him for making her shoot a man, but she couldn't muster the energy to do so. His life was over, and it was beneath her to kick him when he was so far down.

Walking from the barn in a daze herself, Ginny went to the nearby cabin and found Georgia huddled next to it. Her voice was monotone when she said, "It's over. Colby's in the barn." With that, she reached down and picked her sister-in-law up and walked her to the entrance, careful not to allow Georgia inside. She didn't want to cause her naïve sister-in-law any nightmares. Colby walked out as he saw them approach.

"Georgia, why don't you take my horse and see how Vas and Frank are doing. They are only about a mile up the road."

"Why aren't they with you?" Georgia asked.

"Frank took a fall, and Vas stayed with him while I came to rescue you. Of course, Ginny'd already done that."

Ginny heard his words, but couldn't process them. Instead, she relied on what came almost naturally to her now, her medical training. She recognized that she was in shock and her body was shutting down. Fighting the urge to lay down and curl up, Ginny forced herself to evaluate what Colby had just said.

Turning to him, she asked, "What happened to Frank?"

"He was thrown from his horse. He and Vas almost collided."

"Is he okay?" The stress was entering her voice, but she hardly registered it. She needed information, and Colby had it. Ginny simply reacted to her need.

"He was knocked out. He came awake for a moment, but then fell back to sleep again."

Ginny's face must have been incredulous, because Colby asked, "What?"

Taking a deep breath, Ginny was able to pull herself together. "Come on. Let's go see if he's okay." She walked briskly to one of the horses that either Fitzhume or her father had used. Colby just stood like a statue, staring.

"What about your father or the kidnappers?" he sputtered.

Ginny finally mounted the horse after two tries. "I couldn't care less about them. Screw them. Let'em rot here for all I care. I have my family to take care of." With that, without looking back, Ginny took off in a gallop up the road to care for her brother-in-law.

Colby and Georgia exchanged glances, then Colby helped Georgia on his horse and took the other available horse. They soon caught up to the group. Ginny had already dismounted and was talking to Frank. He could see her smiling and brushing his cheek with her hand.

Vas got up and ran for Georgia's horse. She'd barely stopped the animal before he pulled her down and kissed her soundly. Colby heard his sister protest, but Vas quelled her argument. "We're getting married, Georgia. We're allowed to kiss." And so they did, for quite some time.

Colby approached his wife and brother and heard what she was saying. "You are one of the bravest men I've ever met, Frank Miller. It's because of you that your sister is alright. You are a hero, hear me?"

Frank nodded slightly until the movement caused him pain. Then he turned to look up at his brother. "Did you hear that, Colby? I'm a hero."

Kneeling beside him, Colby ruffled his hair and responded, "You got that right. You're a hell of lot braver than I ever was at your age."

Frank took on a contemplative glance. "Is everyone alright?"

It was Ginny who answered. "Everyone who matters." Ginny glanced at her husband. She couldn't quite muster a smile, but her eyes lightened a bit. *After all*, she thought, *this is only make believe.*

Chapter 35

A few weeks later, Ginny was sitting on the porch, cherishing every cool breeze that came along. It was the height of summer and the heat was there to prove it. Since she couldn't convince Colby that there was nothing indecent about wearing shorts, she opted for pants and a light shirt most days. When no one was around, she would roll up the pant legs and find a shady spot to think about what had happened.

Thinking back to the kidnapping, after Ginny had determined that Frank would be alright, it was decided that Vas and Georgia should head on to Cheyenne to get married. They still had to decide what to do about the kidnappers and her father. Vas and Colby were batting around ideas when Ginny made the decision.

"Leave them. My father has nothing left. He won't bother us again. As for the kidnappers... well, I gave them a beating they won't soon forget."

Vas and Colby gave each other a look. In the end, Ginny won out since the alternative was too much work. The five of them headed to Cheyenne. They found a judge who married Georgia and Vas that afternoon and began to head back to the ranch by evening.

Colby felt bad about Vas and Georgia not getting to stay for at least one night, but they agreed that the sooner they got back, the sooner Nate and Nizhoni would stop worrying about them. They got some supplies and set out in the early evening. They pushed themselves to make it to the pass before they had to stop.

They were up again at the crack of dawn and home way before lunch. Nate was crying when he saw that everyone was back. Nizhoni, in her own gruff way, gave everyone a small hug and congratulated her son and new daughter-in-law.

In the weeks since, the group had settled into a routine of sorts. Vas and Colby took care of the stock occasionally bringing Frank along. Georgia set up house in Vas' cabin cooking him dinner on her own, so they could spend some alone time together. Nate and Frank continued their studies. And Colby and Ginny only had sex on Ginny's old bed, then went into their shared bedroom to sleep. Meanwhile,

Colby was working on a new bed frame.

It was just luck that Ginny was alone that afternoon. Colby had taken both boys to fix something or other, then they were going swimming. She was left to think about when she would leave. After everything had settled down, she just assumed it would happen. Night after night, she laid in bed waiting for the crazy dizziness to start, signaling to her that she would be gone. Then she continued to wake up next to Colby.

So why was she still there? With Ian, she didn't leave until she was pregnant. That hadn't happened yet. With Colin, she left almost immediately after they resolved to live as husband and wife in every imaginable way. But with Colby, they had achieved the husband and wife bit, and it was only a matter of time before she got knocked up with the way they were having sex every night. So what were they waiting for?

Leaning back in the rocking chair, putting her feet on the porch rail, Ginny noticed a cloud of dust to the west. Someone was coming to visit, but who? Definitely not the reverend. He'd been madder than a hornet when he found out that Georgia and Vas were married. Not Eloise. She hadn't been by since they'd ran her off for being insensitive. Ginny kept her position as the lone rider drew closer. Finally, the man was in front of the house, dismounting and staring at her with a strange expression.

"How do you do, ma'am." He removed his hat and Ginny saw he was a handsome man. Tall, with broad shoulders and a well-muscled chest. Long black hair framed his square face and strong jaw. He tied his horse to the railing and walked up the steps.

Ginny looked up to his face and smiled. "I do very well, thank you. How 'bout yourself?"

The stranger took the other rocker, put his feet on the railing next to Ginny and laid his hat in his lap. "Been a good day so far. Who're you?"

Ginny lifted an eyebrow at his question, but answered anyway. "I'm Ginny. And you are?"

The stranger laughed. His voice was deep and appealing. "I'm RJ," he said as if that explained everything.

Ginny scrunched her face and knew she'd heard the name before. "RJ?"

"I used to live here. This is my parent's house. Got a few brothers and a sister here too. I haven't been away that long, have I?"

Ginny dropped her legs and sat up straight. Her face looked drawn as she realized that RJ, the missing eldest brother, had no idea that his parents had died, and she would have the unfortunate duty to tell him.

"Welcome home, RJ. I'm Colby's wife. When was the last time you received a letter from your family?" She thought she was keeping her voice even, but RJ sensed immediately that something was wrong.

"Why? I've been moving around quite a bit. I realized that I hadn't heard anything in a long time, so I came home to visit."

Ginny closed her eyes and sighed. "I'm sorry to tell you that your parents were killed last year in a flash flood. Colby, who had been living in Denver at the time, came home to take care of your siblings. A lot has changed since you were last here." She hadn't intended to sound like he should feel guilty, but there was a part of her that thought he should.

As if hit in the stomach with a sledgehammer, RJ doubled over and put his hands to his face. "When, exactly?" he whispered.

"I don't know the exact date. I've only been here a couple of months. Colby and the boys will be home soon."

Turning his head to look at her, he asked, "And Georgia?"

"She's married to Vas. They live in his cabin," Ginny indicated to the log cabin in the distance.

"Married? To Vas?" His voice was shocked to say the least.

"Yes, a few weeks now."

"Everything has changed, hasn't it?"

"Yes. That's what happens. Life goes on."

Shaking his head, trying to clear it, RJ sat speechless for a moment. After a few times of starting to speak, only to stop again, he finally said, "I should have been here."

Ginny took a deep breath as she considered whether to respond. Should he have been there? Probably not. Should he have kept in touch with his family so he could have found out a lot sooner. Most definitely. As the new patriarch of the Miller family, he had certain responsibilities, but that didn't mean he couldn't find his own life.

Before she could try to make him feel better, Ginny heard Colby and the boys returning. She stood up with RJ following suit. Her family spotted the strange horse and bypassed the barn for the house.

As soon as Colby pulled his horse up, he saw his brother standing next to his wife.

"My God," was all he said. Frank and Nate, having caught up, stared without saying a word at the ghost from their past.

Ginny wondered how long RJ had been gone. They all seemed frozen, as if saying anything would make the apparition disappear. Never one to wait for something to happen, Ginny was the first to speak up.

With a false cheerfulness, she proclaimed, "Look who's here guys. RJ." Well, she gave herself points for stating the obvious.

Colby turned his eyes to her for a moment. The look told her that he had a lot of anger towards his brother, and she was not to get involved. Being Ginny, she promptly ignored the look.

Getting down from his horse, Colby turned to Nate and Frank. "Boys, take the horses and bed them down, then come into the kitchen. I'm sure Nizhoni has some treats waiting for us all."

Neither boy moved for the longest time. Finally, they both dismounted, and Frank took Colby's horse and Nate took RJ's. It was obvious they wanted to hear more as they moved as slow as snails toward the barn. Colby walked up the steps and stood next to Ginny, putting his arm possessively around her shoulders.

"Welcome home, RJ. Been a while." Colby shocked himself by keeping his voice even. Inside though, he was seething.

RJ took in the picture of wedded bliss and responded with a sigh. "Too long, apparently." His head dipped and he looked as though his boots were far more interesting than anything else in the universe.

Hearing RJ admit he was wrong to stay away so long took the wind out of Colby's sails. Feeling his wife's arm come around his waist and squeeze, he realized that as bad as his life had been over the last year, it ended up pretty damn good. He had the love of his life to spend eternity with. His brothers got a new mother to cluck over them, and Georgia was happy being a wife. Torturing RJ just wasn't worth the effort.

"So, you met my wife, did ya? I've got to warn you, she's a pistol." Colby smiled as he spoke.

"Yeah, that's me. Don't let them tell you otherwise, RJ. I'm horrible!" Ginny's exaggerated voice made both men laugh.

"I'd like to stay, if that's okay. I'd like to be a part of this family again." RJ wouldn't cry, but his drawn face and forlorn look broke Ginny's heart.

She realized that this was what had to happen for her to move on. The family had to become whole again. Although they would never get their parents back, the rest needed to be together. As Ginny had told RJ earlier, life goes on.

The brothers took the seats on the porch with Ginny sitting on Colby's lap. Nate and Frank came running from the barn, just in time for Colby to tell them to fetch their sister. It wasn't long before Georgia came running across the meadow to see her long lost eldest brother. The family talked for hours, filling each other in on what was going on, where RJ had been and how Ginny had come to be in their lives.

Nizhoni brought out refreshments and to yell at RJ for staying away too long. She told him it was bad enough her own son would take off, but he need not do the same. Vas came back from his chores and joined the family on the porch. Everyone was smiling and happy, the picture of a long awaited family reunion.

As the sun began to set, Nizhoni told everyone to get ready for supper. Everyone else went inside to get cleaned up, and RJ put his things in Georgia's old bedroom. After a minute, it was just Colby and Ginny on the porch watching the sun make its way down the sky.

Cradling her body against his, Colby said, "It's great that RJ's home, don't you think?"

Smiling into his neck where her head rested, she responded, "Of course."

Colby detected something in her voice. Pulling her away from him, he looked her in the eye. "Something wrong?"

Ginny couldn't tell him that the story was over, and she would be moving on. Instead, she asked, "Will you want to go to Denver and work at being a lawyer again?"

Colby turned his lips up in a sly smile. "I thought that was what I wanted. Turns out all I wanted was a beautiful wife, who's a wonderful mother to my brothers and a great friend to my sister. Doesn't matter where I am as long as I have that." With that, he kissed her slowly, deeply.

"We better get washed up for supper or Nizhoni will come looking for us," Colby said, as he stood up with her still leaning against his body. Making sure she had her balance, he slowly let her go.

Flicking her head toward the door, Ginny said, "You go in and get started. I'll be in in a couple of minutes."

Colby smiled and kissed her once more, then went into the house, easing the screen door closed. Hearing it squeak, hearing his footsteps as he went to the kitchen, almost made Ginny cry. Instead, she sat on the rocking chair and stared at the sun as it set on the horizon.

Where will I go next? she wondered. It didn't really matter, because this was where she wanted to be. Frowning, Ginny thought about her real home. When she realized that she hadn't thought much about it in quite some time, she worried. Was she getting too caught up in these worlds that she'd forgotten that she had a perfectly good life in the 21st century? Not wanting to consider it, she pushed it aside. She knew her time was over here, and it was time to move on to something else.

When the dizziness finally came, it didn't surprise her or make her mad or sad. Ginny simply felt numb. She sat against the back of the rocking chair, watching the sun set, allowing the tide to take her away.

For news and extras on the Lesson series, be sure to check out
www.jenniferconnors.com

CPSIA information can be obtained at www.ICGtesting.com

263353BV00003B/70/P